THE COFFER DAMS

NOVELS BY

Kamala Markandaya

THE COFFER DAMS

A HANDFUL OF RICE

POSSESSION

A SILENCE OF DESIRE

SOME INNER FURY

NECTAR IN A SIEVE

THE
COFFER DAMS

A NOVEL BY

Kamala Markandaya

The John Day Company
New York

Library of Congress Catalogue Card Number: 71-75598

PRINTED IN THE UNITED STATES OF AMERICA

THE COFFER DAMS

1

$\mathcal{I}$T was a man's town. The contractors had built it, within hailing distance of the work site, for single men and men who were virtually single by reason of being more than a day's walk away from their women and villages. There was a coffee club and a soft-drinks stall and a tin shack where they showed the films that the Madras Picture Corporation sent up by truck; and there were those long low structures, row after row, like old-time barracks, where the workers lived. Clinton's Lines, the men called them. It was some time before Clinton realized that they did, he was so shut off from the men who worked for him. When it did penetrate he was vaguely pleased: it brought back names of forgotten barracks and squares, names like Clive Lines and Wellesley Lines, hideously familiar to him during the war, but hazed over now with the nostalgic, evocative splendor of the illustrious adventurers they commemorated.

He had hated the war, who hadn't; but it was especially hateful to him because he was a builder, a man who drew his satisfactions from building what would last, who had brought a grim distaste to the task of destruction set before him like a dish of hemlock. It had not destroyed him, this war: he had come out alive; but it had savaged him in ways of which he was hardly aware. When it was over he repatriated himself as soon as he could, turning his back with relief on inept colonies and the succession of shabby little outposts of empire he had been called upon to serve, where he had encountered a chaotic medievalism that offended what was most vulnerable in him, his sense of order and efficiency: where he had learned to raise his voice at the natives, and sampled the piquant flavors of disdain.

In those war days, in his youth and wrath, he had grimly promised alarmed local populations to drag them kicking into the twentieth century by the seat of their pants if need be. But it was not his job; his interest lay elsewhere. He returned to England, forgot the war, took up with avidity the work it had interrupted, founded the firm whose ramifications had become international. Others saw him as a man of wealth and property, worshipped him as a successful man in accordance with the current cult. All this meant nothing to Clinton. He saw himself only as a builder, a man whose conceptions of concrete and steel his highly polished and perfected technical skills could translate into reality. Through what, or where, the pursuit of this reality led him had become a matter of indifference.

A builder. The word ran through his mind with a clear keen pleasure as he walked briskly past the living area to the busy work site, seeing not the welter of men and machines but only his vision, the dam that would arise with blueprint precision at this point, exactly as they had planned it. The Great Dam, it had come to be called. Not by him; he was too absorbed by the work in hand for adjectival excess, but by people of the Maidan and the Malnad, the plains and hill-country people, who had watched with awe the precipitate birth of a town in the jungle.

It was virtually a small industrial town, gouged and blasted out of the hillside. Clinton had sent Mackendrick, his partner, to preside over its creation, this imperative construction of a base from which the whole main project could grow. Mackendrick, not given to excess any more than Clinton, had sworn to himself, hovering in a helicopter above the site of which all he could see was a uniform, impenetrable green. Nevertheless it

had been done, neatly within the time allotted to it. By the end
of the first year the labor force had been assembled, the access
routes mapped, the lines of communication established, a road
cut down the craggy hillside from work site to base camp for the
heavy trucks that brought up equipment and supplies. By the
end of the second the surface installations were in place: work-
shop and work buildings, loading and unloading bays, the car
maintenance sheds, the workers' quarters, the engineers' bungalows, the amenity buildings, the water tower, ice and filtration
plant, pumping and power stations: their bare bones present,
if not all articulated and functioning, and the great heart beginning to beat.

It was a powerful heart, powered to match a project am-
bitious in its scope and nature: a project that looked at the human coin of future centuries, and envisaged harnessing to its
needs the turbulent river that rose in the lakes and valleys of the
South Indian highlands and thundered through inaccessible
gorges of its hills and jungles down to the plains with prodigal
waste.

The people who lived by its waters were grateful, but wary.
They propitiated it with sacrifice and ceremony, and strengthened the banks with clay when the water levels rose. Sometimes
when the rains failed there was no river at all, only a trickle
that did not percolate through to the shallowest irrigation channels of their parched fields. At other times the land was inundated. They saw their crops drowned beneath spreading lakes,
their mud huts dissolved to a lumpy brown soup and carried
away on the flood tide. At both times they prayed to God; they
never blamed him. It was their fate.

All this the planners of the new India, flanked by their technical advisers, had passionately expounded. Clinton listened
with a vast boredom. It did not really interest him, this dreary
sage of a hapless peasantry. He sipped his whiskey and felt hot,
despite the Bharat Hotel's air-conditioning, and wished there
was some way of dodging these emotional preliminaries. Then
it was over. They turned from the woes of the people to a dis-

cussion of the project. Clinton returned to earth, abruptly, disconcerting anew his alienated hosts; and suddenly they were speaking the same language.

Afterward Clinton was to confess—as Mackendrick had in fact known—that he had come within an ace of walking out, of refusing even to consider submitting a tender. Mackendrick would not have been sorry if he had. He had not wanted to tender at all, the scheme had seemed to him to be too complex, not so much in constructional terms but fraught with financial, prestige and political difficulties that made it in his view as brittle as an eggshell. Moreover, he knew that these were precisely the kinds of difficulties Clinton would never concern himself with. He would get on with the job, leaving his partner to untie the knots in long arid sessions in Delhi or Madras.

"Let the Russkies have it," he said to Clinton. "They seem eager enough—and to hell with the propaganda. Or the Americans or the Swedes. They can take the kicks too, heaven knows there won't be any thanks. There never is."

But there was something about the project that had begun to inflame Clinton. Partly because it would be a testing of strengths: his own, his men's, their joint accumulated power against the formidable natural hazards of the scheme. Partly, because others wanted it. The country was full of foreigners— Americans, West Germans, the Russians fresh from their triumph at Aswan, the immense successful undertaking of taming the Nile, the Dutch with their ancient knowledge of dam-building, the brilliant achievement of the Zuider Zee and the Delta Plan behind them—all of them eager, in greater or less degree, to gain a foothold in an expanding subcontinent of vast commercial potential. Both aspects of the power struggle excited Clinton. He was determined to tender, to win contract and last round in the tough battle being urbanely fought in the state capitals, and reported sourly in long memoranda that filled the diplomatic mailbags; and in the end he carried his partner with him. One by one problems that seemed intractable were solved, coolly, thousands of miles away from the scene in a London penthouse padded to keep out the noise of the traffic, later on site under a broiling sun; and when they put their names to the contract, below the heavy lion seals of the Government of India, it was at the end of two years of sweated endeavor.

2

BEYOND Clinton's Lines, on rising ground five hundred yards upstream, in a clearing hacked out of the jungle, were the British workers' quarters. The Indian contractors had built these too, to British specification: neat small four-roomed boxes that housed two, four or six men according to temperament and seniority. Clinton had approved the scale models long ago, far away in London before even the contract had gone to them; but when he came slap up against the colony he had a confused feeling as if a bit of England had strayed on to soil where it had no business to be, as if a section of English housing estate, a scaled-down, whitewashed version, had been improbably lodged in this corner site round a bend of a river in India.

By then the men had been living in for some little while; they had had time to carry their Englishness into the jungle with them. Making his first rounds with Jackson, their chief foreman, Clinton was conscious of pleasure in the orderly scene: the trim square plots of emerging gardens, the graveled paths, the white-washed boulders that demarcated and upheld private property rights. He said as much, and Jackson in slightly different words echoed his views, thumping a huge tanned fist for emphasis: it was indeed like a home from home.

But this was by day. Neither of them alluded to the night. They allowed their thoughts to cross, unable to control the sudden savage leap, and strangled them at the threshold of speech.

By night it was different. The jungle crept back, closing in as the shadows of the huge trees fell across the line where the clearing merged into scrub, and advanced and deepened; and the men grew restless, listening to the yelp of jackals, or the soft furtive sounds of frightened deer, and lurched out to herd together in the canteen or cinema, or the shanty-town-style saloon bar, where the familiar noise and thick blue air, and in the end alcohol, restored the illusion of England.

There were no women here either. It was no place for women. The men were promised home leave, all expenses paid, at the end of each two-year term, and in the meantime fended for themselves. Clinton saw them roistering off down the hill at weekends, packed like sardines into commandeered contractors' trucks. He had no notion where; it did not concern him so long as the work schedule was maintained.

He had even less idea where his Indian labor went. He saw them trailing away down narrow footpaths into the jungle on their leave days, and as far as he could tell the wilderness swallowed them up. He never knew when they came back, whether they came back at all, or whether Mackendrick's efficient recruiting organization replaced one dark wave of humanity by another. They all looked the same to him. Once or twice, anxious to explore the possibility of an alternative access route, he had attempted to follow them and had been stopped by the blank wall of masks that turned to face him. What animated them, what went on behind those black, depthless eyes? He could not ask, there was simply no communication.

Helen, his wife, had no such blocks. Was it, he wondered, because she was half his age? When he asked her she laughed. "It's nothing to do with age. I just think of them as human beings, that's all." He frowned at the equivocal statement, and she added seriously, trying to help: "You've got to get beyond their skins, darling. It's a bit of a hurdle, but it is an essential one."

Clinton suspected that she had had no hurdles to jump, and in the end he got her to admit it. "I expect it's something to do with being born in India in my previous life," she said lightly and turned the conversation, before the uneasiness loitering behind his questions could solidify into resentment.

It was no place for Helen either, Clinton often thought. But the prospect of being separated from her, newly married as they were, a year at a time, was so bleak that he was glad when she forced his hand. She was in love with him, she wanted to be with him: it was as simple as that. Surveying the wilderness to which he was bringing her, he had not been too happy; but he comforted himself with the thought that civilization, such as India could offer, was not too far away. So that she could reach it as instantly as possible he imported a Ferrari 500, cutting through the forbidding mass of import restrictions like a ruthless laser until the gleaming machine stood on the quay at Madras Harbor, waiting for Mackendrick to finish building his road.

Mackendrick had built the road, the bridge, and the bungalows too, but he had chosen the site, across the river from Clinton's Lines and the housing estate, well away from babel, where he and his senior staff could live in peace. "Town houses in a woodland setting," Mackendrick said with a sardonic flourish when the building was finished, and Clinton grinned and agreed. Nothing short of wholesale destruction would have charmed woodland out of this jungle, but the best that could be had been done, the trees lopped and trimmed, the rank lush undergrowth singed to ground level, the bungalows carefully sited so that none overlooked a neighbor. As Mackendrick said, with so much space to spread oneself in, there was no sense living in each other's pockets.

Clinton's bungalow, apart from a glassed-in verandah added at Helen's suggestion, was no different from the other bungalows. There had been twenty in the pilot batch, early that first year, intended for his key men: for Bob Rawlings, the chief engineer, and Henderson, the turbine specialist, and the team headed by Lefevre that ran the soil mechanics laboratory, and

Todd who was the electrical wizard, and Galbraith, the chief technical man and his corps of assistants, and of course Mackendrick, who had been living under canvas and who, unusually for him, made a bonfire of his threadbare tent and danced uninhibitedly on the ashes the day he transferred to his bungalow.

After that they waited to see, as Mackendrick only half-jokingly said, whether the bungalows would fall down; a remark which duly reached the sensitive ears of Subramaniam, the efficient and conscientious contractor who had built them, who thereupon tore up the fresh contract they had sent him for signature and departed, roundly declaring himself unamused by the jokes of the British and determined to have no further dealings with them on any terms thereafter. By then a good deal of the essential building was completed, with the major exception of the British canteen: and by now, also, there were sufficient British personnel available to handle occasional gaps in construction.

Subramaniam's buildings did not fall down, nor did the second batch of fifty that the replacement contractor built; but the latter were distinctly inferior.

"My God, Indians!" Mackendrick exclaimed in bitter despair. He had deliberately relaxed his vigilance in shame and atonement of his earlier unjustified strictures, and these ailing structures seemed to him a poor return for his humanity.

"Slap in the eye for old Mack," said Rawlings, who had said all along Indians were no good at this game, and was glad to have his opinion confirmed. He was also unconcerned, for seniority gave him the right to a Subramaniam bungalow, which by any standards was soundly built and extremely comfortable to live in.

Bailey, Bond, Rankin, Crane, Kershaw, Riley, Richards, Manson, Norris, Shaw—the rest of the younger, less senior officers—were installed in the second batch, of which not one out of the fifty bungalows was entirely free of faults. Walls bulged, roofs leaked, doors warped and rattled in their frames. Bailey, the most vocal, who complained bitterly of the mold that grew on the damp walls and over his boots between taking them off one night and putting them on in the morning, was also the first to admit he had known equal or worse at home. Not everyone followed his lead, but there were thoughtful faces, and the deluge of complaint moderated. After all, they said, they were here for only a specified time: a short length taken from their lives, snip, snip. They could stand it.

Later the wives came out: officers', not men's. Not many; only the few who had been able to resolve family difficulties or who were still free; no children and no problems to consider. Clinton was glad for Helen's sake. He felt it would be company for her, he had never been entirely happy about bringing her to this primitive frontier town that they were roughly hewing into existence. But Helen, he noticed, did not seem to need their company: did not seek it or shun it, but after the merest genuflection toward good neighborliness showed a distinct inclination to wander off alone, enclosed in a rapt absorption for which he felt a kinship, recognizing it as a facsimile of his own. Its nucleus, however, eluded him. He had his work; what had she? Curiosity, not interest, made him ask.

"I have you," she answered him, her body bare and cool under the sheets, lying close to his.

"By day," he said, "when you can't have me."

"It's awful then."

"I've watched you," he said. "It's nothing to do with that."

"What is it then?"

"I wish I knew."

"There are so many things," she said. She was half asleep. He shook her, careless of whether or not she wanted to wake.

"What kind of things?"

"Oh . . . people—all kinds of things."

"Men?"

"Darling, no." He roused her at last. "There are no men."

"The place is crawling," he said, "full of men. Altogether too many sods."

"Then you've nothing to worry about, have you?"

They fell asleep laughing, as closely together as if they were one.

They had been together a month then, after a long separation.

3

IN the long course of settlement the plans for the dam had shuttled between London and New Delhi, design and financing minutely scrutinized and modified at each stage. Clinton traveled with them, an iron will checking his intolerance of any curbs in return for freedom of execution. He was a builder; this was his province: with patient tenacity he wrested it from the hands of the central authority, who in the end were not sorry to see it go. There were nearer problems than the execution of a project a thousand miles away, under difficulties of climate and terrain that they suspected the preliminary plans had only partially exposed.

Clinton did not know, either, what he was in for in full. He went to infinite trouble to find out.

Out of the collated reports of Henderson, Mackendrick, Rawlings, Lefevre and Galbraith—the combined efforts of their teams—the construction plans emerged and were finalized. A year for the diversion channel to take the altered course of the river. A concurrent year for the coffer dams to stem its flow. Two years for the main dam to rise between the coffers.

The time schedule was calculated with precision, the build-

ing program meticulously phased to allow maximum construction between the dying fall of the southwest monsoon and the
summer resumption of the cycle. When it was done, the contract sealed, the plans finalized, the Indian faction demurred.
Not at the Delhi level but later, on the spot, when they were
waiting for the rains to be over to begin.

"They want to speak to you," said Mackendrick. "The new
lot. I've had a try but they're not having me. Apparently it's
God or nothing."

Clinton looked out of the window of his small metal cabin
on the site to the concrete apron where excavators were assembled like the forward thrust of an army.

"Am I God?" he asked.

"You've become," answered Mackendrick dryly, "since, you
see, it is to do with the weather."

Mackendrick's new lot was the band of indigenous engineers
seconded to the British contracting firm whom the government
had rounded up and rushed to the site in last-minute fulfilment
of its contractual obligations. Mackendrick had by then virtually given up all hopes of their arriving: their reception had
not been intentionally bleak. Nevertheless there were deficien-
cies and shortcomings, notably in the matter of accommoda-
tion, which had provoked a succession of disaffected rumblings
from their camp. If Clinton heard he gave no sign, no open
cognizance; there were others whose job it was to deal with
grievances and complaints. He kept his own counsel, preserving his neutrality in silence.

Now they had come up with the weather, either because
they had run out of other grievances, or because the matter was
serious, or for some other reason that had still to emerge. Clinton balanced the probabilities coldly in his mind; but in the
end influences other than any gravity he attached to the views
of his seconded officers led him to summon a meeting.

In the quiet canteen that night he heard them out.

Mackendrick and Rawlings sat with him, while Krishnan, the leader of the Indian delegation, stood up and spoke.

The construction program, he said, in their united view needed modification. The building schedule was too tight. The leeway allowed for natural hazards was wholly insufficient. Allowance had been made for the southwest monsoon but not for the northeast which followed. Cyclones, as anyone who was Indian would know, could make havoc of this kind of peremptory British planning. The question of solar flares had not even been touched upon. And labor troubles were endemic. Any of these factors could upset a schedule as inflexible as this one. It must be amended and a revised date of completion set, now, before a series of delays and setbacks tarnished the whole operation.

"It is not only delay in completion of a dam that is involved." Krishnan's voice rose; the skin over his prominent cheekbones was tight and bleached of its sallow color. "The whole reputation and prestige of the government is at stake."

Mackendrick glanced at the Indian with something like sympathy. In a way he understood—better than either of the Englishmen—the pulsing jealousy and pride that a poor nation could feel and transmit to its nationals: the pride of an ancient civilization limping behind in the modern race, called backward everywhere except to its face and underdeveloped in diplomatic confrontation—a euphemism of sheltering intent but dubious minting and no less humiliation. No wonder Krishnan was concerned, Mackendrick thought. In the other's place he would have been the same, on tenterhooks in case the schedule went wrong and his country was named as the nation that couldn't even build a dam on time. But then the Hindus were thin-skinned: bled at a touch, even before you applied the needle. Not that he had ever felt the need for such needling; watching it done made him acutely aware of his own nerve-endings.

Rawlings' mind followed a different track. He listened to Krishnan's excited, slightly singsong English in growing astonishment, marveling that a qualified engineer could imagine

that at this stage wholesale amendments could be made to a minutely planned, intricately dovetailed construction project.
But Indians, he thought, were an excitable breed, a quality that
diminished rational behavior. Somewhere, too, coursed a thin
stream of feeling that independence nourished these volatile
roots, whose full flower was the grandiose and impractical planning one saw in the new free territories from Kenya to Uganda.
He had seen, or heard from those who had seen. Though of
course one had to be circumspect these days and not broadcast
what one thought.

Clinton felt only that he had heard it all before. But that
had been in Delhi—Delhi which by comparison was cushioned
and air-conditioned. It was that much worse here, shut in a
stuffy tin shed with a crowd of highly vocal, inexperienced
men. Overhead, hordes of insects circled like satellites around
the oil lamps; there was wire mesh at the windows to keep them
out, but they infiltrated somehow, like determined spies. There
was air-conditioning too, but it had failed. The substation,
where transformers stepped down the voltage from the hydroelectric works farther up river, had gone temperamental, alter-
nating breakdowns with spurts of efficiency. He had meant to
order a change of the engineer in charge but it had slipped his
mind. Clinton made a notch in his memory without switching
his attention from Krishnan. Cyclones, monsoons, government
prestige. What the hell, he thought, not showing by a stifled
breath what he thought. His own private prestige was what exercised him: it was, he felt, a man's proper concern, something
of value that he nurtured and cherished in his heart, this reaching for a star and the grasping of it in fulfilment of oaths made
to himself.

Nevertheless he heard Krishnan out without interrupting.

Krishnan, aware all the time he spoke of the cool neutral face
only partly turned toward him, did not believe that Clinton was
even listening. Brush us off like flies, he thought, hurt and insult like splinters under his skin; despise us because they are ex-
perts and we are just beginning. Beginners, he repeated bit-

terly, barred from knowledge and power as from the secrets of a master guild; and the memory of those neglectful years lay in deep accusing pools in his mind. But it's over now, he said to himself. Our day is coming. The day when they will listen to us.

Even if they don't listen now, as this one doesn't listen.

He was wrong, for Clinton was listening. He always listened; it was the final decision that he reserved for himself.

4

AFTERWARD they held a postmortem in Rawlings' bungalow and Rawlings grumbled about Krishnan.

"You'd think he'd know," he complained sourly, "he must know we've gone into it one hundred times before. But no, he's got this kink they all have, that he knows his country better than anyone else—as they damn well ought, but they don't. So he brings up this thing and that thing and expects us to build round them—what the hell does he think we're building, a cowshed?"

Mackendrick listened with sympathy laced with a little quiet amusement. Rawlings' outbursts appealed to him, perhaps because their temperaments were diametrically opposed. *Molaga thanni sahib,* the pepper-water master, was the epithet the laborers applied to Rawlings. What did they call him, he sometimes wondered: milksop sahib? He had yet to discover, and he knew he never would unless it were complimentary. Courtesy was inbred here, among the local labor.

"All right, tropical climates do have extremes." Rawlings rumbled on. "You can't plan for that, you can't afford to: no one can. You work out the averages and you pin your colors to them, it's the best you can do. Of course you can come adrift. So what?

Some fool drops a nuclear bomb right on the works tomorrow: what kind of calculation does one make to take care of a thing like that?"

"You must tell Krishnan all this." Clinton smiled. "He's the one that needs convincing."

"That fool," said Rawlings, "do you think he'd listen? Needs slapping down."

Slapping down, however, found no place in Clinton's thinking. He sent down to base, where the shelves of his office were crammed with notes and memoranda; and presently the figures he wanted—extracted from reports compiled months ago before they had moved their headquarters to the hills—lay on his table before him, closely typed on thick white paper and neatly tabulated.

When he had them Clinton was ready for Krishnan.

Krishnan saw the copious notes on his table, and in a bleak way admired the driving energy that had procured them. He knew even before they began that he was going to be overruled, not tyrannically but logically and with cogent reason and he thought: well, why not, if it's the right thing? We're on the same side aren't we? And Clinton, meeting those dark questioning eyes, for once knew what lay behind them and said to himself, incredulously, what are we fighting each other *for?* We're working for the same thing and we ought to be working together and he knows it as well as I do. But the moment of grace passed. Clinton looked away, and undercurrents of passion between them warned him that what they were fighting for, besides anything they had allowed to surface, was naked and basic: a subtle, savage struggle for domination over the men whom Krishnan presently led, whom Clinton needed behind him.

He shuffled his papers and began.

True, there were cyclones, but they were infrequent phenomena: only four of cataclysmic consequence in the last century according to data supplied by the state meteorological department. Furthermore, cyclones of whatever intensity tended to coincide with the southwest monsoon, which was a known quantity and provided for. The years of such coincidence were . . .

Mackendrick moaned and felt like putting his head in his hands. Statistics going back over a hundred years were, he knew, in Clinton's possession, between the pages of the thick folder he was holding. He tried to settle himself more comfortably in his creaking canvas chair, knowing that nothing would stop Clinton going through them all if need be: certainly not fatigue.

True, Clinton's level tone went on, they had not foreseen or allowed for any disruption of work stemming from the northwest monsoon. This was because the rains it brought were never torrential: he had the records of three hundred rain-gauge stations to prove it. He would cite them, station by station and year by year, back to the turn of the century. . . .

Mackendrick saw the ripple of unrest that this time curled through the audience, like the cringing of oyster flesh under lemon juice, and he felt a little sorry for them as well as for himself. Poor devils, he thought, blinded by figures which they could never have seen before: it had taken them all their time —his and Clinton's and Rawlings', and the Minister's—absolute top-level time—to pry the information they wanted from the dusty archives of this department and that, each more reticent than the one before.

Labor troubles might be endemic. (Clinton was taking it point by point, Mackendrick thought: it was to be a walkover: no more going over this ground, ever again.) But he was confident Indian pride in this project would overcome such troubles—weren't they? Because if they weren't they should never have associated themselves with it. As for increased rainfall linked to minimum sun-spot activity, he was prepared to back his luck on this. Weren't they? Because if they weren't they should never have come here, for all projects like these, always and everywhere, needed an element of luck to carry them through. He conceded it. Did they or didn't they?

Krishnan listened to the rapid fire of question and statement with growing, sullen respect. The art of getting round men, he thought, and in a way he despised them all, himself too, for having been got round.

As they were, the atmosphere of acquiescence was too pervasive for him to mistake.

Persuaded into discarding their own conclusions, dazzled into acceptance of statistical evaluations not independently theirs, and got round by something else too, that he rightly interpreted as pride mollified by this hard, highly skilled Englishman's open admission that he acknowledged the quirks of chance as they themselves furtively did, dubbing it luck where they might have called it the will of God.

Clinton did not care what they thought; but he wanted their strength behind him, without which he knew he might as well pack his bags. It irked him, this dependence on an untried team plus the onus of working what he privately called an international consortium: but specific clauses in the contract insisted on the employment of Indian technicians, strictly limiting the import of his own. Clinton accepted the conditions, because he had not been able to get them scrapped: having done so he was determined that they should not garrot him. Where he would have overridden his own men, who knew him, here he was prepared to coax into being the trust essential to his purpose.

Of them all, only Bashiam clung to his reservations. He was not like the others, products of technical training colleges that were being urged into being up and down the country. He had been born in these hills, had followed the traditional craft of woodcutting until they began building the hydroelectric station, farther up the river, uprooting his family, indeed his whole village, to do so. Bashiam had gone back out of curiosity, and stayed, spellbound by the workings of the strange powerful turbines. A discerning foreman had given him employment, and in the course of it he had learned about electricity and machines, about building and repairing and dismantling, welding his new learning on to an older, part-inherited knowledge of forest and river and hill-country seasons. It was this older knowledge that inhibited him, prevented him falling in line with the others. They made their plans, seduced by statistics: but he had seen what a cyclone could do, had cowered before the storms that swept down the hills to burst in the valleys, knew what mincemeat a rogue monsoon could make in one night of the most careful design. It was not easy for him to shed his misgivings, although his later training made him acknowledge that despite them planning was essential. . . .

Clinton noted the younger man's silence with a familiar stirring of irritation. Bashiam seemed to him to be riddled with fears, in thrall to the spirits of forest and rain like the hill tribesman he still was at heart. Even the other Indians kept him apart, a stranger in their midst, calling him jungly-wallah as he had taken to doing. Jungly-wallah: a man of the jungle. A primitive just come down off the trees, Englishman and Hindu alike looked down their fine Aryan noses and covertly spurned the aborigine.

Momentarily, that day, Clinton wondered if he should stop and give the man his say, but he flicked the thought aside. No modern project could advance if one had first to allay every tribal anxiety: nor did he feel disposed to exert himself to sway a minority of one.

No one heard him say so; indeed he did not; but listening to the cool voice detailing again each meticulous phase of the construction program Bashiam understood what Clinton had meant him to understand: that there was a place for him and another for Clinton, and that his position was not only far below in the power scale, but that the towering and voracious terms of modern commitment diminished him to insignificance.

5

COMING home to a wife was still new to Clinton, the pleasure it gave him unblunted by countless routine homecomings. He did not look forward to it all day, because while on the work site Helen scarcely ever entered his thoughts, but on his way back, crossing the footbridge over the river and following the newly cut path to the bungalow, anticipation lapped in warm waves over his mind and body.

Helen had no great love for routine either, which was one of many things Clinton found admirable in his wife. She did not wave him off tritely from the doorstep each morning, or welcome him back with a peck each night—attentions over which he had endured vicarious excruciation during the long years of his bachelorhood. Nor did she pretend a solic- itous interest in her husband's work: marrying later than most, her cool gaze trained upon her friends' marriage customs, she made, and humanely suppressed, her own acid little comment on these wifely attitudes. Clinton was aware that she had her own interests and into these, suspecting they would bore him, he did not delve. It followed that he did not know where they lay.

Like his Indian labor, he saw her drift off into what Raw-

lings, steeped in African flavors, insisted on calling the bush.
Once or twice he asked where, though he was not really interested, and equally perfunctorily she told him she had vis-
ited one or other of the settlements strung along the course of
the river. These having struck him, during their quest for a site
for the dam, as enclaves of the most primitive and barbarous
squalor, he was relieved that she spared him any advancement
of his knowledge. He warned her not to drink their polluted
water, reminded her they were in tiger country, and thereafter saw no danger—certainly not in the tribesmen whom
Rawlings cited, his eyes full of his querulous extraordinary
fears. Civilized men were another matter. He had questioned
her, his jealousy suddenly flaring, right at the beginning, and
she had laughed and disposed of his fears. *Darling, no. There
are no men.*

He knew it was the truth: felt in his bones he would know
if ever she lied to him.

Helen got on well with the tribesmen. He had seen groups
of them gathered round her in their compound, or accompany-
ing her if she returned after sunset from her wanderings. But
then, Helen got on well with most people, even the housewives
whose sorties down the hill on club or shopping expeditions
she never joined. Occasionally when he wanted her and she
wasn't there he wished she was more like them, ubiquitous,
conformist and predictable. But qualities tangential to these
were what had first attracted him to her, and he knew that they
were still what held and excited him.

Unpredictable Helen. Clinton smiled as he came in sight of
the bungalow. Sometimes she vanished into the jungle, not
even a note for him on the table. At other times she pelted out
of the house, hugging him tightly in full view of interested
bearer and cook, her eyes dark with the misery and memory
of their many separations. On what she called her randy days
she simply lay in bed and waited for him, peremptorily dis-
missing the servants so that later, ravenous, they had to get up
and cook.

Tonight she was quiet, her manner serious and preoccupied. After registering a mild disappointment, because this was not his mood, Clinton fell in with her silence. They dined on the verandah, exchanging hardly any conversation, while the white-robed Das laid plates before them and took them away, his chocolate-colored face cozily aware of the excellent service he gave, his bare feet noiseless on the smooth stone floor. Clinton was content to wait; if Helen had something serious to discuss —and he was not at all sure that she had, it might be only a mood—he would much rather she postponed it until the coffee came. Indeed, he thought, his mind peeling back to past tedium, one of the most exasperating features of the Delhi talks had been the mad stampede into involved negotiations even before the soup. Not that he cared all that much for his stomach: it was a disciplined organ that would scarcely have dared to rumble while there was work in hand. It was simply that he believed that his work deserved his undivided attention.

His work. The dam. His mind slid into the well-loved groove with a sigh of contentment, fastening upon it with a familiar agreeable energy. Construction was going ahead reasonably well, but there were still rough edges that could do with smoothing off . . . the dumping trucks, for instance, that carried away the debris of daily blasting: either the drivers were bad or the tires were poor, they hung in ribbons by the end of each week. The cranes too, there was room for improvement there: perhaps he could have another sent up, to handle the heavy lifting in addition to the smaller mobile cranes in use. Someone good to handle it too, no use handing over expensive equipment to some Stone Age dweller hustled into the twentieth century. Perhaps, he thought, he could have a man flown out, if their quota was not already full . . . he would have to ask Mackendrick, who carried all that kind of thing in his head.

Das brought coffee, and the fragrance filled the room.

"They grow it here," Helen said, responding to his murmur

of appreciation. "There's a plantation not an hour's walk away, it can't come any fresher."

"I expect they hang on to the best and export the rubbish, that's the real explanation," Clinton said. "Not that I blame them if they do."

"They can't afford to," Helen said coolly, and to Das: "Don't wait. It's late for you already."

Clinton looked at his watch. The hands stood at eight and he thought: Millie Rawlings doesn't let them get away this early, nor Betty Galbraith; but he did not intervene.

The silence deepened when Das had gone; even his soft movements had been sufficient to reduce the sounding depths of the still air. It no longer impinged on Clinton, or perhaps only incidentally, as a prime medium in which to follow up his earlier thinking. The crane, he thought, visualizing its powerful lifting jib. But Helen interrupted.

"I found these," she said, handing him a few broken bits of pottery, "not far from here. In fact I found several pieces in our compound alone. They're all over the place, once you start looking."

"What are they?" He turned them over in his hand. "Are they valuable?"

"No, not valuable. Just a few household things, cooking pots and so on. I wondered how they got here, that was all."

"I expect they broke them up and buried the lot," said Clinton, "rather than cart them away. The locals, I mean . . . some of 'em were camped here before we moved in, I'd quite forgotten that little episode."

"What happened to them?"

"They moved."

"Where to?"

"No idea. Just got up and went, like animals. No moving problems there—I wish to God we traveled as light, we could have done this job in half the time."

Helen said: "But they lived here, didn't they? They didn't ask to move."

"No. We persuaded them."

"Why?"

"Why?" Clinton repeated irritably. "Because they occupied a site we needed."

"Were there no other sites?"

"Not suitable ones. It had to be away from labor quarters and near the river and away from the blasting—a hundred things. Then we found this spot—absolutely ideal from our point of view, except for those huts."

"How many?"

"How many? Do you mean huts?"

"People."

Suddenly the warning exploded in Clinton's mind. Darkly, without illumination, like a black sun: an intimation of danger that he was too experienced to discount. Yet he could not place it or pin it down, and struggling to do so evoked a vast irritation that blanketed his other emotions.

"I don't know how many people," he said with a cold distaste. "I didn't count heads. There was an encampment of sorts and it had to be moved and it was. It doesn't matter, does it?"

"Not now."

"Oh, well."

He sat back, watching the glow of his cigarette in the darkness of the verandah. Unpredictable Helen, he said to himself, trying to smile and, eventually, managing it. Presently he touched her shoulder. "Time for bed," he said. "Coming?"

"Not yet."

"Oh, well," he said again. "I think I'll turn in. It's been a long day."

He had nearly said night, he realized. But the nights had never been long, not when Helen was there. He fell into bed tiredly, sending up a cursory wish to heaven that it wasn't to be the forerunner to others like it before he settled into sleep.

Helen sat on alone in the darkness, turning over in her hands the broken bits of pottery. It had been part of some woman's life once, not very long ago: she had filled it with water and scoured it, cooked in it and fed her family—the earthenware was pebble-smooth from use. Then they had all gone away and the vessels had been broken and left behind. Not one or two: enough for several families, the cooking pots of a whole community.

A whole community that had been persuaded to move.

Persuasion, she thought. It was the brand of this century, as livid upon it as the weeping stigma that other centuries bore.

But little more than an episode, which Howard Clinton had quite forgotten, in the building progress of Clinton Mackendrick and Partners.

Someone else had said episode once—long ago. A deep malaise, a sensation of glare, flaring whiteness and pain, brought it back. A room in a hospital, white uniforms, a white bed, on it her father, dribbling, speechless, his disconnected limbs flapping loosely under the bedclothes . . . and the physician, urbane, aloof, speaking of an episode. . . . Someone more human translating what he said. A stroke, a human being cut down by it; it made sense then. But still, an episode.

Helen Clinton laid down the smashed pot fragments on the table for Das to clear in the morning. Perhaps he would have a little more to tell her, she thought fleetingly . . . but he came from the plains and would only, taking great pride in it, disclaim all knowledge of the hill people. Their domain—were the hills their domain? even they were no longer sure—swept away from the bungalow into the darkness, ridge upon ridge, thickly forested. Its density, the rampant furious growth, affected her in a way that the ordered charm of a restrained civilization would never do. After a little she opened the door, and stepped out into the blackness where the shadows of the first trees fell and deepened the night.

6

AT night when machines and men were silent one heard the river. Like a heartbeat: insistent, unceasing, soft when you took no notice, loud when you listened.

Bashiam always listened. He lay on his creaking camp-bed, deliberately awake for the pleasure of listening to the sound he had heard from the day he was born, unconsciously alert for any change in the steady rhythm; and presently, soothed, he slept.

In a very similar bed, in his quarters in the British section a few hundred yards away, Jackson, handpicked as foreman and labor leader, moved his great bulk on the straining canvas and irritably wished the river would stop. By day he did not hear it at all, saw it only in terms of manipulation or coercion, something to be bent or harnessed to the requirements of machinery. By night the river was stronger. Its soft purl penetrated all his defenses, ear plugs and closed door and ticking clock, and hung in heavy oppressive garlands above him until he cursed again and reached for the tablets that made him dream sweetly of the traffic that roared past his doors all night, at home in England.

Rivers were a part of Lefevre's life. Their surface levels,

that moved and ravished other men, meant little to him. His ravishments dwelt deeper, in the sand, clay, rock, gravel, silt and sediment that formed the riverbed.

Long ago—before the men, the machines, the roads, the buildings, the clutter and clamor, while Clinton and Mackendrick still haggled over the contract, Lefevre had brought his team here to the jungle and set up shop. They had one bungalow and one boat, a sturdy little craft with the strength of a tugboat in which they passed the day, hovering midstream and sending down the heavy hollow drills that dredged up cylindrical sections of the riverbed. At night they analyzed the samples, hunched over burners and stills that occupied most of the bungalow, edging them out first onto the verandah and then into tents pitched in the compound that had still to be cleared of scrub.

Lefevre sighed: not for these primitive beginnings, his training in the great modern laboratories of Europe made him profoundly impatient of less than immaculate standards, but for the brief hegemony he had enjoyed. It was still his, in theory; but the growth of the river project introduced other considerations. Men to convince and placate; specialists from the Ministry with opposing views; laymen to whom riverbeds were of such mysterious density that explanations of the most elaborate and stupefying order had to be drafted.

Somewhere in all this the purity of the work and the thought of those long days was lost. Lefevre sighed for the loss, sitting alone in his bungalow with boxes and jars of labeled sediments to keep him company. Most of his thinking was done here, and it was done most easily at night with the river for background.

Clinton dreamed as he slept, sometimes of Helen and sometimes of the dam, and to both the river was accompanist. He heard it distinctly, the gentle gurgle coming to him magnified through the rustling silence of the jungle night, and his dreaming mind enlarged it further until his ears were filled with the roar and he woke. For a while thereafter he could not settle, but presently, deliberately, he concentrated his mind on his dam and slept. Only to be engulfed at the point of dreaming once more with the roar of the river.

By day their attitudes altered. In the robust, prosaic sunlight they reasserted themselves and saw the river dwindle to its proper proportions, like an animal placed in a cage. It was as if the realities of the wakeful night had been queerly distorted, as though viewed through water.

That morning Clinton hummed to himself as he strode along in the sunshine, wearing a topi that Helen derided; and the plans sang a psalm in his mind.

A year to cut the diversion channel, a year for the coffer dams: the two to run concurrently, making one year in time. Two years for the main dam.

Already the marker flags were in place, at points on the east and west banks of the river where the main dam would span the torrent, with further markers upstream and downstream where the coffer dams would rise to block the river flow. It had been his idea to plant the flags: a visible symbol of his belief in this hazardous enterprise ringed with doubts and pious hopes in other men's minds. Mackendrick saw it as a flamboyant gesture —perhaps of pride—though in fact the flags bore no emblems of empire or state but were fashioned from pieces of straw-colored hessian in which the main stores had been packed. He did not say so, it was a small matter; watched, in silence, the day that the holes were dug and the standards planted, the workers shouting to each other in childlike excitement across the expanse of water as the flags unfurled and fluttered. But Clinton had challenged his silence.

"A bit theatrical?"

"Hardly." Mackendrick spoke dryly. "A few bits of old gunny."

"Stagy, nevertheless."

"I wouldn't say so."

"No. But it's what you think. You're wrong."

"It doesn't matter," said Mackendrick. "It amuses the locals, no harm in that."

"It's not done to amuse them," said Clinton evenly. "It's to make them see. Bring out a blueprint and it means nothing to these people. Mark the spot and they begin to build around it. It's something for them to hold on to, and I want them held otherwise they're going to turn tail at the first sign of trouble."

Mackendrick was surprised: there was in the act a quality of imagination that he had not believed Clinton possessed except for structures other than human. If humans had not perforce been interwoven with the structure, would he still have exercised this quality? Mackendrick pondered, and felt he did not know. Apart from their work they led separate lives, and despite their long association there were facets to Clinton that he could not easily envisage.

Months had gone by since that conversation, since the planting of those charged symbols. In that time virtually the whole aspect of the plateau through which the river forged its way in its passage to the lowlands—the entire eastern sector—had been altered.

It ran deeply here, this river whom two thousand men and ten thousand tons of equipment had so far assembled to tame. On either side the banks rose in a steep incline, lichen-covered slopes whose weathered surfaces belied the intractable nature of the igneous rock layers below. Time, the slow aeons that passed in a flash of the cosmic calendar, had hardened and toughened these layers, fusing them at places into granite walls through which the river cut its way on its own measured, implacable course. Here, in the jagged clefts left by that ancient encounter, the waters eddied and tumbled, churned into foam and spume of a blinding whiteness where they cascaded down. Here, too, before the cataracts and between these granite flanks, rising from the solid rock of the riverbed two hundred feet below through its overlayers of sandstone and gravel, Clinton planned his dam.

He had first to alter the course of the river: block its flow at the upstream coffer dam, and deflect the rising waters into a channel cut in the east bank and curving in a wide arc from the upstream barrage to a point north of the downstream coffer where the river would resume its natural flow. In these still waters, the motionless unnatural lake created between the coffers, the main dam would grow.

Clinton had no difficulty in visualizing the dam; not only it, but every detail of its development from conception to consummation. The lag between the two, the grinding years between design and fulfilment, once the power of decision lay in his hands these seldom fretted him. He had a patient mind: vast reserves of endurance over which he presided with pleasure, aware of the iron underpinning they gave to his strength.

So far there had been no call on these reserves. So far, Clinton repeated to himself, making the slight concession to superstition that was the limit his temperament allowed. But there was a long way to go yet, construction had only reached the preliminary phase of the three-stage operation planned. They were working on the plateau now: splitting it open with dynamite to create the channel into which the river would flow at its full strength, twenty thousand cubic feet per second.

"It's an awful lot of water," said Mackendrick. He had joined Clinton on the promontory overlooking the river.

"It's an awful lot of rock," said Clinton grimly. "Real bastard impacted granite."

"The rate of flow quadruples," Mackendrick said, "when the river's in spate. A freak spate isn't calculable, and freaks aren't entirely off the cards. The river's the real bastard."

Clinton smiled. "Bashiam's been speaking to you," he said.

"No," said Mackendrick.

"Then you've been speaking to him."

"Not that either."

Clinton was about to say, something's making you jumpy, but the sharp rudeness of it dawned on him and he stopped. There was, besides, nothing jumpy about Mackendrick or his

calm, rather cool disclaimers. He said instead: "It's not Krishnan again, is it, spreading his special brand of light gaiety?"

"Not guilty." Mackendrick laughed. "I think you've shut
him up for the time being. No, it's the up-river labor gang.
They've been talking to Helen. She passed it on. Apparently the
river's a devil . . . I suppose they ought to know, they've been
here longer than anyone."

The black sun was burning again; burning him. Elusively,
sliding nimbly beyond the range of his vision when he would
have confronted it. So that he could not put it out, crush it
under his heel and be finished with it as he finished with other
things. He said, irritably, "Do you mean the crowd we cleared
off the bungalow site?"

"I believe they are." Mackendrick was a little surprised by
his reaction. "A good many anyway. They came back looking
for work and we took them on. Glad we did, they're good workers."

"They'd be a damn sight better if they kept their mouths
shut," Clinton said harshly. "These bloody scare stories—many
more of them and we'll have the whole crew panicking, Krishnan, contractors and all."

Mackendrick thought, with a minute sideslipping of his
faith in Clinton which he had never experienced before, and
which he instantly corrected, that it was Clinton who was
panicking, and for the life of him he did not know why. He
said:

"Nobody speaks their lingo: none of the other workers. Except Bashiam, he's one of the tribe, and Krishnan, he's gone to
some pains to learn it, heaven knows why . . . and Helen,
of course. Clever gal, picking up a dialect so quickly. Done it in
months, most people would take years."

I didn't know she had, Clinton nearly said, but again he
stopped himself in time. It would be, it seemed to him, a sleazy
parading of the privacies of marriage: a disloyalty to her for
him to reveal there were areas in her life from which she
shut him out. That these areas existed he had of course always

known, but always heretofore the exclusion had been with his consent. That it could also occur without it was a thought he found unsettling, lodged obtrusively in the forefront of his mind. Cumbrous too, and trailing behind it a queer sense of hurt. Why hadn't she told him, he wondered; and could neither subdue nor understand the jealousy that came in spasms. What *of,* he asked himself in exasperation: of a tribe whose outstanding characteristic in his view was the severe retardation of its civilization? Or of the glib communication she had established with a people who presented to him only the blank opacities of their total incomprehension? But he could not track it down. The maze of introspection was nearly always beyond him, and one that, by choice, he rarely entered.

7

WHAT had grown into a town was also a colony, with an establishment which the colonizers had not deliberately contrived, but which grew from their needs and fears, from tribal memories and anxieties of which they were hardly aware, from a nostalgic harking back to a hierarchy that, more or less, worked at home.

The officers and their wives. The technicians, the subordinate cadre. The men. Each cluster kept to itself, neither seeking nor wishing to enlarge its ambit, but nevertheless drawing together and presenting an indivisible front when faced by a new category, the native labor.

From within the invisible white stockade thus thrown up the new colonists peered at the vast sprawling enigma that they felt India to be. Some, like Clinton, with a total lack of interest; some, like Helen Clinton, with a great, pulsing curiosity and effortless identification; some uneasily, reluctant to advance into territory whose strange codes and values made them as unsure of themselves as pigeons roosting on anti-pigeon jelly; but most of them with rising tides of superiority lined and laced and made heady by fear, a nameless unvoiced fear that to step outside was a hazard whose culmination would be a total, terrifying absorption of identity in an unknown ocean.

Mackendrick, with that odd quirk of vision that enabled him to look at two worlds, might have acknowledged the fear. To Rawlings, Henderson, Galbraith, Todd—and Clinton when he troubled to think about it—nothing so complex existed. Their cohesion, they chose to believe, was a straightforward matter of sharing the same background and speaking the same language and consequently finding each other's company, relatively speaking, congenial.

Jackson, penned in the men's canteen, put it more succinctly. "We like keeping ourselves to ourselves," he said. Even Lefevre, born in an era that looked sardonically on empires, totally unschooled in prejudice, found it easier to retreat within the charmed circle. He had made, in the beginning, overtures of friendship; but his choice had been unfortunate, alighting on Krishnan who, unlike most of the other Indians, had lived through and been soured by imperial insolence. Krishnan, mistaking friendliness for condescension, had snapped at him, treating him to a lecture on the wind of change that was blowing across the continents, making all men equal.

Poor Lefevre, who made no distinctions and needed no corrective drafts, retreated; and another little prevaricatory pennant fluttered up to proclaim the impossibility of decent relations between the races.

In Millie Rawlings' mind whole strings of similar pennants were already in position; their flapping made it difficult for her to envisage any kind of relationship, apart from overseer and serf, between colonists and natives. Prewar Africa had molded her, and her African light adventures, turned overnight by Mau Mau into a grim and bloody business, had rendered the model cast-iron. In a way her clear-cut attitude was the easiest to sustain. With no leeway either side there were no strains imposed. She was spared the bewilderment of Lefevre, the conscientious embarrassments of Mackendrick, the self-assertive exertions which Jackson in his off-moments confessed exhausted him. Phrases that hardly anyone else would have used, except perhaps in their own enclave, rolled off her tongue in a mixed environment in generous measure. "He works like a nigger," she would say, in fond pride of her husband which never manifested when they were alone; or, categorically, oblivious of human emotions, "Never trust the blacks. That's my motto, and I stick to it."

Mackendrick called her an extreme case, but his wide tolerance easily accommodated Millie.

Helen Clinton liked her too, although she offended against her every canon and instinct; but not to the extent of keeping her company. Perversely, Millie Rawlings sought her out; she did not lack for company, the other wives were happy enough to join the activities she organized, but there was something about the cool poised Helen—whom she could not accuse of unfriendliness, yet from whom she felt herself held at arm's length—that created its own attraction.

"She's got class," she said to Clinton one day, oblivious of Helen who sat near. "You can tell, can't you."

Clinton grunted; he did not like public discussions about class, or about his wife; and besides his relations with Millie were reaching the point where he reacted against almost anything she said. Helen's reactions were saner. It was not Millie against whom she recoiled, it was the kind of activity she proposed to embroil them in. Coffee parties. Shooting. Jaunts to the nearest town that possessed a civilized club that possessed a dance band, a bar and imported one-armed bandits. Shopping in the big city emporiums where smooth Indian shopkeepers, who knew how to treat vintage memsahibs, flattered and mulcted her shamelessly, their suave faces showing nothing of the contempt they felt. To Helen, a detached and interested observer, it was a strange pursuit, an extraordinary and endless preoccupation with trivia. To Millie it was the only answer to living in the tropics: a constant and feverish activity to prevent them all being engulfed in the creeping tide of Eastern inertia. The fact that the working of the dam site, with its enormous demands upon laboring men and machines, had already routed inertia of whatever origin, in no way modified her thinking.

"We're behind them here, you see," she explained to Helen. "We drive 'em along . . . well, supply the drive, if you prefer . . . but they'd soon slide if we let them, believe me. I know you'd hardly believe it, but then you are new to the East, dear, aren't you. Now if you take my advice—"

Millie's advices seemed to Helen redolent of the suburbs: stiff little fences erected by silly old women afraid of the rape of their minds. If she refrained from saying so it was only because she did not think Millie would understand—not from any consideration for her feelings. There was a ruthlessness in her which matched Clinton's—which he recognized and saluted in her—which Millie had not yet grasped. Perhaps it was because Helen was too lazy to exercise it often; perhaps the good humor with which she was rejected deceived Millie. She often felt balked, but believed it was merely a question of chipping away at Helen, at a childish obstinacy that had no real foundation: whereas in fact it involved the altering of a whole carefully chiseled-out, scrupulously evolved evaluation of living.

"Care to come down to Sandie's with us?"

Sandie's was a guest house upgraded to a hotel, fourteen hours' drive down the hill, full of the new technical people— Germans, Swedes, Dutch. Helen shook her head: "I'd love to, some other time."

"They're throwing a party. Lots of booze, a dickie bird told me . . . are you sure you can't come?"

"I'm afraid so, yes."

"Got something better on?"

"Something else, yes." Helen smiled; Millie's heavy sarcasms amused her, her harping disenchantment with what she called their damn camp living which she dodged as often as possible, racing pell-mell down the hill to Sandie's or Joe's or the Gymkhana Club in her escape bids, which, she knew, the season would soon foil.

As the weeks went by and the rejections mounted, Millie's tone grew sharper.

"You haven't really got anything else on, have you?"

"I have, really."

Millie's hands tightened on the wheel of the jeep she had driven up to the bungalow.

"What?" she asked.

"I'm going out."

"Where?"

"That's my business" was too easy; besides Helen, like Mackendrick, knew how quickly rancors could build up in an unnaturally constricted community, wanted no part of it. She said: "To one of the villages. I find them—interesting."

"Do you? Beats me what you can see in them."

"Each man to his taste."

"Seems so odd."

"Depends on how you look at it."

"You're not," Millie paused, so that she could rivet Helen's wandering attention, and looked her straight in the eye, "you're not going native, dear, are you?"

Helen sighed; she leaned against the jeep, and felt its hot metal side, and wondered if she could have heard correctly.

"I'm not," she said at last, "but it's not from lack of trying."

It was not even a bad joke: it was something one did not joke about at all. Millie's face tightened, accentuating the erosions of late middle age which the morning sunlight had already exposed. She let out the clutch fiercely, and the trim little jeep bounced away in a swirling funnel of dust.

Afterward, not immediately, stray tendrils of guilt ruffled the equanimity with which Helen contemplated her morning. She could perhaps, she thought, have watched her tongue: matching her tactlessness to Millie's brand was an exercise in the unspeakable. But she had not meant to wound: a surface scratch, intended to stop at that, had gone under the skin. Perhaps the skin was too thin. They were all, she thought, a little like that: thin-skinned, or getting that way. As if something in the country was acting on them like sex or an allergy, sensitizing them, honing their sensibilities to needle-point, quivering awareness.

From the bungalow came a faint tinkling. Das, with his penchant for time-keeping initiated by some long-departed memsahib, was gently percussing a teacup with a teaspoon. He would have preferred a gong, she knew: one of those Benares brass things from which he could have coaxed shimmering sounds. He had told her so, deprecatingly, commiserating with her on the hardships of camp life that deprived her of gongs and other memsahib essentials. He himself lived in a godown, a tin-can structure that filled with smoke and threw him out whenever he cooked his rice. Now he cooked only on alternate days, keeping his rice in a covered bowl on the lowest shelf in her refrigerator whence it emerged in a cold glistening slab, but eatable. Das, Helen thought, she would never get inside *his* skin, never more than hazard a guess as to what went on in the mind behind his polite chocolate face. Howard, she knew, understood him perfectly. They spoke the same language, even if it sometimes had to be pidgin. It was his native laborers that Howard found both dense and impenetrable, which Helen by climbing into his shoes could understand, although it was an exercise of which she grew increasingly impatient.

The tinkling sounded again. Five minutes past eleven. Five minutes past coffee time. She did not feel like having coffee but she went in. Das liked her to drink coffee. He hovered over her attentively while she drank, as he hovered over every other meal, his polished face bestowing accolades on her that she did not merit, for she was little attuned to his correct ordering of days and lives. In his rigid attitudes he seemed to her like Millie. A dark-brown Millie, she thought, and was consumed by silent ribald laughter.

8

HELEN'S initial excursion to the up-river village had been alone. This was partly intentional, for she liked keeping her first impressions uncluttered, her visual images free of tags like interesting or charming that the formulae of conversational exchange might have slung round their necks. Partly it was involuntary, because there was no one in her circle who wanted to accompany her, and, in the beginning, no one with whom she could communicate outside it. But there was this path, which led over the brow of a hill to a shallow dip in the land beyond, an inhospitable rock-strewn basin within sound of the river, and because it was there she took it.

It was a rough track, more the result, she thought, of feet wearing down forest than any deliberate effort at road-making. At the end of it was a clearing with a huddle of flimsy huts in the middle and around them a stockade which a dog of the lowest caliber could have leaped. There were several of these, thin animals with dusty yellow hides that yapped hysterically and slunk away as she approached, as well as chickens, pigs and children. Brown, potbellied, they surged on her from all sides, their shining faces clearly expressing gratitude for any break in their ordinary day, even the timid thumb-sucking ones turning out in their anxiety to miss none of the fray. Helen liked children; she smiled at them amiably, leaning against the perilous bamboo palisade while she waited for her day to develop.

Very soon dogs, hens and children were cuffed aside by inquiring adults, men and women almost as naked as the children who stared at her in vivid surprise, slaking their curiosity without a vestige of embarrassment until from somewhere a well-submerged sense of hospitality surfaced, and then with a good deal of chattering goodwill they ushered her in.

Helen went back—by invitation, slaking her curiosity as uninhibitedly as she knew how, learning from them as she went and discovering natural springs of intercourse that for the time being satisfied her as much as it did them. Delighted her too, opened up new acceptances, filled a want that was in her, quiescent but ready to flare. Something in England had starved her. Its muted tones perhaps, or the softened edges of its living which she registered with the same cool detachment as she did Millie's foibles, measuring with a steady eye the point where it slopped over into slackness and indifference. Suddenly, here, there was color and confusion, and outflowing warmth to which she responded, matching the flamboyance on offer with a deep quiet pleasure which the tribesmen, after initial agony and heart-searching, correctly interpreted as the most extrovert display open to an Englishwoman.

There were other settlements too, to which over the months word spread, where she found herself welcomed; but they were too distant for regular visiting, and her first incursion became her stamping ground. She played with the children, rubbed flea powder into the dogs' yellow coats, watched the crops grow, watched men and women at work, sated herself with watching, and most of all she marveled that such full and rounded-out living could go on, on so feeble and flimsy a footing. The fragile huts that a man and a boy could put up in a day or a determined wind demolish in less: the primitive patches of surface-root crops of a community with one harvest in

mind, rather than the recurrent cycle of growth: the hap-
hazard clearing, overshadowed by encroaching forest: on these
impermanent, flyaway foundations, whole people built whole
lives.

Early on, when they were all new to the environment and
new to each other, and relationships had not yet shaken down
into any kind of pattern, she had remarked on the paradox to
Krishnan, the harsh-faced engineer who dominated his group,
to whom questions in any Indian context were as if by natural
choice directed. Krishnan knew of the existence of the tribal
settlements, but had never ventured into one, knew the oddity
he would have been in the tribesmen's eyes if he had. He
even despised Helen for thinking that he, as educated, more
civilized than she was, could be familiar with any aspect of the
half-savage hill people's lives. Nevertheless he said, grimly,
closing the Indian ranks as decisively as Jackson or Millie, "Of
course they seem flyaway to you, you are used to better things.
Unfortunately our people are not. They've become used to
being done out of their rights."

Helen fell silent. She caught the rebuff intended, but its
source puzzled her, the barbed reaction to an ordinary remark.
She could not trace it back, as perhaps Mackendrick might have
done, to its sour origins in past and present, from the noxious
emotional caldron that Britain the ruler and India the ruled
had kept on the boil throughout the term of an imposed over-
lordship, to the humiliations of being an underdeveloped and
pauper nation. History, for her, still lay largely between the
covers of a book: intellectually assimilated, but dissociate
from impassioned human reality. It was only now, lodging on
Indian soil, that the first intimation came that between them
Howard Clinton and Krishnan, and Bashiam, Rawlings, and
Mackendrick as well, were illuminating the pages.

But if Krishnan was forbidding, there were others who were
not. The camp was, after all, full of Indians: most of them well
disposed, most of them inclined to be friendly. Shanmugham,
for instance, Krishnan's voluble young assistant, who fell over

himself to be helpful, whose affability waned and grew nervous
only when Krishnan loomed near; or Gopal Rao, the trainee
blossoming under Lefevre's wing, who cheerfully referred to
himself as the mud inspector; or Ranganathan, whom his foes
called the cement mixer—much to his annoyance, for as an
executive of Asoka Cement he was well past these raw stages.
But all of them came from the South Indian plains. Helen
wanted someone local, someone whose breath and bones had
been formed in these hills—not for introduction and entree,
which she could manage quite well by herself, but for interpretation. So she cast around, and eventually found what she
wanted virtually on her doorstep in the person of Bashiam.

Bashiam, the hill man whom they called jungly-wallah, or
even more disparagingly the *civilized* jungly-wallah. He became her link man, providing the information she sought of a
country and a people who intrigued her, whetting a curiosity
with which she had always been liberally endowed. The curiosity grew with each encounter: no longer satisfied with watching, but wanting to know: entry achieved, now seeking per-
formance.

He helped to quench her wanting to know, and she gave him
generous credit. He firmly declined it.

"One learns if one wishes to learn," he said, "about people or
machines."

"One gets by," she rejoined, "but it's harder work and it
takes longer."

It would in fact have taken much longer, for the language
alone presented formidable difficulties, different in rhythm
and structure from any she knew. Here, too, she would have
got by, but sign language and a smattering of a few words that
she might have achieved—the thundering hodge-podge of *jaos*
and *jaldis* with which Rawlings and Mackendrick bewildered
their South Indian labor—would have fallen short of her standard, the minimum fluency without which, in her view, communication degenerated into grinning goodwill and one-syllabled

monotony—a degeneration which, also in her view, had begun to set in.

"Sometimes we just gape at each other," she said to Bashiam. "It's a shame really, there's so much one could talk about."

Bashiam privately doubted it, but he withheld his view. If she found interest in a village, for whose standards and acceptances he had little left but a near contempt, who was he to dispute her curious predilection?

So he went with her, in his off-time which was limited and which he would have preferred to spend on site with the machines that Clinton Mackendrick had assembled like a panzer army. In his own secretive way he doted on them as passionately as Clinton. The skilled precision that man had imparted to metal, the extreme functional beauty of each working part, the powerful action of steel tongue in oiled groove, of whirring flywheel and cog, all these soothed and satisfied his own brand of wanting, the void each man creates in himself and spends his time filling, cramming his industry like a sop in the face of the life that has come to him with such terrifying unknowingness of jail and intention.

"You almost love your machines," Helen said to him.

"I believe I do," he answered.

"It seems a little—curious."

"Why?"

Helen felt herself flush; it was not an easy question to answer except brutally, and she felt no particular itch at this moment to exercise brutality. It was simply that one expected people like Bashiam—a backward people—to be content with natural things like hills and woods and a water pump or two, and this expectation made any further desire on their part smack of effrontery. Perhaps they contributed, with their humble acceptances; perhaps they were easily contented; but sometimes their loves and wants extended beyond and why not, she thought: they were creatures of the nuclear age however much it had bypassed them. It was ludicrous not to acknowledge it, to delude oneself that no one among them hankered for the offerings of the age to which they belonged.

"I forgot," she said, "when the world goes round we all go round with it. There is no reason why you shouldn't like cars and cranes as much as my husband does. Or anyone."

Later he took her up, and was as honest as she had been.

"Machines are to me what they are to your husband," he said to her, "only more. They have given me another way of life."

"A better one?"

He nodded at once. He had no doubts. The old way of life held nothing for him. The paradox that intrigued her, the pathetic granules around which whole lives were built, the ramshackle fly-by-night structure of the settlement that excited Helen's pity and Clinton's scorn—as Bashiam well knew there were valid explanations for these, but they did not dispel the horror that dwelling on them infused in his mind.

"And yet it must have been peaceful," she said, and the evocative phrase drew from her mocking mind a view of the Thames at Marlow—was that what she meant by peaceful, and could that orderly scene have any relevance here? "It must have been quiet," she amended, "before we came, before the blasting began."

"It was," he agreed. "Naturally."

"More tranquil," she pursued, crushing the mocking minions her mind so liberally conjured up.

"It was," he said, "in patches."

But he could not really remember. The mainstream of memory was clogged with sharper happenings, with storm and rain, the long drought, a periodically overflowing river and precipitate flight from it. Confusion and disaster, he thought with wormwood in his mouth, the distaste for such things he had learned from his masters, the men who built and controlled; and despite the long ribbon of time that stretched between he shivered, remembering the sodden huts, the cold, the uncertainty, the comfortless ritual of departure, the incantations of a bewildered clan to an immune god. And she thought with vicarious horror only of his present life, the peripatetic shuttling from site to site, the strange rootless life of a man who trailed after these grunting mechanical marvels up and down India, and of the times when there were no machines to man, only bleak returns and spells of waiting in these hills to which he had become an outsider. Hill or plains, forever an outsider.

Bashiam seldom paused to analyze his situation. He knew he no longer belonged in the tribal huts of his birth, but his brief returns to them he did not find too irksome. Equally there was no sense of belonging to what they called the jiffy towns, the tin and canvas camps the contractors rigged up at breakneck pace for their labor, but he did not look for it. No one did, none of the workers. They left their families behind to answer the call of the wealthy building and contracting firms that took on men in tens of thousands, and when the work was over they returned to their roots, razing to the ground the temporary structures they had helped to build in a jiffy at boom time.

Bashiam's roots were attenuated: his homecomings were uneasy surface affairs, but not being given to dwelling on lacks and losses he made do. And in the camps while the work lasted it was good. What it was he could not easily say. A feeling. A richness. Somewhere in the midst of the rubble and the chaos around them, on a definite day they could look back on, though none could tell when it would come, a fusion took place. From then on there was a one-ness, and once it happened problems and hardships were never as destructive as before.

Bashiam explained it to Helen, stumbling over the words. If it had been a man he would have described it in sexual terms and found no difficulty; as it was he shied away from such verbal intimacy, finding it impossible with a woman. Helen listened, hearing the echoes of another conversation: Howard, covering the same ground, describing it not to her but someone else, an overheard conversation. "You work up a team spirit," he said in the clipped language of his upbringing, "if you can, and if you can't it's bloody hell."

Team spirit. A feeling, a richness. Helen understood what both men had said, but it seemed to her that Bashiam's nebulous words came closer to the heart of the matter. They frequently did, she had begun to discover. Perhaps it was by contrast: by contrast her husband's idiom, which was after all her own, seemed framed by caste and convention to move only at skin level.

It took some time—several weeks—before Helen discovered that the up-river tribesmen were precisely those whom the Mackendrick bungalows had ousted from their land. No one exactly told her. They examined the pottery bits she dug up in her compound with interest, skating skilfully round the questions she put, until suspicion seeped in and presently it was all there, the whole knowledge of a nefarious transaction.

Bashiam had proved as reticent as any. His ability to reach the heart of the matter, she further discovered, did not always coincide with a desire to unveil it. One day she said to him, "Do you know what they call you behind your back?"

"Jungly-wallah," he said at once without hesitation.

"Do you know what it means?"

"A man of the jungle. An uncivilized man."

"What it really means," she said cruelly, "is someone who doesn't count. Someone who gets kicked around and doesn't do anything to stop it."

He was puzzled by her vehemence, saw no reason for it. He said slowly. "Do you mean me?"

Her anger began to scale up, crossed and compounded by a sense of shame. She controlled it and said, quietly,

"There used to be a village where the bungalows are . . . where our bungalow is. A tribal village."

"A small settlement, yes."

"When they were told to go, they went."

"Yes."

"Without protest. Just got up and walked away, like animals."

"I suppose you could put it like that."

His calm unnerved her. Was her own passionate reaction the right one, she wondered, perhaps for these people it wasn't? These people, *these people*. It jarred her, the ominous, monotonously familiar phrase. So it's getting me too, that old indestructible India bug, she thought with an icy dismay. But these people aren't different clay, they're like me, like people like me. What is for me, is for them, there's no other kind of yardstick that's worth anything. She said, half asking him to be on her side: "You were—you are—a member of that tribe. It was their land. They didn't want to leave it, they were persuaded. Why did they allow themselves to be? Why did you? Without even protesting?"

It was past history, it did not rouse Bashiam. He said: "When one is building a dam—"

"It wasn't a dam they were building. It was bungalows with a view."

But he wasn't with her. There had been too many moves, under different pressures, divine, man-made, and natural, for him or his tribe to wear themselves out with protesting. Apart from which he had been too long with men who were molded like Clinton, he could no longer accord human beings the status he gave to their creations. Prudent men make way for machines, he thought, and it struck him as a wise adage for the century they were living in. He did not tell her so, however. He had learned not to argue, like most of his clan; and consideration for Helen, moreover, made him disinclined to pursue the matter.

9

THE morning shift came on at eight. By then the mechanical workshops and maintenance sheds had been operating for two hours, overhauling and servicing equipment for the first shift. The second shift worked from two in the afternoon until eight in the evening, under artificial lamps if the light failed early. The workshops functioned throughout the night, when necessary; otherwise they finished with the first shift.

The schedule was going well, Clinton thought, pleasure murmuring in his veins. It was a physical feeling, a sensation of humming along, when men and machines swung into line. None of those infuriating delays, now, that had dogged their early days, labor gangs waiting upon maintenance men, and maintenance for spares, and expensive equipment laid up for want of trained men to repair and operate them. They could handle most of the repairs on site now, even the major ones; had refitted and expanded to be able to do so. The maintenance sheds alone spanned an acre of ground, extending from construction site to Clinton's Lines and eating into jungle on the west bank well beyond the original area of clearance.

Rawlings dealt with the other problem, running what he called on-the-spot crash courses for what he called underdone

Bengali babus. Into these classes the babus were crammed, whence they emerged smoldering and resentful, but turned out to a pattern of efficiency that satisfied Rawlings.

"These classical engineers," he sneered to Mackendrick, "think they can play it by book. By textbook. What in hell use is that do they think in a place like this?"

What he wanted was versatility: men who could strip down a gearbox, retemper a drillhead, dismantle and reassemble a machine, turn their hand to anything; and this kaleidoscopic skill was not in the beginning available, or only in limited quantity.

Mackendrick was sympathetic, but not openly so. He did not want to encourage Rawlings to further denigratory sarcasms, fearing a wholesale defection of technicians for whom he, and Clinton, were responsible, and for whom he alone would have to find replacements. He merely said, "I wouldn't call them Bengali babus. They're not from Bengal anyway, and the babus are clerks down at base."

Rawlings thought Mackendrick was soft, where Indians were concerned; but he did not say so either. Mackendrick guessed; it made him wonder whether he was, because he did not care to see Rawlings exercising his wit on them, and the raw eager young men still wet from their technical schools, withering and stiffening before him.

The system worked, the physical side of it. What happened at the border where flesh became spirit Mackendrick did not know and Rawlings would have been astonished to think that anything might. Clinton, watching the end product with narrow vigilance, was satisfied: the validity of intensive systems lay in their results, he scrapped or retained them wholly by such palpable criteria. Krishnan also felt satisfaction. He had no need of a crash course, he was part of the nucleus of trained and experienced men as skilled as Rawlings could call for. He watched those who were not go in, saw how they looked when they came out, applauded their new skills, noted the inward hardening with private appeasements. Like Rawlings he had no patience for amiable weaklings, and the wide arc of his vision swinging beyond the encompassing hills saw no place for them in the power game that the world was playing. Strength: one spoke only from strength. The West understood no other language. The sensibilities that handicapped other races, the finer modulations of thought and behavior, all had been ground away, leaving only a superb act of public relationship to fill the void with the belief that such qualities abounded. Well, thought Krishnan, there was no game under the sun that two could not learn to play. He brooded, his dark unlined face like a carved god's, while his subtle Brahminical mind delicately picked up and dissected the Western techniques of seduction, persuasion and coercion. It was the new guiding trinity, as piety, gunboats and the way of Christ had been the old.

Clinton, insulated by his skills, had little interest in power games and power politics. They existed, he knew. No single contract, outside or internal, had ever been signed without their hidden or open intrusion. It filled him with loathing—a bitter loathing that went far beyond a subcutaneous irritation into acute mental spheres. It was as if something glutinous and evil by touch and intention were laid upon his structures, tainting their fundamental purity.

No one, not even Mackendrick, who did the negotiating, was more profoundly thankful than he when that side of it was over. Looking back from the calm of construction Clinton felt he had come close to suffocation, those months in Delhi and London. Hell, he thought, sheer and flaming. What it was now by contrast he could not easily have said, heaven being an abstraction of peculiar embarrassment that he tried to avoid; but there had been a time, working on a hellish site east of Suez, when they had had nothing but Evian and Scotch. When they tasted water again, it had been pure and cold and sweet, like something they had never drunk before. A taste of that nectar returned to him as he stood with Mackendrick on the hill overlooking the shattered valley.

It was nearing noon. In the phased rhythms of the day the bore-holes had been drilled and explosive charges laid. The valley lay empty now, the jagged cavities torn in its rocky flanks exposed, open to the sun and deserted except for a handful of men checking the fuses. Presently they too were done, the six ants that were men scurrying up the escarpment to safety. A great silence began, suspending itself like a gong over valley and hill until absurdly dissipated by a shrill piping of whistles.

"Ten minutes to go," said Clinton, shading his eyes against the heavy glare. The sun was almost directly overhead, he could feel the heat on his shoulders, penetrating the thin aertex shirt he wore. In the distance, along the granite ridges, red flags flickered like warning tongues.

"Five minutes," he said, and as he spoke the sirens began, the rise and fall reverberating across the valley.

"If anyone's still there," Mackendrick shouted above the booming backwash of sound and echo, "he must be bent on suicide!"

Clinton hardly heard. He waited, absorbed, his heartbeat accelerated, as the minutes ticked by.

The first explosion came with a great roar, singly, followed by the others in twos and threes, impacted blasts that rocked the ground on which they stood. Automatically, as one might a striking clock, Mackendrick began to count. Eleven . . . fourteen . . . sixteen . . . twenty. Twenty explosions, close on twenty-five tons of dynamite splitting open the valley in symmetrical calculated pattern. As the dust clouds rose Clinton looked down at his watch. It was exactly noon.

"Going like clockwork," Mackendrick said.

"Yes." Clinton felt his heart cycle resuming its normal rhythms. He stretched, relaxation like bland unguents within him, reviving rich memories and the need for speech.

Mackendrick noted Clinton's reminiscent smile, and from the debris of his own disastrous day tartly prepared to listen.

"That rat hole," Clinton said, "off Djibouti. The day the

water came. Christ, the taste, it almost made you believe in God."

"I remember the rats best," said Mackendrick. "Desert rats. I never believed in them until I saw." He stopped: it was like a mechanical joke: some jackass of a robot speaking, the real man listening to peculiar metallic accents.

"Spiny backs," Clinton said, "like small wild boar. Out with it, Mack."

They had worked together too long, Mackendrick thought: each with a private nucleus the other could not pierce, yet above it extensive, sensitive fields of communication and interpretation. He said: "Pilfering's got serious. Every third drum in the reserve store is half empty. Jackson reported this morning."

"Who was it?"

"Jackson didn't know."

"He wouldn't. He's too wrapped up in Smith."

Mackendrick frowned. "Well anyway he didn't cover up for him this time," he said. "Smith hasn't been affluent in weeks, which means he hasn't been flogging anything in town. Jackson must have brought the chopper down hard."

"Jackson's a good man," Clinton said dispassionately. "One can forgive him his Smith."

"One can forgive a man anything in this climate."

Clinton's persuasions were less ductile, but he did not choose to go into it, suspecting the distances that separated them. "If Jackson doesn't know," he said, "Krishnan probably does. Biggest born snooper this side of the Atlantic."

"He thinks it's the coolies. But he hasn't any proof."

"What do you think?"

"I haven't any proof either. I wouldn't care to name names without."

"I wouldn't worry too much if I were you," Clinton said, "about that. Dock their pay. It's astonishing how often the loss of a week's pay produces the culprit." He paused: "Or if you're squeamish, I'll give the orders."

Mass fines, mass punishment. For Mackendrick, twenty-five years later, over this slight matter, they still carried the charnel-house odor. He said: "I'm not being squeamish. These days one has to think of the unions."

"Their writ doesn't run here," Clinton said comfortably, "in practice. We could sack the entire coolie labor force overnight and have a queue a mile long by morning if we wanted and they know it. Organized casual labor—it's almost a contradiction in terms."

"It has been done."

"Not by these people. Not in a hundred years."

In a hundred years, Mackendrick thought. In a generation, less, they've been sprung from Stone Age into Space Age. Why not? Nine months takes anyone from coelacanth to human being. He only said, "It'll hardly be worth the rumpus. Dock their pay and you'll have them wrapping themselves round your feet." He grimaced in distaste. "You know what these people are, live from hand to mouth."

"Not on what we pay them. They're affluent, by their standards."

"There's the government, as well."

"They're on our side. They want this thing finished on time. And one's got to stop the rot somewhere."

"I suppose so, yes."

Both men were silent, each clamped to his own view. He's right, Mackendrick thought. Clinton was nearly always right, it was just that he seemed to miss out somewhere on the human level. And Clinton wondered what there was in the Indian air that could induce disharmony even between such close associates as they were.

In the valley below the machines were screaming again. The silence that had preceded the blasting was gone: it only fell once by day in the valley, and would not return until nightfall. Now the excavators coughed and grunted, biting into granite torn loose by dynamite. South of the main excavation area, where the riverbed would lie, drills and shovels worked with precision, chiseling away rock in the natural cleft to take the gates that would control the flow of the river. On the rugged incline of the improvised escarpment leading to and away from the site the dump trucks were assembled; at two-minute intervals they rumbled down the slope, paused beside the diggers, took on their granite loads and lumbered away, their heavy engines laboring. Five tons, every two minutes, carved from riverbank to create the channel into which the river would run, and tipped into the river along the line of on-shore markers and floating buoys where the rock-fill coffer dams, still under water, were rising.

"At the rate we're going," Clinton spoke with a quiet elation, "we ought to finish smack on schedule."

"I was going to tell you," Mackendrick said, with a spasm of regret that he had allowed the more important matter to marinade until now. "Part of that last shipment has gone astray, the part that was coming up by rail. Somewhere between Bombay and us, that's the nearest I can get out of them."

"Including the Avery-Kent?" asked Clinton, naturally.

"I'm not sure," said Mackendrick with an equal lack of emotion. "I've been on the phone half the morning trying to find out."

10

ONCE a month on Saturdays Millie Rawlings gave a party at her bungalow. It began at sundown and finished when the drink ran out, which was usually fairly early in the evening.

"Just when the fun's beginning," Millie would say, pouting, lugubrious, manner belying her age, the drag and dissatisfactions of her colonial years pulling down the corners of her mouth. Or, her face suddenly naked in its wanting, "They won't even let you get drunk in this bloody country. Damn them. *Damn* them." Inveighing against them, the veins in her neck thick and gobbling, for she felt about it passionately.

Clinton could have helped if he had cared to. He knew he had only to ask, and he knew when Indians said this one thing they actually meant it, especially the upper, older echelons, who would put themselves out endlessly to meet the wishes of guests on their soil, suffocating their consciences if necessary to do so. But he did not care to ask, he wanted nothing by favor, only what was due as a right. Moreover in his view the liquor quota was adequate, and it prevented the evening degenerating into what he detested, a mawkish all-night session like a planter's sabbath.

Millie, after several attempts to enlist his aid, gave up what she dimly sensed was an unequal struggle. Howard Clinton, she said, extracting a few bedraggled shreds of victory out of her rout, is as straight as a die, they don't come like him in this lousy place, and as a final compliment (in a mixed gathering, half a dozen Indians and as many embarrassed Britons), "He's white through and through," she said, ignoring the contempt which nowadays Indians showed if they felt like it, her mind hauling indignantly back to a time when hurt, insult, insolence, all had had to be contained under closed countenances, and pale faces no longer knew nor wanted to know what dark faces were thinking. That was how it ought to be, thought Millie, forgetting that in the end it had been surprise, surprise, all over the world one ludicrous awakening after another until finally no one wore veils any more. You could see, or you could prefer not to see, unless you were blinded by habit. Millie was not altogether blind; when she did sometimes see, as now, it made her stiffen against—what? She did not really know, but she raised her chin a little, as they had all learned to do when the sun went down in Africa, and the contours of her face grew hard.

That Saturday Clinton forgot about Millie's party. His mind was on his equipment, a fair slab of which was apparently adorning some siding near Bombay, and particularly on the Avery-Kent, the crane that had been ordered and specially modified to meet the specific requirements of the valley project. Some little clerk, more likely an army of them, had bungled the affair, and now, he thought with a growing irritation, it was Saturday, they would all have gone away, glad of the excuse the weekend provided to do nothing. Bloody country, he thought, forgetting other frustrations, elsewhere, in England too, for which like pain there was no total recall.

Helen had forgotten too, but Millie who guessed she would had sent a card to remind her. It was propped up conspicuously on the table, a pasteboard card with balloons that Millie had painted on it and a line in her childish hand intended to be gay and enticing: "We girls are at a premium. So come on, girls, let's join the boys and have some fun!" Helen was not enticed, but it moved her, the faint leer under the bold words with its hint of a suggestion of orgies in the offing which did not square with the truth. The truth lay elsewhere, in the fervid imagings of bored women, in the guilty huddle in the shadow of a verandah, or a hasty impromptu or two in the back seat of a car. Millie would not see it that way, but then, Helen thought, why should she? Life would be untenable, but for the gilt one assiduously laid on, each of them scraping a different pot. She turned the card over, noticing only then the urgent little P.S. "I've borrowed Das," Millie wrote. "You not being there I couldn't ask you of course, but was sure you wouldn't mind. Many thanks for loan."

In the valley sirens were blaring, modern muezzins announcing the end of the working day. The distant humming slackened, like a run-down dynamo. After the daily pounding, blasting and drilling the air seemed strangely still, the tremors that traveled up from the valley and were felt even here, finally subsided. In the mounting silence the purl of the river grew stronger. Helen listened equably, undistracted by the incompetent ferment of the cook in the kitchen. Then gravel crunched under Clinton's heavy step and he came in blinking from the darkness outside.

"All alone, Lennie?"

When something went wrong, or he was tired, he called her by the old pet name that dated from their first meetings. She warmed to him, returned his kiss warmly.

"All alone, darling. Except for cook."

"Can't stand the man. Where's Das, Das!" he shouted. There was a timid scurrying in the region of the kitchen, but no reply.

"Millie's borrowed him," Helen said.

"What for?"

"The party."

"What party?"

"Millie's."

"My God," he said, "do we have to go?"

"Only if you want."

Clinton never wanted. Why then, he asked himself, did he go? He would have preferred to sit in the darkness of his verandah, worrying at some problem in peace until the kernel of the trouble lay exposed in his triumphant palm. Or to lie in bed with Helen, who seemed to recede from him a little farther each day. To take possession of her, to know her, know this woman who was his wife carnally, spiritually, wholly, as he felt he did only by night when they lay together and loved.

And he went in to her, and he knew her.

It had been a flat, slightly abstruse statement once. It had acquired depth and clarity since, especially in those bleak moments when he reached out and encountered sometimes a stranger, worse still a casual ghost.

"Do you, darling?" Helen's eyes had darkened. In response to his mood? He could not tell.

"I suppose so," he said. "I suppose we ought to show the flag."

"What flag?"

"Heaven knows. I'm quoting Millie."

But he did know, though the knowledge was amorphous, a feeling that in a foreign land it was essential to consolidate one's position by getting together exercises such as these. Or was it, he wondered suddenly, in fact, basically, a demonstration, banners and a banging of drums to impress a hostile army? Yet what hostile army? Britons and Indians were collaborating, he thought, and felt the familiar sense of incredulity prickling under his skin. It was Helen, her cool probing, and Millie with her flags and banners who were, he felt irritably, inching him down these barbed alleys of thought.

"Millie has her points," said Helen, over the unruly voice that chanted, name them, "but a party today is rather the limit."

"Why?"

"With the laborers on short rations."

"Are they?"

"They've had their pay stopped," she said, and saw him

stiffen. But why? He must know that she would know. "They live hand to mouth. Poor devils."

Clinton watched her narrowly, but she gave nothing away. Hand to mouth, the phrase was familiar, Mackendrick's, he had used it like a lash. What was her intention? Again, he could not tell. He got up and poured himself a whiskey, listening to the tap of insects beating themselves to death against the wire-mesh frames that barred them from the lighted room. What did she know about his labor, and how much? It was not her province, he thought, resentment sparking, to know about his labor. He said sharply, "Coolies don't eat canapés, do they? You're close enough to them, you ought to know."

Helen looked up: "They eat," was all she said. Baldly. Neutrally.

"Do you mean," he said, and took a grip on himself and spoke carefully in case he was wrong, in case the neutrality was real, not a shell that housed live accusation, "are you trying to tell me they are facing starvation because they've been fined?"

"Oh, no," she answered at once, "no one will starve in a week. They'll have to eat less, that's all."

"And whom are you blaming for that," he asked heavily, "them? Or us?"

Before she could answer, the door opened a few hesitant inches and the cook appeared in the slit.

"Memsahib wanting dinner for memsahib and master?" he asked nervously, demoralized by the fear that they might and an awareness of scamped and half-hearted preparations for it which he had based upon the certainty of their going out this evening.

"No thank you," said Helen, glancing at Clinton for confirmation. "We shall be out."

While memsahib was changing the cook returned to his kitchen. He got out a loaf from the larder, and butter and cold meat from the refrigerator and, mindful of Das's parting instructions, made a neat pile of sandwiches, trimming away liberal margins of crust and meat which he ate. On the top shelf in the larder was a sheaf of fresh-cut plantain leaves, come up by truck from the foothills that morning. He extracted two, spread the smaller on the table, placed the sandwiches on it and flanked them with his hands. Then he relapsed into a state of vacancy, his eyes glazing, only his hands on the leaf showing, in case anyone came in, that he was alive and about to be busy.

Presently he heard the gravel crunch as master and memsahib went on their way, and the sound reanimated him. The sandwiches he finished wrapping in the glossy leaf, tied the parcel with string, put it in a plastic box whose efficiency he distrusted, and replaced it in the refrigerator. Then he untucked from his waist the crumpled checked duster with which he had earlier dusted the kitchen, spread it on the table, placed a second leaf on it—a large double one this time—and on this laid a half-loaf, a liberal dollop of butter, four small newspaper cones, already prepared, each containing a few spoonfuls of coffee, tea, salt and sugar, and two boxes of matches. He folded the leaf over these, moved the parcel into the middle of the dirty duster and knotted it, and disposed the final bundle carefully under his coat. It was rather bulky, but he was satisfied it would not show before he reached the safety of the servants' godowns. The quantities were double what he usually considered cook's perquisites, but rumor was rife in the camp that lean times were coming, and it was up to each man to look after his interests.

11

THE Rawlings' bungalow, always well lit, was a blaze of light when they gave their parties. The company's labor mustered in strength to watch the display, gathering in bunches around the flood and fairy lights disposed about the compound in intriguing pattern. Bob Rawlings was proud of his lighting effects: they were a testimony to his own skill and designing ability as well as the efficiency of the electricians who, under his directions, had wired them as permanent outdoor fixtures—so far without mishap. To Millie they were essentials to gaiety in an area of darkness; she saw the lovely lights, and averted her eyes from the intense blackness they created beyond the illuminated circle.

Mackendrick, averse to the scheme from a fear of overloading and breakdown which would have plunged the whole camp into darkness, now that his fears had been proved groundless still found fault with it. What was the point, he wondered, of attracting insects by the million out of their jungle fastness, as if one were not sufficiently plagued by them already? The real point he did not state, which was that the days of obstentation were over—gone with their proponents the British, and their lesser copyists, the maharajahs. It was the day of the com-

71

mon man, and the common man was done with flummery. He
might gape at it, it was a free show and that was the custom, but
nevertheless one grew conscious of narrowed eyes, resentful
minds that speculated on how many paise each light bulb
burned, what it all cost. Mackendrick had no strong feelings
either way, but he was not walled off from the feel of the country. Anyone, he knew, who adopted the panoply and pomp of
an English archbishop would find himself heartily jeered in
any Indian town. Indeed one of his more excruciating memories, which made him wince even now, was the gale of hoots and
laughter that had greeted some mummery in Parliament, shown
in a newsreel at a Madras cinema. Mackendrick sighed—not
for the old days, which he did not lament, but because he did
not feel in tune with the new. Something always gave—a slight
sideslip that put one out of true. Somehow one no longer belonged in India—the reserved place in it was gone. Was it also,
he wondered, because one no longer owned, no longer came by
right as an owner, but strictly by invitation only? Mackendrick
slapped at his cobra boots, which were chafing him, and envied
younger men like Bailey and Lefevre, who despite rebuffs
rubbed along with the new India better than he or his generation could hope to do.

Lefevre, still at half-past eight in his bungalow, waited impatiently for Gopal Rao to arrive. Millie had said, in a postscript
to her invitation, any friend of yours will be welcome, and Lefevre could think of no one who was more of a friend to him
than his trainee and assistant. His growing friendship with Gopal Rao, over the last few months, had opened vistas which he
found fresher, and distinctly more appealing, than the limited
view which fright and older counsel had ushered him into taking. Frequently, now, he sallied cheerfully out of the stockade
into which, in those early days, Krishnan's saturnine strictures
had contributed to send him, shrugging off the jabs, when he
felt them, administered by those who still believed in tribal reservations, his retreats confined to occasions when religion, language and ethical codes combined to settle on him in great oc-

cluding clouds. Taking Gopal with him he did not consider
such a sally, he would never have skirmished using a friend as
a weapon; in fact he did not even think about it, merely acted
naturally.

Gopal Rao was even younger than Lefevre. He was twenty-
one, a slim man with delicate features and brilliant eyes who
had courteously declined the affectionate nickname of gecko,
or lizard, which Lefevre had originally bestowed on him. Lefevre meant well, the name was a respectful acknowledgment
of his neat, quick and efficient gecko-like movements. But Gopal was a Brahmin, to whom the consumption of flesh, blood
and carcasses was a necrophiliac activity unfitting for human
beings, and he did not care to be associated with geckos, whose
transparent stomachs grew black with the insects they bolted.
Lefevre took his point and gracefully gave way. Their association bounded happily along on this give-and-take basis.

Lefevre saw the flickering flashlight coming up his path and
to save five seconds rushed out to meet it.

"Come on, man, you're late! If we don't hurry there won't
even be soda water left."

"So sorry." Gopal panted a little, having run all the way.
"Krishnan was having a meeting, he said only come for the
beginning, then he forced me, my dear fellow, to stay right to
the bitter end!"

"Just like him," grunted Lefevre, "old misery. Can't see what
you see in the chap."

Gopal did not reply, because Krishnan was always charming
to him, he could be really charming when he tried.

They loped in step out of the compound and along the path
that led to Millie's bungalow.

Millie saw them in her garden, floodlit, advancing up the
drive, and rolled her eyes to heaven.

"Look what the lad's brought in," she said, long-suffering,
not too sotto voce, to her husband.

"Well, for heaven's sake don't make a scene about it," said
her husband, his sotto voce ringing in the patch of silence that

had fallen. Then a little lame conversation started up again, the guests laboring to cover up the patch, their own embarrassment, the edgy exchange between husband and wife.

Bob Rawlings strode to the verandah to meet the latecomers, holding out his hand to Lefevre, flattening palm to palm in a *nameste* to Gopal Rao. Gopal, who had expected to have his hand shaken, withdrew it and returned the *namaste*. He could not say why, but he felt the gesture was unfriendly, though he could not put his finger on it. He wondered whether he was being a little too pernickety, or a little too percipient, by feeling this. Soon he forgot all about it, for Mackendrick had come up—dear old Mack as everybody called him—to lead him to the revelry inside.

Clinton, early on, had taken up a stand, back against a wall, a well-filled glass in his hand, which he intended to keep to the end. He felt he had done all that could be expected of him by being here, and he proposed to enjoy himself in his own way, which did not include charging around among Millie's guests at her behest. She had a driving energy, she was that tiring kind of woman, he thought, drinking her liquor steadily. Liquor did not affect him, he had a good head; when it did, or he could not stop when he wanted, he knew he would give it up because he would never be anything less than his own master. Not like poor old Henderson, whom they carried to his bed night after night, whose fleshy face was already puce-colored, the network of facial veins ruptured and blotched under his yellowed skin. Or Bob Rawlings for that matter, tied to loud Millie. He liked his women low and cool, understated, like Helen. How elegant she looked, he thought, searching her out in the crowd; bare-armed, tanned, in an ivory linen shift that made the other women look overblown and overdressed. That fondness for florals! Women seemed to think they were just the thing for the tropics, bought them by the armful. But they were not; the light made a hash of the colors, and the flower prints merely seemed fatuous in a land that sprinkled orchids by the wayside.

"Darling, that thing's gorgeous on you. Where did it come from? It makes you look like a bride."

Millie was addressing Helen, her voice rang out. He saw them between bobbing heads and passing trays of food and drink borne by bearers at shoulder level.

"Does it? Really?" Helen was smiling, relaxed. "I'm simple, I'll take it as a compliment."

"My dear, it's meant as one! You're positively blooming."

"It must be the climate. It agrees with me."

"Well, darling, obviously *something* does. That's plain for anyone to see."

Suddenly, Clinton was alert. He saw the faint flush on Helen's face and pushed his way to her side.

"Hello, Lennie. Enjoying yourself?"

"Loving it, yes."

Except for her heightened color, which would easily have been due to the crush, Helen was in no way discomposed. Had he then only imagined that the words were spiked?

But that inflection.

Well, darling, obviously *something* does.

No, he thought, no mistake.

"I trust you're enjoying yourself, Howard." Millie turned to him. "We hardly see you, at least I hardly do. As for Helen, she's quite a stranger. I'm sure she has better things to do, but—"

"I'm sure she has," said Clinton smoothly. "You'll have to ask her, my dear Millie, to initiate you some time, though I can't promise you'll find it an enjoyable exercise."

"Anyone care to sample my brand of mysteries?" Helen was laughing—laughing it off, Millie thought. Her brightness did not fade, but rage and confusion unsettled her. Did he mean she was too old to have fun? Or wasn't up to Helen's standards sexually? Or what? Allowing his wife to run about the country letting the side down, she thought belligerently, then coming here, swigging my whiskey, insulting me under my own roof.

A good part of the pleasure she genuinely took in parties began to turn rancid.

Gopal Rao, for reasons other than Clinton's had been, also had his back against a wall.

"It is all a misconception, I assure you," he was saying, pinkly, to the English who ringed him. "Aid to underdeveloped countries is not a free gift, there are strings attached to it, for instance all the equipment here, we have to buy from Britain with our loan."

"But you don't repay it, do you, boy." Henderson wagged his heavy, liquor-logged face loosely in front of Gopal. "So what does a loan become? I ask you, what does it become?"

"We pay interest," said Gopal unhappily. He was not too sure about his facts. He wished Krishnan, who knew all this kind of thing, had come with him: or that he had not come at all.

"Interest," said Henderson. "What interests me is capital. What happens to that, that's what I'd like to know. Right, I'll tell you: it gets gobbled up, boy, that's what. A great walloping mouth opens and it all goes down. Lock, stock and barrel. That's all. Sunk for good. Not a penny in return."

"No, no," cried Gopal. He did not care to be called "boy," it was what one called one's bearer, but the feeling was swamped in a larger agitation. "I am sure you are wrong, we pay back all we borrow—"

"On the never-never," said Mrs. Henderson.

"Only one never," said Mrs. Galbraith.

"The taxes we pay," said Mrs. Henderson, "simply to make these 'loans!' "

"Beats me why we do," said Mrs. Galbraith resignedly, helping herself to a passing vol-au-vent. "No mugs like English mugs, they say."

"But not only we, you also have taken from others. Like Elgin marbles," croaked Gopal, dim, other people's memories stirring in his mind, "or Koh-i-noor which is biggest diamond in the crown of your queen—"

"Will you please leave her out of it?" said Mrs. Henderson ominously.

"—which you took from us and never paid for it," finished Gopal rapidly. He felt a little hunted and looked about for Lefevre, but Lefevre was talking to a planter's pretty English daughter whom Henderson had invited (she had motored up from the neighboring coffee plantation and was what Millie had had in mind, rather than someone like Gopal, when she said her friends' friends would be welcome). Feeling Gopal's eyes on him Lefevre hunched his shoulders and engrossed himself still more in her, thinking, why can't he behave? Everyone can see he's quarreling and showing it too, the silly ass. (Afterward, on their way home, he said critically, "Why did you pick on those old bags? There were two other girls at least you could have spoken to."

(Gopal did not answer; he had not picked on them, they had picked on him; also he did not wish his friend to know he was unused to chatting with girls and would not have known where to begin. But he liked the way Lefevre had dismissed his countrywomen. Those old bags, he had called them. Old bags, Gopal repeated ripely, his wounds healing and the warmth he felt for Lefevre fanned to a glow.)

Mackendrick observing the same scene thought, he's cornered like a rat, but fighting back . . . and Henderson like a bulldog, those jowls. . . . Sure as sin, he said to himself, they're talking politics. Or economics, it comes to the same thing. It was politics twenty years ago and they're still at it arguing who bled whom. He wondered in passing if he should rescue young Gopal—in passing because his mind was on other things—but the thought slipped away.

"Strange," he said to Rawlings, "no one's out looking at your lights tonight."

Bob Rawlings suspected he was gloating: old Mac had always been anti his illuminations.

"Who wants them to?" he said, falsely. "Can't stand coolies hanging around the place."

Mackendrick fell silent again. Outside in the brightly lit compound insects swarmed, heavy revolving orbs around each light. The compound itself was empty. They've stayed away, he thought, staged a protest against us in their own way, that subtle underhand way Indians specialize in. Damn them, he wanted to say, but small nagging devils would not allow him. We've treated them badly, he came round to thinking, as if they were guilty en bloc which they're not. It wouldn't wash at home, we wouldn't even try, so what happens to us when we come out here that we behave as we do? We're bastards, he said under his breath, and with self-castigation the little devils went, yielding place to bigger ones that wondered whether the work schedules were going to be maintained in the present mood of the workers.

Mackendrick's preoccupation communicated itself to Clinton and he felt he ought to be concerned but Millie intruded. What the hell had she meant? He tried to make out it was nothing, watching her across the room dancing with Bailey, having her good time, watching his wife framed in the embrasure of the window laughing at some joke of Lefevre's, but it would not work. Blooming. Like a bride. Women wore that look when they were satisfied, Helen had borne it since the day they were married, he had drawn his own rich satisfactions from the way she looked. So what extra dimension did Millie perceive to make her remark upon it now? He cogitated, and the widely dispersed field that the dark rays scorched began to narrow down.

Nearing midnight the party was over. Headlights flashed in the darkness, returning planters to plantations, plains people to plains which many would not reach until morning. They went in convoy because of the jungle, but careless of its sleepers roared helter-skelter down the hill sounding their horns in communal merriment.

In Millie's bungalow the servants contemplated the debris with heavy eyes, waiting for memsahib to retire before making for their godowns which was the rule. Millie however was not ready yet. Parties left her in euphoric mood; she hummed little snatches of tunes they had played and picked at the food that was left until the lights in the garden, which her husband controlled, went out. Then she lay in bed waiting for Bob who was too drunk to come, listening with heightened heartbeats which she could not control to the padded sounds the servants made as they walked home in bare feet in the darkness.

12

IT was a bad week, everyone agreed.

On the Monday, as Mackendrick had predicted, the labor force broke up into its human components and each of them, or so it seemed, came to him and wrung its hands and protested innocence and called him its father. Mackendrick was nauseated; and the nausea was as much for himself as for his demeaned fellow beings. *No shame, no dignity,* his assaulted senses cried; but his fellows beings, bred to simplicity of emotion, understood no need to conceal what they felt.

"Some of you may be innocent," he attempted to bring reason to bear, "but some are guilty. The oil did not flow away on its own. If you shield the guilty you have to take the consequences."

"Sahib, we go hungry."

What kind of answer was that?

"It will spur you to honesty," Mackendrick said ruthlessly.

Only the words were brave; the day drained him. He could have gone to Clinton and said: *you* did it, now you deal with them; but this was not the way they functioned.

Krishnan also felt slightly nauseated, for reasons that began like Mackendrick's but then flared widely. Cattle, he thought.

Look at them! Lined up like passive cows at a backstreet Christian butchery! He had tried not once but thrice, to call a strike and each attempt aborted. He shouted, he even pleaded though this went against his nature. The labor gangs listened uneasily and shook their heads and dispersed; and Krishnan saw the power, that might have been, fragmented before his eyes. No organization, no discipline, cowards! he flung at them; but afterward in his meticulous way he worked out what else was true. That the oil had not flowed away on its own, so that the detritus of guilt prevented a total confrontation. That the two wings of the labor force—the lowlanders, and the local recruits from the tribes—did not always articulate together. That strike-breaking machinery existed, in the shape of an under-employed army that would swarm up the hill at first beckoning by Clinton Mackendrick, the company that paid by far the healthiest wages in the area.

Clinton calculated coldly too. He would take time off to coax his technicians into line, they were organized and educated and hard to come by, and he needed their strength behind him. Labor was another matter. Expendable. A second thousand to be had for the picking where the first thousand had come from. Emasculated, furthermore, by awareness of their crime. Strange, he thought, how much strength, conversely, people drew from flagrant injustice: muscles and sinews grew where puny arms had been. Well, that particular genie was still stoppered in its bottle. It had been a straightforward transaction, a correct balance struck, loss set against loss, in which there was nothing he could see that could justifiably affect the backing he wanted from the men. Which as far as it went was true.

Helen, that week, vacillated between daily visits to the settlement bearing food and sympathy, and studiously staying away. Unenchanting Lady Bountiful pictures, inexplicably tangled with legends of loaves and fishes, quickly decided her against the first. Bashiam, more or less, dissuaded her against the second course.

"Why do you feel they hold it against you?" he said. "Besides, a week's deprivation is nothing, they are quite used to it."

"Which is why they kicked up such a fuss," she said flatly. "Delegations in relays to poor old Mack."

"We are an emotional people," he answered. "The spirit has been bruised as much as stomachs."

So she went, taking with her a carton of sweets which, perversely, she asked Das to pack. Das did so, banging the carton and tying vicious knots in the string to show his disapproval. He did not, she knew, like the tribesmen. By the refined tenets of his training they were outside the pale, people of whom—in a different time and environment and bearing a different skin —he might have said, victoria plums rather than acid in his voice, naked barbaric savages.

There was something else too: a curious osmosis by which the sahib's feelings seeped into his, making him resent memsahib's excursions to the village. Helen was aware of it, but so far without active resentment.

Only, now and again, she had this desire to torment him.

"Ready, Das?"

He nodded as if to an equal, his ultimate in impudence; and was mortified when she did not notice. In fact she had noticed, and debated whether to please him by speaking sharply, but could not bring herself to assume false roles. Poor old Das, she thought, he ought to work for Millie, he's as satanic on protocol as she is, they'd both be much happier. . . . But it could not be done. The appointment of servants, she had discovered, was governed by strict rules. The best man in each cadre—cook, bearer, sweeper—went to the chief executive and so on down the scale until someone like Bailey ended up with a teen-age houseboy who thought nothing of shining up master's shoes with master's best handkerchiefs. Nothing short of a holocaust could dismantle the rules and generally speaking who wanted holocausts? Hardly anyone, she thought; they all shared in the acceptance which seemed to be India's collective unconscious.

"Memsahib wanting coffee?" Das spoke wistfully, watching her shoulder the carton.

"No, thank you," she said with a matching regret. "I shan't want lunch either, tell cook, will you?"

"Shall I call coolie, memsahib?"

"What for? Oh, for the box. No thank you, I can manage."

It baffled her, this rigid assumption that she—all Europeans —were above certain tasks. Poor old Das, she thought again, warped to meet some alien standard. Why did Indians do it, had they no integrity of their own? Krishnan, fed on bitter aloes, said the British had eaten it away during the centuries when they were the rulers and Indians the ruled: it would take a century to form again. But Gopal Rao, who had suffered only minor modification, had a more hospitable explanation. "You are guests in our country," he said with dignity. "We like you to be comfortable so we adapt ourselves to your ways. Would you not," he asked with a shattering innocence, "do the same for us in your country?"

The tribesmen, whom she had thought the stalwarts—even they, it sometimes seemed to Helen, and never more forcibly than in that week of strain and tension, were changing. A backward people, whose primeval ways had exasperated successive governments, monumental impediment in the path of progressive companies and administrations, even they had felt the glancing blow of social change. On the surface, little showed. Surveying the village, that morning, standing in front of its palisaded perimeter, she was struck more by its sameness than by any difference. Women sat in the sun, pounding grain or kneading dough. Children played in the dust. A group of men in breech clouts—throwouts, unable to hunt, forbidden to fish in the requisitioned river, unable to find work with the Company—squatted round a cockpit, grooming bright-feathered, peppery little gamecocks. Nearby the tribal chief ruminated, his jaws working over a wad of tobacco: an old man, with fine white hair and beard, and dark corneas rimmed with the milk-blue of age.

"Can you hear them moaning?" His voice, a shrill bark, came surprisingly from a shriveled larynx.

"No," Helen said, squatting down beside him. "I heard them in the camp. Here it looks different."

"It looks. It is not." The chief was full of his disgust. "They moan here too, they miss the money they have not had. Money, money. They are becoming as money-mad as you foreigners are."

"It is a useful commodity."

"Useful," the old man was roused. "Useful you say. What for, I ask you: for that rubbish they buy from the camp shops? Tin cans and cardboard boots, and scented pigs' grease to plaster on their hair. For this, they moan."

"I have heard differently," said Helen. "There are other causes for complaint."

"Ah, yes," the old man confirmed with asperity, "they are short of food too, whose fault is it, the jungle is full of game, if they relied on that and not on the money which comes and goes —but what is the use of an old man talking. Keep away, I told them . . . I am their headman, I have to say these things, someone has to say them; but no. Now they are punished and are hurt, like small children. Like fools. Whose fault, I ask—"

The shrill barking went on, gathering strength as it rooted for defects. She had never, Helen thought, heard him speak so freely, usually he was taciturn, a silent figure in gnarled wood. It had been months before he would address even a few words to her, and though their relationship had advanced since then she had never suspected a capacity for such crisp sustained monologue. Dwelling on iniquity, she thought, was a good tongue-loosener . . . but whose iniquity, was he separating the strands in his mind?

"Soon," she said, in a lull, "when the work is done, we shall be gone, you will be left in peace."

"A peace full of moaning," croaked the chief, whose voice was going, "and pining for trash. But before that they will learn what is real and mourn what is lost. A score or more before they bend the river . . . the great Dam will take them, the man-eater will have its flesh." He stopped, his voice had given out. There were beads of sweat on his forehead and she thought poor man, poor old man, on an impulse of pure pity undiluted by progressive or atavistic proddings.

Rawlings, meanwhile, had gone in pursuit of the missing equipment.

"It calls for a man on the spot," he said to Clinton. "What's the good of telegrams? Half these johnnies can't read!"

Barely able to face daylight after his high weekend, nevertheless he departed on the following morning. Loss of altitude, and sudden encounter with the humid heat of the plains, laid him low in a matter of hours. He had forgotten what this particular combination could do, especially after the cool climate of the hills. Reminded, he prudently cosseted himself, so far as anyone could, in the shuttered gloom of a railway retiring room. Forty-eight hours later he emerged, out of sorts and in no mood for inefficiency, and pushed on to Bombay, clerks and officials feeling the rough edge of his tongue en route.

In the end they kept out of his way, dodging agilely round corners when they heard his step along the corridors.

At officer level it was hardly better. Senior officers sent their deputies, and deputies their assistants. Rawlings brushed them aside, together with despatch and delivery notes which lay in tottering piles on tables. He wanted men he could talk to, not underlings: the goods, not excuses wrapped in reams of paper.

Slippery Customers Passing the Buck, he wired Clinton. Creating Bandobust in Hope of Results.

Whether by bandobust or persistence, he got his way. Urbane men confronted him proffering formal assurances.

"We are doing all we can to trace the consignment."

"Will you say what?"

"Everything, you may rest assured . . . there has been a slight mishap but everything possible that can be done is being done."

Sweet damn all! Rawlings interpreted angrily. Answer, *answer*, he felt like shouting, but he knew it would not do and restrained himself. Both parties restrained themselves and silent rancors wreathed through the air, settling on their heads like unhappy laurels.

"But surely," Rawlings leaned forward—it was the third day of his mission—"mishap or not a thousand tons of equipment can't just get mislaid?"

Disdainful eyes surveyed him. "My dear sir, ten thousand tons of equipment are passing through our hands each day. From Rome, Cairo. Moscow."

Rawlings understood this ploy; it was one he often used himself.

"Well, God help Rome, Cairo and Moscow," he said bluntly. "And this country," he added as an afterthought.

When Clinton received Rawlings' wire it read: SLIPPER CUSTOMERS PASSING BOOT CREATING BANDOBUST IN HOPE OF RESULTS.

Some telegraphist, he thought, had done his worst; whereas in fact the man had done his best to make sense of the message.

The boot, Clinton pondered, these days was it wise? But Rawlings was his man on the spot and he scrupulously thrust all such thoughts from his mind. The kernel of his message, however, was clear enough: another of those infernal delays which they could still absorb, but which, cumulatively, contained the power to disrupt the meticulous clock that governed the construction of the dams.

Rawlings had by now lost sight of the larger objective—the delivery of equipment at a carefully calculated stage of operations to meet the requirements of each planned phase of the project. He waged a private battle, which revolved around locating, instantly, an assorted quantity of bulldozers, excavators, pumps, tires, dumping trucks, barges and a high-load capacity crane. Sometimes it seemed to him that the country was maliciously bent on informing him it did not work that way. In the heat and dust, the soulless air-conditioning of innumerable offices, he felt the massive weight of inertia pressing on him— processing him, he thought with sudden fright, to its own lethargic mold. He reacted forcefully. Immediately, he demanded, without further delay.

But the matter was not one to be opened and buttoned shut instantly. A river had overflown, sections of line were awash. The goods train carrying the equipment had derailed, the forward trucks remaining upright but the rear two overturning. In the general confusion, and the urgent need to clear the line, the goods had been off-loaded, reloaded, and shunted to nearest available sidings to await onward transit. Scattered like birdseed, Rawlings thought furiously, which it was nobody's business to pick up. But he made it his business, and it was done in a fortnight which to him felt more like a year.

ALL ITEMS EQUIPMENT LOCATED NOW EN ROUTE he wired Clinton jubilantly.

Clinton, receiving the message intact this time, felt the knot of tension that had worked up in his system smoothing out.

By now January was ending.

13

EVENING mists swirled in shallow drifts as Clinton came up
the jungle path to his bungalow. He could not see his feet; from
the ankles down they were lost in the soft eddies that smoked
up from the ground. The sky had darkened early and the forest
followed, green turning to lead and bronze and black as the
light faded. Should have brought a flashlight, he thought, switching vigorously at shrubs and grasses that overhung the path:
they did say these damp vapors brought out snakes. Not that he
was particularly afraid of them, anyhow no more so than he was,
say, of tigers. Still, there was no denying the heightened degree
of repulsion most people felt for them, like sturdy old Mack,
who would not stir a yard without his cobra boots, or Jackson
who simply went berserk, flailing to death anything that slithered along the ground even if it was only a blindworm or a
harmless green snake. At least Helen said they were harmless,
but she was going by what the tribesmen told her. Clinton
frowned. Helen, he felt, went too much by what they told her—
even after allowing that very likely they did know a certain
amount about the country they were born and bred in. But
what weight if any, he thought with contempt, could one attach
to the words of a people who worshipped birds and beasts and

probably snakes, decking the forest with scruffy hutches which they knocked up out of driftwood and crammed with leaves and flowers for their deities? Himself, very little; but Helen, that was another matter. Images rose in his mind of closing wings, and traps whose jaws were biting, as he strode through the darkness slashing left, right, at the rampant growth that tore at his clothes as he passed.

Helen was changing for dinner—a relatively infrequent event for them—given to still a nagging awareness of largely unrequited hospitality on her part, in reluctant recognition of the need for good public relations on his.

Clinton lay on the bed, his arms crossed under his head, soothed by the sight of his wife, and watched her. It was funny, he thought, how much pleasure it gave him to see her as she was now, arms and throat and shoulders bare, in a lacy black dress against which she seemed to glow, her skin lambent under the peachy tan. No doubt it was the rarity: he was more used to seeing her in jodhpurs and khaki shirt which she had made her daily uniform, or wearing one of those checked lumber-jack shirts that the canteen shop sold.

"Lennie, you look delicious," he said. "You ought to wear these things more often."

"Perhaps." She smiled. "But if I did you wouldn't notice."

"Perhaps I forget," he said, "what a beautiful wife I've got."

He got up and came round and clasped her shoulders, slid down the straps of her dress and the cups of her slip until her breasts were bare, and gazed at the lovely sculpted bust reflected in the looking glass as if it were another woman's, or he were seeing her for the first time.

"Beautiful," he said, and bent and kissed the perfumed cleft, and pulled up the dress again and dropped his hands. "I ought to take more care of you. Lock you up, as wise men would."

"But locked up things go mangy, like captive animals," she said, and he thought, anxiously, we're double-talking, she doesn't mean what she says, she means something else and she

knows I know, we're like people tied in an uneasy marriage
. . . but the thought was unreal, without cause or foundation
as far as he could see and he put it down to the imaginings that
had plagued him of late. I'm run down, he thought, wrestled
with the proposition and abandoned it, substituted another.
The country's getting me down, he said to himself, and was
presently reinforced in this sentiment by a view of the puce-
fleshed Henderson.

Das liked entertaining—vicariously, that is. The last enter-
tainment—on his account, so to speak—had been some twenty
years ago when he was married. He wished master and memsahib would entertain more often, then he could please them, and
himself, by practicing the arts which all the previous memsahibs whom he had served said he had learned to perfection.
He sighed. Present memsahib was the only one—but no, that
was not just, she also appreciated everything he did and said so.
It was simply that her heart did not seem to be in it, he did not
think she really *cared* whether things were done in the proper
manner or not, which grieved his soul, being part of his vicarious lot in life.

And, of course, present memsahib kept low company. At this
point Das clapped his hand over his mouth as if he had uttered
heresy, and began harassing the sweeper who rose sullenly from
his corner and started sweeping out the already swept verandah.

When they were in their bedroom, after the guests had gone,
Clinton could hear Das (in fact it was the cook ferreting) moving about in the kitchen.

"Collecting his perks," he said grimly. "God knows the man's
well paid. I don't know why you women put up with it."

"They all do it." Helen shrugged. "It's too small to fuss about
anyway. I prefer to go along with custom."

"But you don't always, do you?" He had not meant to say
that, the words had slipped out. But he was not sorry.

"Do what?"

"Follow established custom." If only you would, he thought, keep away from those bloody aboriginals and behave like the other women on the station do! What then of the nonconformity, the unpredictability he had loved in his wife?—well, these qualities were still important to him, it was just that they belonged elsewhere, to another time and country. Not here, it did not work out here. But it was a silent dialogue that went on in his brain, he could not find acceptable, suitably stripped words to fit.

"No," said Helen. "You wouldn't want me to, would you?"

"It might be easier," he said, "if you did."

"In what way?"

"Well," he said, trying to keep his tone light, "for instance if you didn't hobnob quite so much with the tree men . . . even Das disapproves, you know."

"I know." Helen's voice was light too; he could not be sure of the undertones. "Servants can be the most terrible tyrants, can't they. If one lets them."

There was a silence, stretching all the way to the kitchen. Ears pinned for bedroom gossip, Clinton thought with irritation, and he shouted peremptorily to Das to lock up and go home.

Helen was already in bed, her face shadowed by the mosquito curtain. It was pale pink netting, not the usual white; he had had it specially dyed to mitigate the first-sight shock of the drab forest bungalow for her and then it had not been necessary, she had been delighted, not shocked, by everything including the bungalow; but the pink had faded from sunlight and dhobi-washing, and the holes in the net were clogged here and there with streaks of black and rusty red where someone— no doubt the excellent Das—had swatted mosquitoes, mingling his blood, hers, the mosquito's, in those murky smears. Part of the curtain, on Helen's side, was untucked. He padded round and tucked it in, following his nightly routine, before climbing in himself. Helen was awake, the sheet up to her chin and her eyes on him. He had a feeling that she was about to say something to him and he waited, but there was nothing. Presently he reached up and switched off the light.

He slept badly and woke late; the 8 A.M. sirens were sounding. Helen was not in the room. He dressed and went out onto the verandah, expecting to see her at breakfast but she was not there either. Das was hovering with eggs and toast and he asked,

"Where's memsahib?"

"Memsahib telling gone jungle, sahib."

"Already?"

"Yessir, gone early," said Das, "for trapping birds."

"Birds? Are you sure?"

"Yessir, master. Gone with jungly mens."

Das, clearly, would have liked the conversation to continue, but Clinton dismissed him. Trapping birds, he thought, it seemed a singularly unpleasant pastime . . . but he did not dwell on it. The fresh batch of equipment was due up the hill by noon, Rawlings had informed him with pleasure: a pleasure which he shared, without showing or expressing it. He finished breakfasting quickly, pushed back his chair and rose. The whole lot could be inspected, overhauled if necessary, and in operation on the site by—when? Before the end of February, he thought. Sooner, if he and Rawlings and Mack could make it sooner, for there was that infernal delay at Bombay to be wiped out.

By now the entire range of his vision was occupied by the river and the dam, and the machines that were to manipulate them.

14

BASHIAM was an outsider—de-tribalized, he had heard them say of him. Sometimes, without undue agonizing, he acknowledged the truth of it. He also knew in his bones that, however de-tribalized he might be, birth and upbringing within the tribe gave him race knowledge and instincts that could never be acquired by the real outsiders, those who had never been inside. That was why they came to him, the delvers after knowledge, accessible as he was because of his English, asking him questions and recording his answers in notebooks or on tape.

Helen Clinton never recorded anything, except possibly in her head. She did not come to him because of his English either, for her grasp of dialect made her independent of him. It was more to do, he felt, with the divergent channels they had carved for themselves—he the skilled and competent technician away from his jungly-wallah tribe, she the No. 1 memsahib who refused to bear the memsahib's load—so that there was an acreage of common rebellion which both were stimulated by and respected in each other.

What he particularly liked about her, Bashiam often thought, was that she was not like the other memsahibs, even these latter-day ones, whose outlook barred them from allowing their interest to be sparked by anything; nor was she like those others, the recorders, the authors and researchers who alarmed him by taking down everything he said for use in the books they were going to write, attaching an importance to every trivial detail in a way that first bewildered and then tired him out. She could tire him out too, because alienation from his people made it an effort for him to trace back and supply correct information; but she was robust about what interested her and what did not, so that he did not have that exhausting advance across a broad if amiable fact-producing front.

Sometimes their interests coincided.

It coincided over bird-trapping.

Helen had seen the birds, flapping frantically in the onion-shaped split-bamboo cages that they suspended from a pole near the cote where the fighting cocks roosted. Sun birds, bulbuls, finches, hill mynas, a kingfisher or two—a dozen other kinds she could not name. The mynas were very popular with the British; the men bought them and put them in cages near their bunks and lovingly taught them to swear in English. The bulbuls went to them too, for their sweet voices, they sang their sweetest just before caging killed them. The labor block was full of bird song.

"How are they caught?" asked Helen.

"Very cleverly," said Bashiam.

"Can you?"

"Only a bird-catcher can."

"Can one watch?"

"If one wishes."

Besides wishing, one had to be patient and persistent as well, for the bird-catcher was a shy man, jealous of his skills and reluctant to display them, an itinerant who demarcated the jungle according to rules known only to his own guild, working each sector in rotation so that none was overcropped. One waited for him, and he waited for the right time and season.

"When will he come?" she asked the village chief, but the old man did not know, he shook his head sadly, for at each visit he exacted tribute from the bird-catcher who was an extramural member of his tribe.

"When the young birds rise," said Bashiam, repeating parrot fashion what he had heard and stored, hazy about when or what that might be.

But because it was for her he made it his business to find out and arrange a meeting.

"Tomorrow, before first light," he said to her, "the bird-catcher will wait for you."

Helen thought of the dinner party they were giving and found it irrelevant; a late night, no sleep at all, never stopped her rising when she wanted to.

"Before first light at the bridge over the river," she confirmed.

Later that night after their party, she thought she would tell Howard, but he spoke of other things and after a while lying under the pale-pink net watching and listening she felt a hardness come into her and she no longer wanted to.

Bashiam had second thoughts too. Imaginings. A meeting at dawn in the jungle between her and this bird-catcher, a man whose supple hands fashioned crafty bird-nets, whose low sweet voice enticed them. He involuted it, saying it was not safe for *any* two to walk in the forests alone, that what did he know of this man, could he swear to his control in such vulnerable closeness and situation? But the flame came at him alone, licked over him, over his limbs and mind.

Helen switched on the rose-shaded light so that Howard might wake and if he did she would tell him; but after a restive night he was deeply asleep, there was a line of white where the lids pressed tightly together. She kissed him lightly but he did not wake; pulled up the rumpled sheets and tucked in the mosquito net as he had done for her, dressed without feeling the pre-dawn cold, and went out into the night.

In the darkness at the bridge there were darker silhouettes —two instead of one. Bashiam, she thought, who was on early call but who had given up his sleep to come; and something in her shifted, very slightly like a few grains in a sand hill whose movement indefinably alters the whole structure.

A match flared as she approached, then another and another, before the lamp was lit; the river created erratic drafts here, flowing over boulders between steep banks. She huddled beside the men, next to the hurricane lantern, feeling the cold now, while the wild fowler instructed them in sharp whispers.

"Follow closely, except when I tell you. No sound, no light. Watch for the fireflies when you cannot see me. Now."

They rose. She was shivering. Bashiam said, "Are you cold?" and without waiting for an answer put a shawl around her, draping it over her head and shoulders. A heavy dew was falling, chill and clammy, she was grateful for the rough warmth. When they moved off she felt better. The bird-catcher led the way with the lantern. He had a thin black cord looped over his wrist in coils which he paid out as he walked; it did not rope them together but acted as a guideline which she found she needed despite the radiance of the lantern swinging ahead of them.

Once past the bridge they stopped to douse the flame and the darkness intensified, concentric rings of black and green pulsed in front of her eyes. Through them she became aware of a curious pattern of phosphorescent light, three specks of luminous green in the form of a triangle that moved ahead of them like some bizarre minified road sign. These, she realized, were the fireflies, squashed or gummed to the fowler's back, somehow still emitting a luminous glow, and felt an illogical pang for these three that she could not feel for the insects that perished in their thousands at the wire mesh each dusk. There were no insects at this hour, except for the fireflies; perhaps they slept near dawn; but the night was lit and sparked by the fireflies, the darkness was full of their dot-and-dash flight.

By now they had advanced well into the jungle; the undergrowth was thicker, the lianas that hung and twisted down from the branches not easily thrust aside. There were no votive altars

here either, such as were found on the outskirts: those minute pagodas that the tribesmen lit with a candle and left
glimmering in the forks of trees for their forest gods, whose
unexpected and decorative quality invariably filled her with
pleasure; perhaps even jungle dwellers set a limit to how far
they penetrated into jungle.

Here and there from all round them came the squeaks and
rustlings of disturbed animals, but the night was vast, it swallowed them all, sucked them into its absorbent vaults as if they
had never been. Even their footsteps: she could not hear the
man in front or the man behind, and even her own, clumsy
from inexperience, were muffled. How long had they been
walking? She could not have said, time had detached itself from
existence. There was only this awareness of herself, and the triangle of light that she followed, and of the man who followed
her: a sharp awareness this, that ran along the connecting
thread between their hands and lay warmly against her breastbone.

Presently they stopped. The darkness was easing, the shapes
of bushes and trees emerging from amorphous black like
sculpted forms out of marble. From somewhere above the
canopy of matted creeper and interlocked branches a pale in-
determinate light seeped down. They were in a glade, a clearing whose stubble had felt the sun, it was wet with dew but not
sodden and dank with decaying leaf-mold. Clumps of gorse and
thorny evergreen shrubs dotted and ringed the area, and the
bird-catcher crouched beside one of these. He was carrying a
sack, which she had not noticed before. From this he extracted
an earthenware pot, a reel of twine, several reeds and nets.
All the simple, ordinary instruments of disaster and death, she
thought, as he set them out neatly in front of him. The pot contained a thin shiny fluid—a bird-lime, she realized, it looked
more like spun glass or sugar as he spread it along the delicate
filaments of his net. When this was done he rose, gathered the
folds of the net in his arms and flung them from him in a wide
arc that settled on the scrub as lightly as a butterfly's wings.

At intervals there were pegs of green-painted wood that looked like fishermen's floats. These he thrust into earth and stubble, crawling around the perimeter of the snare to do so until they were invisible. The net had vanished too, she could no longer be sure where it lay: only a few feet distant, yet the mottled strands of netting were lost in the undergrowth.

And still she did not know why the birds should come—numerously, as she had seen from the cages—to this deadly limed patch, when the whole jungle lay open. The wildfowler had enjoined silence, and she did not break it.

Now the light was changing, dove-gray shades in the dark-gray sky, and somewhere distant a hint of rose. It seemed like a sign the fowler had been waiting for. With a finger he tested the glue; it had grown viscous and tacky, apparently the consistency he wanted, for he motioned them down. Then he selected a reed, split it with a thumbnail and put it to his lips, curving his fingers around them.

In the silence a bird called.

Another, and then another. Low, isolated calls, like birds' first stirrings out of warmth and sleep. Islands of quiet between.

Lying in the stubble, waiting, she began to quiver. Long shudders that came up from the bone and scored her flesh, but invisibly. Inwardly. The tremors not communicated to the coarse shawl that swathed her or the rough grass cradling her body, but only in her. When it grew, and she could not contain it any more, she reached out for him, lying beside her in the ebbing dark, and it was like being on the edge of some truth, only without him she could not advance any more, and he, after a while, very gently withdrew.

Outside the colors grew: a pale-gray and dark-rose dawn. The birdcalls came frequently now, pure low notes rising from the ground beside them, answered from bush and branch, and she could not have said which was bird song and which the luring reed. After a little she found she could sift the cries, distinguish in the general chorus the delicate arpeggio of particular species, of partridge and cuckoo, and the exultant bubbling trill of bulbuls. Singing, she thought, as if their hearts would burst, as presently they would, those who obeyed the siren song. For that was what it was: a coaxing and a caress, and one came and then another, flocking down as if the ground were sown with birdseed but there was nothing except the sweet urgent summoning that poured from between a man's lips and a split stalk.

The sack bulged but still they came as if they could not see what went on in front of their eyes, and the bird cries rose on shrill notes as the lime gripped and the delicate claws were ridged and rippled with blood from straining against the net. She wanted to—but what? She felt she knew, and would be able to tell if only these molten assaults against her rib cage would stop; but they did not. She glanced at Bashiam and his eyes were brilliant, lust lay like a heavy bloom on his lips which were parted over sharp white teeth like an animal close on quarry and she knew then that she was like that too, that that was how she looked; and it was not a judging but a recording.

Then it was over. It had not been so long after all. The bird-catcher stood up and stretched, working his fingers and blowing out his cheeks to relieve the cramp. As before he inspected his catch, wrung the necks of the common kinds neatly with two fingers of his hand and one swift dislocating thumb, thrust the rare and the dead into the sack and tied its mouth. The limed net he buried, scraping earth and leaves carefully over so that it would never ensnare again.

When they were ready to go he spoke for the first time since they had set out. "It was a good haul," he said briefly. "God was kind."

They went back as they had come. All three fireflies were dead, their fitful pulsing had ceased. Overhead the sun had begun to ignite the topmost fringes of the trees, reminding Bashiam that he was late for the machines to which he had given his life, recalling her husband to Helen.

15

MOST of the equipment came up under its own steam, the rest by road transporter. They drove the truck-mounted crane to the foothills and towed it from there, the head section of its jib folded back neatly alongside the heel, with red flags fluttering fore and aft. It was a lengthy and strenuous operation which Rawlings, on guard against further misadventure, personally supervised. He felt nothing when it was over, he was too tired for anything except a hot bath and bed; but when he saw it resting in the marshaling yard next morning he felt rather pleased with himself, felt, moreover, that he had every right to be.

Clinton experienced no such elation; he had looked forward to an effective addition to his work force, and all he saw now was a damaged piece of costly equipment that would clutter up the servicing bays for weeks on end.

"My God," he said. "What happened?"

"Don't ask me," said Rawlings. He thought, rancorously, that's a bloody fine thing to say to a man, all he'd have but for me is a sou's worth of scrap, and his rancors built up as he thought of what he had been through, slaving away at a thankless job in a thankless bloody country. Clinton noticed the angry mottling and disliked it: he preferred angers to be

marbled and contained, like his own; but it did not perturb
him, he knew Rawlings, as they all knew Rawlings, who would
vent his spleen upon the country, allow it like an unconscious
bloodletting while he banked his strength for the issue in hand.

But the crane. He walked round it, Rawlings, Mackendrick
and Bailey with him, a small silent group of engineers following them, sizing up the damage. A main boom twisted. The
hinge section, and the plates that bolted them together,
slightly bent. A window in the cabin smashed. It could be
worse, he thought, but as the mold of acceptance poised about
to settle on him he thrust it away in a flurry of impatience in
which Rawlings had been caught for weeks. Why should he,
he thought: he wouldn't stand for this kind of thing in England so why in this damned country?

"Silly buggers!" Rawlings fulminated, catching his mood.
"Must've tried to winch it up, you can see where the sling's
slipped . . . suppose they had to scrape it up off the track after
that, don't ask me how . . . block and tackle, probably, as if
it were a load of lumber! Christ, a job like this, humped like a
lot of lumber."

"It's a bit of an awkward brute," Mackendrick said, running his gaze along the eighty-foot length of the jib, "not easy
to handle."

Rawlings turned his close-set, dust-reddened eyes on him.
"The more awkward the brute, the more carefully you handle," he said bitingly.

Mackendrick nodded, offhand. "The rest of the equipment,"
he said, "seems in pretty good shape?" Only the slightest upward inflection of his voice conceded that it was a question,
not a statement.

"Pretty good," Rawlings agreed.

"Unscratched?"

"Virtually."

Mackendrick nodded again, an advocate who had made his
point. In truth he was nobody's advocate, cared little about
scoring points, but he had seen the faces of the Indians behind

him. And swore at them silently, a little sickened by the humiliation that rippled across those faces because somewhere
in the wilderness a lone Englishman with a loud mouth called
someone else—a lot of someone elses—silly buggers as they
ripely deserved to be called.

Rawlings had no such complicated thoughts. He twisted
his lips and said to himself, nigger-lover, a simple sentiment
that covered all the animosity he felt toward Mackendrick
whom otherwise, and on the whole, he liked.

Clinton's thoughts were fairly simple too. In England, in
similar circumstances, one did this, and this. It was a straightforward procedure, especially for a powerful firm like Clinton
Mackendrick. But who the devil did one sue here, how long
did it take, and if they agreed to replacement how long
would that take, in a country whose all-out effort churned up
a dozen power-driven cranes per annum or whatever the figure
was? A shudder went through him, not the febrile tremors that
had shaken Helen, but similar nevertheless, passing somewhere near the bone.

Your beloved dam, Helen sometimes said.

In his mind it now became true.

Then he came out of his preoccupation, grew conscious of
the men who surrounded him. Who waited and who looked
at him. Those eyes. Black as the pit but flat, where were the
depths? With an effort he turned away, toward Rawlings, felt
the hold break and was able to say, crisply,

"How long will it take?"

"To have her functional?"

"And working on site."

"A couple of weeks." Rawlings stroked his chin. "As a matter of fact she's functional now. A competent crane man
could work her."

"Get one."

"Get Smith," said Rawlings.

In the barrack block where Smith slept, the reluctant emissary poked at the bare shoulder above the crumpled sheet on the camp-bed.

"Rawlings sahib calling," he said.

"Tell him bugger off," mumbled Smith, and sank back into the heavy and torpid sleep of mid-morning.

"Where the hell is Smith," Clinton demanded, waiting impatiently on the tarmac.

"Not on duty," someone said.

"He's sleeping."

"He was working last night."

Clinton frowned; unanimous solicitude for Smith, he thought, that sprang from Smith being Jackson's angel. Jackson of whom everyone was afraid, who became an avenging fury if a hair of Smith's golden head was touched. Still, one couldn't expect a man to work night and day. He said: "Who else is there?"

"Bashiam," said Rawlings. "He's as good as they come, here."

Anywhere, amended Mackendrick, silently, adjusting the scales of justice oscillating in his mind until they leveled to meet his exacting standard.

They waited for Bashiam, who should have been on duty but was not, while the scouts went out and his name came over the loud speakers in puny blasts between the thump and clamor of heavy machinery, and Clinton could feel the fretfulness that linked the three of them working up between their white-skinned shoulder blades and taste the sweat that formed at the corners of his mouth.

Bashiam heard the summons as he neared the clearing and in obedience to his training began to lope toward it although he was tired, but then an older discipline supervened and he thought, philosophically, that a few minutes would make no difference except to his health and serenity and he reduced his speed to a walk.

Rawlings saw the lone figure following the curve of the valley. "Don't hustle yourself, will you," he cupped his hands round his mouth and called, some of his ill-humor lifting at the nervous titter this raised, "we've got all day, even if you haven't!"

Bashiam grinned to himself. Rawlings, he knew, would bawl him out and he accepted that: it was sly sniping, Henderson's kind, that was difficult to sustain.

"Where the hell have you been?" Rawlings scowled at him.

"In the jungle, trapping birds," said Bashiam. "I lost count of the time." He could have said: I overslept, the sirens didn't wake me, which could happen to any man, they were all on the overworked side; but he did not feel like lying.

"Trapping birds," said Rawlings. "Well, next time see that you don't—"

"Did you say—trapping birds?" asked Clinton. He turned and looked at Bashiam, and saw him then for the first time as a man, and the eluding and fragmented obsessions that had harried the edge of his consciousness crystalized, took on form and a figurehead. Bashiam, he thought: the man with whom Helen went, someone with whom one had to reckon. It was a queer sensation: he had not thought to come face to face with what had been a faceless cog in complex machinery, or to find it impossible of dismissal as a ludicrous adversary.

"Yes sir," said Bashiam, meeting the older man's eyes. Blue, cold, lightening as if windows were opening, with which dialogues were possible. Then he looked away, remembering the exiguous role far down in the power scale to which Clinton had assigned him, long ago, in the beginning.

Then they all waited, while crosscurrents wavered between them which they could not grasp or name, like fur on pelt erecting softly in face of uncertainty. And Clinton for once could not control it, could not bring his authority to break the overlapping silence in which his flesh had become involved. It was Rawlings who did so, Rawlings who felt crosscurrents too, but made a habit of never giving a damn for them unless he was forced.

"Since you've condescended to join us," he said, elaborately,
to Bashiam, "do you think you could turn your attention from
birds to cranes?"

The Indians smirked politely, they could see it was meant to
be some kind of joke. Bailey gave a loud guffaw, childishly
pleased because there was another meaning to birds which he
knew and the others didn't that made it a sort of in-joke. Bashiam, with other involvements crowding him, could not take
in what was said. He grew confused and stammered, and Rawlings began to shout.

"There, man, there!" He gestured, an arm outflung crane-
ward. "Warm her up, you can do that can't you? Up in the cab,
boy, and get her moving."

Bashiam grew more confused still. He wanted to put his
hands over his ears and shout back that he had to concentrate
when English was spoken to understand it, and he could not
do this when people spoke in the way that Rawlings was doing.
His face went blank in self-defense, and Rawlings to whom the
look was familiar felt like throwing his hands in the air and
giving up, or flinging his topi on the ground in despair and
jumping on it like an old-time comedian and both images were
vivid in his mind but he restrained himself, suddenly aware of
Clinton and Mackendrick, not that he stood in awe of them, no,
but between them they had this chilling, dampening effect on a
red-blooded man like himself.

"Get in that crane and make it work," he said. "Savvy?"

He spoke simply and carefully, spelling out the words as
if to a child of limited intelligence so that Bashiam might understand. Bashiam understood; it was Rawlings who could
not fathom out the sudden anger that darkened his eyes as he
swung himself into the cabin.

But Bashiam's anger died as quickly as it had flared. In his
cabin twenty feet up from the ground, the levers and dials that
controlled the immense strength and finesse of a superb piece
of machinery ranged before him and awaiting his touch, a peace
crept over him that muted the people below, neutralized the

hidden and verbalized strife that irked him. Though he did not know it, it resembled the peace that, of all of them assembled there, perhaps only one other experienced: Clinton, who in conception and contemplation of his creations knew it too, felt his energies concentrated and encapsuled along a single hard beam that annihilated the raucous and the external. Only in Clinton's case the cutout was total. Or had been.

16

OF the thousands of tons of equipment, including cranes, that they had assembled for the building of the dam, none, Clinton thought irately, had created more disruption than the Avery-Kent.

"Why the hell can't Bashiam keep on operating it?" he snapped at Rawlings. "He knows exactly how it handles."

"Smith can handle it," Rawlings spoke doggedly. "He's a crane man, knows them all from A to Z and in my opinion he's the better man."

"Smith hasn't operated an Avery-Kent mobile. Whereas Bashiam"—Clinton smacked the file lying on his table—"according to his record sheet has had two solid years operating nothing else. He's the best man for the job we have."

"Look." Rawlings leaned forward. "It's taken us three weeks to fix her up, put her in good running order after the bashing she took from those ignorant sods. Are you just going to hand her over to jungle johnnie? Yes I know some of 'em are pretty good, they learn quickly I'll give 'em that and we use a lot of them—we have to, there aren't enough of us to go round. But the real know-how? You think it comes in two years? Or ten? Our chaps, it's in the bone. This lot, you never

know which way they're going to jump." He paused. "I
wouldn't trust one of them farther than I could throw him.
That goes for Bashiam especially."

"Why Bashiam?"

"Because he's too clever by half."

"It's not a question of trusting. It's putting a skilled man
to a skilled job," said Clinton. Why, he wondered, did he insist? Let Rawlings have his way, maybe he was right, anyhow
there was little to choose between the two men . . . but he
knew the fact of the matter, which was that he had to persist
so that he could not, afterward, accuse himself of allowing
his judgment to be twisted by his emotions. Dark emotions.
Turmoil that ratcheted up and took its grip somewhere behind
his throat. Clinton passed his hand over his eyes.

"Well, if you feel strongly—" he said.

"I do," said Rawlings.

Over in the British labor quarters beyond Clinton's Lines,
in the four-room block which he shared with Jackson, Smith
said: "Burra sahib says I'm for the Avery-Kent."

"What, Clinton?" said Jackson.

"No, burra sahib Rawlings," said Smith.

"What'd you say?"

"Told him I'm not."

"What'd you want to do that for?" Jackson sat on the edge of
the camp-bed and roared for the boy allotted to the block.
"Gundappa, you idle sonofabitch! Where's the char? You gone
to sleep or something? Bloody heathen, can't even tell the
time!"

"Yes, what," said Smith. "I'll tell you. That job, she come
up busted, right? So they take her into works and they fix her
up, good as new, right?"

"Right," said Jackson. "I seen to it myself, like I seen to
the workshops, built them up from nothing as you might say.
Finest job this side of the Pacific."

"Atlantic, don't you mean?"

"If you say so. Anyway this side of home."

"Maybe it is. It is a fine job, I'm not querying that so don't get me wrong. All I'm saying is she's not been tested and according to regulations she ought to be."

"What for? Nothing's been altered."

"Who says so? The gate's been recast hasn't it?"

"We had to, all twisted it was, wouldn't hinge back proper. But done according to specification, you're not denying that, are you? You've seen for yourself."

"I seen her," said Smith. "The plates don't look the same to me. What's more the lugs are square, what I seen before they was triangular."

"Well maybe," said Jackson. "They didn't have none of them others up in spares store, we had to use what they bloody well did have. Stands to reason if you ask me."

"If you ask me," said Smith, "they ought to have been cut new."

"Cut new!" Jackson's eyes bulged. "This country, you've got to improvise. We haven't got home facilities here, you know. Where d'you think you are, home sweet home?"

"My way of thinking, it ought to have gone down to base," said Smith, "to one of them Indian workshops what would do the job proper."

"Who says so?" said Jackson.

"I do," said Smith. "What's more I told his lordship."

"What'd he say?"

"Blew his top, he did."

"What'd you expect?"

"Makes no difference to me," said Smith. "I've told him, and I'm telling you, it's no go."

Jackson ruminated. There was a lot more he could say, oh yes. But then Smith might take umbrage, he might even go away, and then he, Jackson, would be alone in those four rooms again, and hear the river gurgling in the darkness though it was five hundred yards away, and there would be no sleep, the river and the jungle would see to that. He glanced at Smith,

Smith who was tall and slim and lithe, well-muscled and bronzed and everything he liked his men to be, whom he liked by him and whose body could dissolve the fears that engulfed his mind at night. He decided that he would not say it. "Gundappa!" he shouted instead, ill-temperedly, "Where's the char, you lousy bastard! If it's not up pronto I'll do you, you hear me?"

"Coming, saar, coming," Gundappa shouted back, and he bent down and blew through the holes in the charcoal *sigri* to hurry the fire along. At the first wisp of steam from the spout he lifted the kettle off, holding it by a grimy wet rag which he wound round the red-hot handle, and poured the water into the teapot. He had been told not to do this, but he dare not wait any longer for the kettle to boil, Jackson master was already in a state he could tell. The tea leaves floated to the top when he poured the water on and he eyed them doubtfully, but it was too late to do anything about it. Perhaps, he thought as he bore the tray in, Jackson master wouldn't notice, he seemed to be taken up with the other master who was fair and smooth and beside whom (especially when he wore only a singlet and you could see most of his great hairy body) he looked like a gorilla. Gundappa gave a little private snicker. They often called him gorilla among themselves, almost as often as he called them black apes, and there were other diverting matters too, such as the bed that the masters shared, details of which he, Gundappa, was in a privileged position to divulge. All these matters ran through his mind and bolstered him, while Jackson's invective rang round the block.

So Clinton had his way, though he had not actually wanted it; and Rawlings, with ill-grace, gave way knowing he could not fight both Jackson and Smith.

Bashiam, shut off from these conferences, yet knew long before he was told what had come about. That was the way it was in the camp—in all camps, in his experience. Word got around: one had almost to be mute if one didn't want it to, and that was impossible because there wasn't much else to do once one finished work. Despite the canteen, despite the cinema, despite the games room and the coffee shop and the bar. They had crowded into them, in the early days: still did, for that matter: but now if one wanted to avoid a quarrel one did well to keep away, but that was not easy to do either, they still had this drawing power; and, sometimes, quarreling was a way of letting off steam. Bashiam sighed, but it was not for himself that he did so. He had no cause for sighing—not just now, with the Avery-Kent going to him.

The Avery-Kent. In his mind he saw the towering structure, burnished by the sun where it stood on the escarpment, dwarfing everything else on the site. The long extended arm, eighty feet of steel and strength. The silk-smooth controls, and the precise, formidable power that resided in them. Long before the whispers reached him, while the dismantled jib was still going through the fabrication shop, he had itched to lay his hands on them. It was a growth and extension of the feeling that had flooded him when he first swung himself into the cabin of the crane with its shattered upper window, in its turn an echo of the pride he had felt that long-ago day of his triumphant graduation, when after years of weary second-fiddling they had allowed him to put away his badge of tribal backwardness and take on a responsible role.

That time, too, it had been an Avery-Kent. Devi, he called it now, Goddess; and contentment sat like a pearl in the center of his forehead. Sometimes the pearl grew cloudy, but this was only when he recalled the way Clinton had looked at him, making him wonder, uneasily, about the basis on which that look had built up.

17

MARCH came, and the mornings were no longer cold. The winds blew warmer across the valley, and Clinton's thoughts, narrowly intent on maintaining the time schedule, leaped forward to June when the monsoon would break and the river would be in spate. By then the cutting of the channel and the installation of the control gates would have to be finished, ready to receive the deflected waters of the river at full capacity; at the same time the coffer dams, now well above the waterline but not yet at the three-quarter mark across the river, would have to be completed and in place, to hold the pressure of the river building up against them. If not, if the gaps had not been closed by then, the floodwater would pour through them, taking with it substantial portions of both the upstream and downstream coffers.

That gave him three months: three months in which to complete and pit the strength of his structures against the river and monsoon. Well, he thought, it had to be done and it would be: perhaps with a step-up of tempo; but more onerous datelines had been met by Clinton Mackendrick before.

"I'd be happier," he said to Mackendrick, "if we worked round the clock."

"So would I," said Mackendrick. "I like a few weeks in hand, to toss over the side if I want to. We'll get the night shifts going, soon as we can."

"Hope there won't be trouble."

"Only from our men." Mackendrick grimaced. "They hate the place by night, it twists their guts."

"I cannot think why."

"Well . . . strange places do have an effect."

"They've been out here a year," said Clinton. "Two years, some of 'em. One can scarcely call it a strange place."

Mackendrick shrugged. "Is India ever anything else?"

The soft warm March weather Helen found delectable. It came as a surprise, after the long session of brilliant cut-glass days and freezing dawns and nights: another surprise that the country seemed to hoard and suddenly drop like a jewel into one's lap.

"Memsahib like?" asked Das, his plump face benignly creased. Their relationship had moved on. He was no less critical of the memsahib's ways than he had been, but nowadays he found if he closed his eyes he could slice off that side of her and think of the things that pleased him.

"Memsahib like very much," said Helen. "It's lovely, a lovely change."

Das agreed. He had come out of the huddle of blankets and rugs in which he swaddled himself each night before retiring to his icy godown, in which he was never really warm. Against his better judgment he had tried lighting a fire once, nearly kippering himself in the process, after which he had resigned himself to his fate.

"You can't stand the climate," Helen, watching the white-uniformed figure lumpy with memsahib-discarded cardigans, unable to alleviate his misery, had said to him. "You should never have come up here. Couldn't you find a job in the plains?"

"Plenty jobs for best servants like me, memsahib," Das answered with dignity, producing the bulging packet of chits

which testified to his excellent buttling and were the acknowledged passes to a good job; but the truth of the matter
was that the demand for his kind had dwindled to almost nothing—a truth that (his mind chattering with fears of the sack)
he could not bring himself to voice.

Millie Rawlings was more forthright. "Only a few left now,"
she said. "The memsahibs, I mean. Not the ones from Russia
and Sweden and Salford, they're there all right, inheriting our
earth . . . I mean the real mems like us, dearie, there's precious few of that breed left. When it's extinct, they'll follow."
She jerked her head at Das, "An end to them, and an end to
the superb service we've had from them and shan't ever have
again till kingdom come. Eh, Das, you old rascal?"

Das gave a discreet smile and went on making miter shapes
out of the luncheon napkins. He knew he was not really being
asked for his opinion, it was not his place to give it and he knew
his place, none better; but he increased the grace of his movements and comported himself even more respectfully than
before to show how ardently he agreed.

"Poor Das," Helen said one evening when Das had been
borrowed by Millie—this had become a recurrent loan. "On
the scrap heap when we've gone."

"I suppose so, yes," said Clinton, turning his attention from
the rows of eyes glowing green in the jungle darkness. The
deer came every night—shy creatures one never saw by day—
despite the dam, the clutter of machinery, the floodlights,
drawn by what he could only conceive was insatiable curiosity.
A doe-eyed, unafraid curiosity that he found unusually moving.

"It seems a shame," she said.

Clinton nodded. He didn't want to commit himself to anything, because he didn't know what she wanted of him: grew
wary, these days, when she raised the subject of some Indian,
any Indian, even one like Das who was far more attuned and
allied to him than to her. She seemed to have become prickly

about them, he thought, pouncing on ordinary reactions for reasons that he could not follow, in a way that he recognized permeated their whole relationship adversely though he could not have explained exactly how.

"Couldn't we give him a pension?" She watched the deer too, not twenty yards from the glassed-in verandah. Bailey had shot one, though they were a protected species; he was very proud of the spotted skin, which he used as a bedside rug.

"When we leave," Clinton said, "there are going to be hundreds of labor out of a job. Are we going to pension them all?"

"It swamps one to think like that," she rejoined. "Let's not. Let's just think of one."

"All right."

"Of Das."

"All right," he said again. "We'll make him a pension, if you like."

But that was not at all what she wanted: she wanted him to do it because he cared, not because she liked, and he could not.

It was as if they were walking on different levels: he on the overpass, she on the under. He had, as he said, an overall vision. She saw the detail: Das, and the birds, and the passions below. We go our different ways, she thought, and maybe his is as valid as mine; but could not drum up much conviction and it remained an intellectual exercise.

The birds were Jackson's, a pair of hill mynas bespoken by him that the wildfowler, who went in fear of the burly foreman, refused to sell her out of the morning's haul despite the outrageous price she offered. The rest she bought and released. An empty gesture, she knew: what of the countless birds that she would not free, for a trade that she could not block? Yet it was valid for her and it had to be made, and at the end when she saw the birds go, fluttering on cramped wings and then soaring up in headlong flight, the academics lapsed and she simply stood holding the empty wicker basket peppered with bird droppings, conscious only of a stretching and a smoothing out of what had been crimped and in spasm within her.

Jackson kept the pair in a cage on the verandah until someone told him neither would sing or speak unless in solitary confinement, and so he gave one away. Sometimes Helen went to see the one that was left. Jackson was very pleased when she did, or when anyone did, he loved showing off his glossy black myna.

"Some beauty, miss, eh?"

"It's a beautuful bird."

"Hear that, sweetheart? You hear what the lady says? Here you are, Lovey, see what Daddy's got for you." And he would pick up a worm from a tin which Gundappa scrabbled about and filled each morning and hold it between the bars, cooing, and sometimes the myna would take it, more often not.

When it didn't Jackson would coax it. "Come on, Lovey, just to please your daddy," standing patiently beside the cage.

One day she bumped into him, literally, for he was blundering along the path outside the bungalow.

"Oh hullo, Jackson," she said. "I was on my way to you."

"That's funny, miss," he answered slowly. "I was just coming to see you. To ask if you had something what would do for Lovey, wrap her up proper like."

"For Lovey?"

"She's dead, miss. Gone, see. Must've happened in the night."

Jackson's cheeks were wet, she saw him bending to wipe them on his sleeve, awkwardly because of the dead bird he had in his hands.

"Me and Smith," he said, "we looked, but we've not got nothing what would do. Not for Lovey. She was a beauty, eh, miss?"

Helen looked down at the bird. Its claws were shriveled but its feathers were still bright, a brilliant gloss. A beautiful bird, she agreed. She had on a cream silk scarf with a knotted fringe and she took it off and gave it to him.

"Will this do?"

"Do beautiful," Jackson said, squatting on the ground and arranging the shroud. Presently he looked up. "I want her buried proper," he said in a strained way. "Where we are them savages might have her up, their rites and such what we don't hold with. I wouldn't like that, miss, not for Lovey, but they wouldn't here, would they, being as it's the burra sahib's. . . ."

"I don't think they'd dig up a dead bird anywhere," she said gently, "but if you'd like . . ."

So they buried the myna in a corner of the compound, and presently Jackson marked the grave with a cross. She was glad when he did, in case the gardener's spade did bring up the bones, confirming Jackson in his fears and prejudices. But Clinton was not too pleased. It marred the view from the bungalow, and was not the kind of symbol he liked to see implanted in the home ground of the head of Clinton Mackendrick & Co.

18

TWILIGHT fell perceptibly later as April went by. The evening shift that ended at eight, having worked the last hour by artificial light, came out now to crimson and copper skies which killed the powerful glare of the arc lamps. In minutes the sunset colors faded, the brilliant streamers thrown across the globe retracting to a leaden pool poised on the western horizon; and the workers who walked up the hill slopes framed in nimbus were silhouettes in the landscape before their ascent was complete.

With the sudden, peremptory plunge into darkness the arc lights grew strident again. The harsh explosive glare, like flaring naphtha, cut out and lit the whole scene sharply, giving it the blue-sheen edge of steel. Rocks and ravines assumed dual roles, their plane surfaces bathed in bluish light, the folds and pleats of the granite structure jet-black by contrast, impenetrable and unknown. The river glittered, reflecting the agglomeration of lights in the valley except where the cliffs closed in over cascading waters in the narrow gorge. In the shattered plateau, dwarfed by the debris left from blasting, men were at work; blue flame leaped and spurted from the machines they wielded, the electric shovels and diggers that bit into and gouged out rock.

The silence that came once in the twenty-four-hour cycle, enfolding the hills and valley at nightfall, was now permanently fractured. At dawn, at noon, by night, machines thundered and pounded; land and air vibrated spasmodically to the dull crump of explosions, the shock waves traveling to the barracks, the bungalows, the leisure blocks and the tribal settlements. Men slept through it: those who adapted quickly or who had come off duty exhausted, or who raided the medical stores for sleeping tablets, or those whose lives had had acceptance ground into them. But the cradling quiet in which they recuperated, body and mind and spirit, that quiet was gone.

"Gets on your nerves," said Millie. "You can't hear yourself think."

In fact her thoughts buzzed quite audibly in her head, and were about big cities which she could picture revolving to her needs and desires. Not London, no, uppity London where every man imagined he was as good as the next . . . but Cape Town say, or even Bombay or New Delhi where social order had not been torn down wholesale and you knew where the tiers were and, more to the point, so did other people.

But Cape Town was too far, and Bombay and New Delhi would soon be like ovens . . . Ootacamund on the other hand would be cool, but it was not the same, people said it had been infiltrated, even the clubs. . . . Millie sighed, and tried not to think of the half-naked coolies, and the cocky half-baked technicians, and the tribal savages among whom her present lot was cast, and to help her forget began a desultory affair with young Bailey. Yet though she plugged the gap, interstices remained of which she was barely conscious, into which seeped background stresses and strains, the noise, the dust, the fretfulness. They had done so for many months, and she had employed different plugs. But now, suddenly, it all seemed that much worse.

The village, up-river, felt the onslaught most, the hill at whose base the tribesmen were encamped acting as a peculiarly effective baffle-board, bouncing sound and shock waves off the shallow, boulder-strewn basin where they had pitched their huts.

"Why on earth don't you move? God knows you haven't much to carry!" Helen said ill-temperedly.

"Where to?" the village chief asked tartly.

When their mutual irritation had subsided he explained: there were no reasonable moves left to them. Depending on water, they were tied to the river. But downstream the ramifications of building requisitioned the riverbanks until the terrain grew untenable. Upstream beyond the sheltering hill, they and their huts would be in the path of the southwest monsoon winds. Those fragile huts, that would take off like kites at very first puff. Backs against a mountain, she thought, they had been pushed as far as they could go. Physically speaking no further retreat was left. So they stayed where they were, while the bed of the valley quaked, and dust flew through the thatch on their ramshackle huts and settled grittily in every nook and cranny.

"It's a bit hard on them," Helen said, and Clinton thought, she's at it again, why them only? If it's hard on them it's hard on everyone. He said: "Nobody likes a lot of noise. It's no worse for them, is it, than for anyone else? Sometimes I can't sleep either."

"But their huts don't take it," said Helen, glancing at the solid walls of their carefully sited bungalow, the double insulating glass, the excluding mesh at the window. "They're rattled around like peas in a tin."

"They've been rattled around for some considerable time," said Clinton. "They should be used to it by now."

"But now it's worse. The nights are. They feel it more."

"They'll get used to it. People do when they have to."

Helen held herself tautly. She could feel his detachment working in her like solvents and suddenly despite herself they were gone, all the controls, and she flared at him—senselessly she knew, for neither he nor anyone could stop this modern juggernaut that was on the move. Yet if only he would say something in sympathy or exculpation, she thought in the calm plane above her ignited emotions, even if nothing could be done . . . but Clinton was silent, astonished by her intensity over this trival matter, and in the silence a loneliness washed over her and she despaired, crying, "Can't you care? Don't human beings matter anything to you? Do they have to be a special kind of flesh before they do?"

Clinton, bewildered, face to face with forms of violence he had not suspected in his wife, had nothing to say. In him was the same battered refuge to which from time to time they all had recourse, and into this he retreated. The country's affecting her, he told himself, it's getting on her nerves: well, she's not the first person it's happened to nor by any means the last. Get the job done, he thought, get back quick, home to sanity, that's the drill.

In the British canteen the ceiling had cracked, all over like a breakfast egg tapped with a spoon. They surveyed it solemnly over their beer: Smith, Jackson, Wilkins and Wright.

In the valley they were blasting, at each thump a minute puff of pulverized ceiling wafted down as if an atomizer had been squeezed, depositing specks on the termite-proof, Formica-topped table. Not only their table, all the tables; but although the canteen was full Wright was the sole complainant.

"This rate the whole ruddy thing'll come down on us one day and that day not far off," he said, covering his beer against the drifting dust. His hands, he noticed, were trembling. He could control it at work, usually; it was more difficult when they laid off, sometimes impossible.

"Bloody contractor's effort," said Wilkins. "Botched the job, lined his pockets, shoved off leaving us with it."

Smith waited until the bearer was out of earshot. "Wasn't no contractor," he said. "Our lot built the canteen, top to bottom. Old Subramaniam, he was good, built all the burra sahib bungalows, but he went off in a huff, him and his men, having had words with the bosses. So then Mack says to us, get on with the canteen will you, you got to have a canteen, he says, it's essential. So we did."

"First I heard of it," said Wright.

"You wasn't out here first," said Smith pointedly. "You come out with the replacement draft, after we got it cushy for soft arses, so how would you have got to hear?"

"Cushy my arse," said Wright. "You call this cushy. Ask me it's a dump. A man can't even have his beer without having the ceiling fall in."

"I heard enough of that," Jackson brought his fist down hard, disarranging the neat pattern of dominoes on the table. "It's a temporary structure, see? You don't build temporary structures to last unless you're off your nut, do you?"

"I'm sure you're right," said Wright, retreating.

"It's the blasting does it," said Jackson, rearranging the dominoes, flicking an end one round in his favor. "Days only, that's one thing, days and nights, that's something different. Ceilings, they got to rest same as us otherwise there's bound to be trouble."

"Who're you kidding?" said Wilkins, giving a loud guffaw.

"Similar to metal fatigue," said Jackson, his brows laced together menacingly.

Wright put his head between his hands. "Ought to be a law," he said, "against nonstop working. Fair gives you the willies, going out there day and night, especially night."

"Suits me," said Wilkins. "Triple time for night shifts, I'm not grumbling."

"Gets the job done quick, you want to get shot of this dump soon as you can, do you or don't you," said Smith, thinking of his little doll of a wife, putting her down in front of him and making lewd comparisons between her and Jackson whom he called Jackanapes in private conversations he had with himself.

There was a pause and in it their homes grew alluring and

the sense of longing rose, as strong as the tropical scent of blue gum and arum lily blown in by the April wind.

"All those in favor say aye," said Wright, weakly, raising his hand, which was joined presently by the other three.

That evening Mackendrick stayed late on the site. As he walked home he glanced in at the Indian canteen, which as usual was half-empty (they're not good clubmen, he remembered someone telling him, and smiled to himself), and then at the British canteen which seemed to be bursting its seams. Declining the offers of a drink which rained upon him he waved a cheerful good night, crossed the bridge and took the path to his bungalow. He had forgotten his cobra boots and he walked carefully, using his flashlight to cut wide swathes in the darkness, so that he had not gone far when he heard the accident: the scream of brakes, the crash, the jangling ricochet of heavy metal bouncing off jagged rock. He waited until he heard the wailing sirens of the emergency services, and then he went on. There was nothing he could do. Henderson and Krishnan were on site, they would do all that had to be done. In the morning they would tell him—not that he didn't know. In his time he had seen most of it: the casualties of war, to whom they put up those rearing obelisks, and the casualties of peace —but who ever thought of building them memorials? They died horribly, some of them. He had seen men chopped to pieces by their own machines, fished out suppurating from chemical vats, electrocuted, strung up against the high-tension cables like burnt-wood effigies, crumbling to cinders when the current was cut. He had never developed a stomach for such sights: accepted them of course, as did Clinton, Henderson, Jackson, anyone in the game you cared to name, as part of a way of life: but never without a chill recoil, the stealthy shadow of mortal dissolution towering and pressing closer.

After a while Mackendrick walked slowly on. By morning the report would be on his desk, they would hold an inquiry if the facts warranted it. And the loam would be freshly turned

in the British cemetery, which they had faithfully copied from
the home model so that the dead could lie easy . . . if the
dead were British of course. The Indians preferred not to lie
and molder, carried out the funeral rites punctiliously, then
sent their ashes bowling merrily along on the river. One did
not have to write those difficult letters for them either. There
was a grapevine, which worked as efficiently as other systems,
which summoned and informed relatives. Mackendrick halted
these thoughts and took a grip on himself. One did not choose
who should or should not die on the extraordinary basis of
how troublesome their deaths might be. Or, taking it further,
on the equally extraordinary basis of their group or race affili-
ations. If one did, it was a symptom of unease, of disease,
of some inner damage. . . . For the second time Mackendrick
stopped himself. He was, he thought, allowing the accident to
play altogether too much havoc with his nerves.

19

AS the dam advanced the river began to rise.

Imperceptibly, edging up its banks, appropriating territory inch by inch. Along the watercourse, now, one saw the tops of scrub and evergreen rising in incongruous tufts above the waterline, surviving briefly despite inundated root and stem. Through the narrow gap that still remained the river forced its way, foaming and churning round the coffer dams that were rising to block its path.

Sometimes, watching the river lashing and writhing around their handiwork, aware of the sweep and strength of its currents, Lefevre felt a chill fear closing round his spine. At these moments he had to look back, return to the long strained months in which he and his team had assembled, patiently, collating and testing, piece by piece, a knowledge of the river— its flux and flow, the structure of its granite flank, the depth and formation of its bed, the nature of its sludge—a knowledge which controlled fear, and upon which they could base their design and building. When they had finished they knew as much about the river, from bedrock to high-water line, as anyone could. They never said they knew it all, they knew too much to say that: but as much as trained and experienced human beings could. What was it worth, this knowledge wrung like blood out of stone? Lefevre knew to a quite precise degree, turned to it again and again for that vital underpinning to his faith when he looked at the cascading water and felt himself shiver, when the river liquefied his strength, as it could.

In the bungalow laboratory, keeping pace with construction, was a part-finished model of the coffer dam. They built it carefully, Gopal Rao and the team whose head Lefevre was, week by week to match the work in progress, using the same material, withdrawn from the river and its environs—the granite, river-silt, gravel, rock, clay and cement—as was incorporated in the actual structure.

"So that at every stage we can see exactly where we are and what we're doing," said Gopal when initiating the project.

"You've only to stroll a few hundred yards out of your compound to see for yourself," grunted Lefevre. "Alternatively, you could consult the design models, all fifteen of them."

But Gopal persevered, and before long Lefevre conceded that the totality of concept emerged more plainly here, in the clean lines of this miniature dam advancing inexorably across a ribbon of mica, than in the unrelated clutter out of which two coffers and a main dam were to spring.

"Not far to go now," said Gopal one evening—it was long after the conversation that had launched the model dam. Picking up a ruler and a pair of dividers he carefully measured the distance between riverbank and dam. "Four centimeters," he said, on a note that was deliberately toned-down, "and it will be done."

"Not forgetting expansion to scale," said Lefevre.

"But the machines are bigger," said Gopal, and was aware that his pleasure was matched in the other.

The reality lay outside, and its patterns grew steadily clearer.

Across the river, ridge-backed dinosaurs, strode the twin coffers. At their west-bank sections the spine had been broad-ened and smoothed to take the continuous stream of dump trucks, the heavy vehicles that backed slowly along the double lanes, tipping their granite loads to heighten the crest of the dams.

On the east bank, unless one noticed the heightened flurry of water flowing over submerged obstacles, there was no sign of dam. Only the rows of moored buoys, dipping and bobbing like garish balloons, showed where, below water, the foundations were being laid. Foundations of coarse sand, compacted by vibration, laid on the silt of the riverbed; a mattress of boulders and gravel molded over it; rock-fill above, consolidated with clay and cement.

They were working the rock-fill now. Mechanical sieves lining the riverbank graded and sorted rock for the waiting barges, rotating with an abrasive, metallic falsetto like teeth being filed—giant teeth on pitted enamel. At regular intervals barges detached themselves from the waiting flotilla and maneuvered into position alongside the sieves. The rotating griddle stopped in obedience to signals, flaps in the cone opened, and rocks and boulders slid down polished steel chutes into the holds of the barges which lurched away, in water to their gunwales, to dump their loads at the site of the marker buoys.

It was a smooth operation, satisfactorily accelerated since the arrival, thought Rawlings with some complacence, of the additional barges and rotary sieves he had shepherded from Bombay to base, from base to their present sites. The barges, particularly, were proving ideal for the job—their new design a distinct improvement on the original batch—with their cavernous holds, the skilled craftsmanship that kept them buoyant and maneuverable while under heavy load and low in water.

The sieves, he reflected with some irritation, were a different matter, developing one fault after another which were put right soon enough, but which were nevertheless a thundering nuisance—especially with the monsoon hanging over them like a blight. These teething troubles weren't behind them yet,

Rawlings knew. Jackson had reported intermittent jamming on two further machines, and a third had seized up completely. So far as he could see, though (he had come especially to see) all had returned to normal functioning. Squinting in the diffuse light, he checked the line again, and this time spotted one that was still out of commission. Once seen it stood out, a small pocket of idleness in the general activity, surrounded by workers and two figures—he couldn't be certain who from this distance—tinkering with the rotor.

Rawlings lowered the strap of his topi from brim to chin to anchor it in the gusty wind, and strode down the escarpment. As he came closer he saw that it was Bailey, who together with the new man Wilkins was working on the flaps inside the cone, while Wright stood by the controls. He gave them a cheerful wave and Bailey waved back—it was his last natural act. Then his arms shot up and pinned themselves against the metal wall of the machine in the gesture of a man at bay, his mouth opened in a wide incredulous O as the rotor began to turn.

Rawlings raced toward them. There was a lot of shouting competing with the machinery, rising with the whine of the rotating sieve and spiked with horror as the spin increased. He could see the two men, poised on jagged rock, falling to their knees, recovering, falling again and this time disappearing from sight beneath the rim of the cone. He shouted hoarsely, and the rags of sound floated away, uselessly, lost in the uproar of rocks jostling and rearing at the mouth of the open flap before toppling onto the chutes. It was finally obliterated by the rock-fall.

The men in the barge had seen the danger too. Two of them, farthest from the outfall, jumped clear; two others, flung in the river by the impact, escaped with their lives. The rest were overwhelmed where they stood, struck down like ninepins, some with the surprise of it still on their faces, some with the split seconds of realization scored on their features.

Unmanned, the laden barge began to swing with the current, taking with it the two men clinging to the cringle ropes, until a quirk in the flow lodged it momentarily in the offshore sludge a few yards from the crowd that had collected.

Rawlings went in first, water up to his armpits as he grabbed the mooring ropes, hauling on them frenziedly before the barge and its load could be swept away to destruction on the downstream cataracts. The labor gangs followed. Shouting and wailing, in a welter of noise and confusion, they fell in raggedly behind him, passing the heavy, waterlogged coir coils hand over hand down the line to the bollards, winding and making fast.

Then the uproar died. The men were silent, and the machines were quiet too. Rawlings knew they were waiting for him to take command and he knew that he would, it was the role assigned to his country and through it to him; but momentarily the impetus was gone. He stood where he was, heavily, his limbs dragging him down like weights. Then he heard a low cry, like a puppy whimpering, and turned, and above the heads of the crowd saw that it came from Wright. He was alone, slumped at the controls of the killer machine, large tears rolling unchecked down his cheeks, his throat working, heaving out those choking sounds. Those awful damned sounds, thought Rawlings with a violent, gritty rage, nerve gone and showing it, the bastard, letting the side down and doesn't care who sees it, bastard, bastard. . . . His own weakness lifted, and he shouldered his way through to Wright and hauled him to his feet.

"Clear out," he said distinctly, without raising his voice. "Get back to your quarters and stay there, do you understand?"

He waited until Wright had shambled off, before returning to the scene of the disaster.

The day, unconcerned, developed as usual: only Rawlings, under stress, had neglected to allow for the fact that it would. A sudden lurch of the barge reminded him. He saw then that the waves, fanned by the freshening wind, were lapping stronger, realized that in these conditions the barge would not remain afloat as long as he had assumed. Already it had be-gun to list, dipping farther at each slap of the river, shipping water at each wallow, the top-heavy pile of rock shifting and grinding in its hold. She'll be gone any time, he thought un-easily, waiting for the heavy lifting gear; perhaps an hour, not much more . . . and she'll take them with her, Bailey and Wil-kins are still there, somewhere under that pile. . . .

"The barge is going to sink," someone said at his elbow and he turned and saw it was Krishnan, and turned away again and ignored him.

"We should tow it to intended site," said Krishnan, "and open the tip-chutes before it sinks."

"The current's running strong, we shall never recover the men if we do," said Rawlings curtly.

"No matter," said Krishnan. "They are dead."

"We like to give our dead a decent Christian burial," said Rawlings, passionately, "whatever your pagan beliefs, Mr. Krishnan, enjoin upon you."

"They teach us that the body is nothing, it is the spirit that matters," replied Krishnan. "Are these beliefs, Mr. Rawlings, not also yours?"

Rawlings passed his hands over his face. He felt them sting and he took them away and looked down in surprise. The palms and the roots of his fingers were raw. The coir ropes had rubbed off the skin, and the wound was smarting with his own sweat. Our blood, our sweat, he thought: what for? It's not our bloody country!

"We do it my way," he said furiously.

"As you wish," said Krishnan, openly sneering.

Mackendrick, appalled, listened to the exchange; the words were like pebbles, scooped out clean and hard from the gen-eral hubbub. At a time like this, he thought, how deep the division goes . . . but the young ones, he thought again, sane ones, Bailey and Lefevre and—but he's gone, he thought incredulously, Bailey's gone . . . and his stomach began to heave, though his visible muscles, his face and his hands, were still.

By now the lifting gear had arrived, coiled hawsers, cable-drums, cranes and hoists, the men to man them. What had been chaos was already being transformed into a smooth rescue operation. Side by side Smith and Bashiam worked the mobile derricks, going in alternately, the steel hooks poised above the mountain of glittering, mica-encrusted rock, descending, lifting, slewing and landing in a rapid, continuous rhythm. Minute by minute as the load in the waiting trucks grew the rock pile in the stricken craft reduced and the barge rode higher.

We'll do it yet, muttered Rawlings, if the wind levels out, if it veers only a little, and he licked his finger, childishly, and held it up and felt it dry instantly in the gusts of wind that swept south and west down the ravine and whipped peaks in the surface of the river.

"Not long," said Mackendrick.

"No," said Rawlings, and was grateful for the sympathy underlying the remark, as well as the strength he sensed in the other.

"It's that much worse when you see it happen," he said.

"I know," said Mackendrick.

The barge was half empty now. Once more the valley was quiet, a hushed, unnatural quiet. Except for the rattle of chain-slings and the unwinding drums.

"They can't be far," said Rawlings, and almost as he spoke both men saw the protruding limb.

They worked quickly after that, came quickly to Bailey and Wilkins. They lay close together as they had fallen, their faces pulped and indistinguishable one from the other. Their bodies were raw; the abrasive cone had flayed them, rubbed up the flesh in swollen purple ridges. In parts the shredded flesh had fallen clean away from the bone. Serum, from some depleted source in the body, dripped slowly down on the rocks below.

Once more it came: the hiatus between the training, and the discipline and the drill, and the intrusion of frail, human emotion. It fastened on them like a clamp, excluding, denying the right of all action in face of what had been so terribly branded *finis*. Then as suddenly as it had crippled them it was gone. The barge on the river lurched, accentuating realities and urgencies, and halted energies began to course again.

On shore, Rawlings bawled at the men; but now they were anticipating him, forestalling his orders half of which were carried away by the wind. Alone in his cab, waiting while the bodies were trussed in canvas for lifting, Bashiam heard the roared directions and exhortations and the curses, sometimes muffled, sometimes swelling, and was not offended. None of them was offended. Because of the hour and the occurrence nothing Rawlings said could cause their spirits to rise against him.

The gusts grew stronger as they worked.

Bailey and Wilkins had been brought ashore. They lay, neatly sheeted under canvas, on the shelving bank overlooking the site of their labors. In a row beside them, in equally blind contemplation, were the bodies of the men whom the rock-fall had overwhelmed, whom they had taken from the layers below. Crushed and suffocated, but not savaged to death.

Not that that should matter, thought Mackendrick, but somehow it did. He bent and straightened a corner of canvas that had flapped back in the high wind, noticing that the smashed face below still wore a look of surprise. Gone out like a light, he thought, not even time to be afraid, but no time to make one's peace either. With one's god, with oneself. Would one want to, he wondered, and felt that Bailey and Wilkins, at any rate, would have plumped for a quick death as he himself would have done. The others—well, they were not Christians, their faith was whole and deep, not strewn in fragments. They feared death too, who didn't; but they didn't scuttle sideways at the sound of the word, they composed themselves and waited, like that desiccated headman in the village. Perhaps the hills bred that kind of courage, he thought, and machines manufactured their own special brand.

Bashiam, up in his cab, also thought of death and the method of it and the one he would choose but was kept too busy to tease the matter long. One goes when one's time comes, he thought dismissively, sinking himself in the routine of working the derrick. Rawlings' urgent voice was borne up to him and now and then he let it intrude, thinking, he's worried in case the barge goes down but it's too late to tow it out now, he should have done it when Krishnan told him, it was then or never. . . . He worked steadily on, not hearing Rawlings at all toward the end until the last rock boulder rose clear of the barge leaving it still afloat, and then he did hear him, cheering loudly and leading a muted applause, and detected in the sound a note of triumph over and above that due to successful completion. Victory over the river, he thought, placing it at last, but victory over Krishnan too, ah yes, and that first. But by then he was too near exhaustion to care.

"In the end what he really cared about," said Krishnan with contempt, "was that he should be right and I should be wrong."

His assistant Shanmugham, who was chewing *pan* because it was the end of the day and to quiet his jumping nerves, grew very still.

"It is important to them," he said at last, "not to lose face."

"The question is," said Krishnan, "how far will they go to save it."

Shanmugham did not answer. He did not want to talk about it now, although over the past months they all had, someone noticing something here, and someone something else there, until the disturbing picture built up. But the silence would not be contained and at length he said—the emollient less for his bruised skin than for Krishnan's—"It is of lesser consequence . . . it is the final outcome that matters. To them as to us."

Both were silent now, their thoughts on the outcome, the dam to which they daily committed themselves in little bits—

their body, their mind, the unknown quantity that they called the spirit. All of them: not just one. All of them working toward a common end. Yet at every stage, under the smooth skin stretched over their community of purpose, these savage break-away strands of internecine struggle. Which everyone knew, it was a sap and marrow knowledge which had percolated over the months by a species of osmosis, and this being so they were at pains to see only the surface.

20

AT dawn on the morning of the interment Clinton left his bungalow and went to look at the coffer dam. All work on it had ceased, the machines stood gaunt and idle in a way they had not done since commencement. There was no sign of anyone except for a solitary watchman, a palmleaf cloak doubled round his shoulders, sheltering behind a truck from the wind. The man rose as he passed, the stiff palmyra scraping his scraggy back like a bow drawn across a cheap fiddle.

"Bad business, sahib."

"It was," said Clinton, and walked on. Past tense, over now and almost done with.

A few yards on, at the end of the orderly line of equipment, was the mechanical sieve in which the men had died. Halted and impotent now, impersonal, its jutting contours concealed under khaki-colored tarpaulin. The killer machine, he said aloud: he had heard them calling it that. He had heard it many times over many years applied to many different kinds of machine and it had never seemed anything but meaningless. Men were the only killers. Of themselves too, sometimes, following through a wish for death without knowing it themselves. Like people who asked to be murdered, bearing on their forehead the invisible mark of Abel. Like Wright, who had allowed the country to shake him to pieces, his overwrought nerves triggering the careless, lethal act which could as easily have cost him his own life. It still could, which was why they would ship him off home as soon as they could, they didn't believe in taking risks of that kind. Then, dismissively, he put away the shaking, white-faced hulk that was Wright from his mind, and made his way to the cemetery.

Unaccustomed hat in hand, Mackendrick waited in the little shaded British burial ground to conduct the burial service. It was a duty that had devolved upon him, more by adroit sidestepping of the others than from any wish of his to play padre. At one time, of course, there would have been a padre: one shipped them out with the rest of the outfit, or borrowed one from outlying mission or church. Now they had been dispensed with. Like doctors, Mackendrick thought, his mind weaving backward and forward in time. In the old days each set-up had its attached medico, but their grasping propensities, their preoccupation with money and their own dignity didn't go down too well with anyone . . . so instead they laid in a store of modern drugs and streamlined the access to an efficient hospital and invariably it worked out better. Not that anyone, neither hospital nor medico, could have done much for poor Bailey, not once the lever handle fell. . . .

Presently, through the trees, he saw the pallbearers approaching, walking with the stiff, paralytic gait considered appropriate for the dead. The coffins were teak, rough and unvarnished. The carpenters had knocked them up in record time, and hadn't, he thought, made too bad a job of it. Usually they carried a discreet reserve store of two or three coffins, which was the British fatality figure; but recently there had been rather a run on it, a spate of accidents making up for the long stretch they had been blessedly without. . . . There were some twenty crosses in the cemetery now, arranged in tidy rows like a small lost regiment. How many more, he wondered, and felt the gooseflesh rise, softly, along the ridge of his spine.

At the end of a line, beginning a new one, were the two open graves, great gaping slits that waited for Bailey and Wilkins decorously encased in their teakwood coffins. Rich dark loam, heavy with leaf-mold, lay piled in mounds alongside each pit, giving out the dank buried odors of newly turned earth. Mackendrick, his nostrils reacting against the smell, his mind against the loss, the looming sense of decay, those long dark holes waiting to be filled, wished they would hurry. But he also knew that that was not the way it was done, and turned his attention to the setting sun, strung like a blood orange at the rim of the horizon.

At length they were all assembled, Clinton and Rawlings and Millie and Helen, and of course Bailey and Wilkins the main performers, who had had to tout round for someone to wash them and lay them out, so peeled and unpleasant were their corpses. In the end it was a tribeswoman, the hereditary undertaker, cautiously offering her services in case she was not good enough for the sahibs and they had fallen on her withered neck in gratitude. A group of the tribesmen had come to the funeral too, stood in a close pack shuffling awkwardly, visibly paying their last respects. Decent of them, Mackendrick thought, considering their repugnance at this consignment of the body to moldering decay . . . but Bailey had been popular, had got through to them without difficulty, though they had nothing in common, not even language, except this willingness to connect.

The pity of it, Mackendrick thought, open Bible in hand, the pages bright in the tumbling sunset colors; the great rending pity of it.

"The Lord gave," he read, "the Lord hath taken away."

But would Mrs. Wilkins take it as placidly, suddenly bereft in her tidy council flat holding the telegram and blindly watching the telly?

"Ashes to ashes, dust to dust," he read. It was moving and sad, subtly put together to make you weep, but taking care not to kill any hope. It was dangerous, that: nothing to put in its place except thought, which bred revolutions in church and state. Better to weep, be borne along on the loose overwhelming tide.

Millie was weeping, quite openly, past caring. For whom, he wondered, for Bailey, for herself, the woman of fifty pleasured by a handsome young man as she could not hope to be again in her life? Would not have been, except in this far-flung hothouse station that impinged upon them all, strangely, sometimes delicately and sometimes murderously like some enlarged and poisonous sea anemone.

He closed the leather bound Bible and the coffins went down on the ropes. There were Union Jacks stenciled on the lids: Millie, he guessed. How maudlin one became about dying in a foreign land! Perhaps because one had to be so brisk about it at home? With the hearses in and out of the crematoria at twenty-minute intervals, and once, on the M 4, belting along with the best of the traffic. The fact of the matter, though, was that they were done with the trappings of death, as they were through with the romantics of war. It was only in these extended limbs of Britain (as India still incredibly was, though not in name) that some of the old blood still flowed, injected with pickling fluid by memsahibs like Millie. What, he wondered, did she really think about it all, deep down, alone with herself, if anyone could be said to think who could stencil flags on coffin lids? He shifted his gaze from the coffins, up the earth sides to the right side of the grave, edged by the feet of the mourners. Under lowered lids his eyes slid over them, the neatly shod pairs. Clinton's prominent in the prominent position at the head of the grave, then Helen's standing very close to him, was it for show? Then Rawlings' and next to him Millie's feet, and suddenly he was moved by the sight of her shoes, a young woman's fashionable pair and the telltale leather bulging over the middle-aged bunion. Poor Millie, he thought then, with a desperate sympathy.

Clinton read the prayer, scrappily as the light was failing.

Clods of earth, held together by severed threads and rootlets of the distant trees, clumped heavily down on the coffins. No one had brought flowers. The simple graves, in the shadow of the towering jungle, were suddenly forlorn and pathetic.

21

A WEEK went by and one night over a whiskey in Clinton's bungalow Mackendrick said: "The strain's telling on them."

Clinton looked up. "It's a strain on everyone," he agreed. "It often is, working to a tight schedule."

Mackendrick swirled the whiskey in his glass; there was a midge paddling frantically in it and he rescued it on a thumbnail before he spoke again.

"It may be only an impression," he said, "but sometimes when I look at the men it seems to me they're half-asleep. They're working, but bits of them have taken time off to sleep. Not all, of course, some . . . not all the time either, but enough. . . ."

"Enough for what?" Clinton, who also preferred not to look, because of the nakedness of eyes, watched instead the little gecko cupped to the ceiling on its soft suction pads, a tiny upsidedown creature.

"Enough to make a difference," said Mackendrick.

Clinton stirred. The grip created by suction was not always proof against gravity. Sometimes it loosened and the creature fell, its body which was like putty making a horrible plop.

Which knocked it out, you could see it gasping, and the pitted belly, before breath came back. But it recovered quite soon. He had not seen one which did not, and the bungalow was full of geckos. He said: "People have an extraordinary capacity for revival."

"But need a pause," said Mackendrick, "to reflate."

"And have it," said Clinton, "or as much as it is possible for them to have. Since the schedule has not been affected."

"If that is what one goes by," said Mackendrick.

"That is what I go by," said Clinton, and hardened, his own words an ossifying agent. "I would not know by what else to go. Perhaps I'm not imaginative enough. Perhaps you are too imaginative."

Then Mackendrick, who being roused was past avoiding eyes or truths, faced him, "Those last accidents we've had," he said flatly, "there's no real reason why they should have happened."

"They happen in the natural run of things," replied Clinton, "as you know."

Mackendrick faced this knowledge too, and struggled.

"These were above that," he said.

"Do you think so?" inquired Clinton, coolly.

"Think," repeated Mackendrick, who felt his certainties shrinking, and wondered if perhaps he had inflated them, so that now they were reducing to size. "I can't think," he said, and heard the gecko's tck-tck-tck. "When I do it slips away, I can only feel. What I feel is perhaps we ought to ease up now, catch up later."

Clinton rejected it, but knew he could not do it out of hand. He had to persuade and carry with him, especially Mackendrick, his weight being what it was; and he looked round for some pillar against which he could brace himself, only then realizing Helen's presence, which she had allowed to be effaced from both men's consciousness so quiet was she in her niche by the window. But a quality to her silence, which he now perceived was stone, out of which pillars might be fashioned—not for him, but against those certainties whose essential nature was abundantly clear to him. When it was necessary to preserve the view, or perhaps the vision, without those obtruding stumps whose threatening lineaments were already forming. Then Clinton began to feel the tiredness that lay in wait for him, the seductive tiredness so easy to slide into in this lotus land where, he said, the handgrips and toeholds have never been installed. And drew back sharply.

"We couldn't catch up later," he said. "There wouldn't be time. We're into May now, we've got till June. You know what a monsoon's like, it's make or break by then."

"I know," said Mackendrick, quietly. Persuaded it seemed, though one would not have sworn. "Only sometimes one needs to hear it said."

Over in her corner against the window whose glittering jet reflected the moonless night, Helen felt Mackendrick's uneasiness combining with her own, sensed the quality of wrongness he had sensed, and snuffed out with the breath of reason and expediency. With words that her mind repeated, coldly. Make or break, she said, chilled; make what, break what? Dams, lives, men? Pride, time, money? One had to chip away until one's hands were raw, to expose. Then she dragged herself up, out of the silence which had been easiest.

"There's time after the monsoon," she said. "It's not an irrevocable date. Unless one chooses to make it so."

They turned. They had, she could see, forgotten her, and were unhappy to be reminded.

"The choice was made when the contract was signed," said Clinton. He could hear his voice, overriding and formal, which he could not alter; and he would like to have seen her point of view and been reasonable by whatever alien standard was hers, but he could not do that either. Soon he did not even wish to try. My work, he said, from mounting conviction, which loomed tall as a mountain now; my dam; my business. And grew resentful, walls between these, and his wife, being essential to him and to his side of their marriage.

"If the choice was wrong," said Helen. "One could go back on that. It would be wrong not to."

Pursuing it. Unable to take the easy road, to let things lie. Though, if he looked, he would have seen her laboring.

"The choice was the right one," said Clinton.

"There was a silence, until at last Mackendrick took pity.

"It would be difficult to go back on now," he said gently.

"But if it means pushing," said Helen, and stumbled over words, which his kindness had done. "It would be easy, if they were not. But they are men. If they are pushed. It is a killing pace," she said, sweat running. "You think so yourself."

"I would not," said Mackendrick, and thought of the years that she lacked, during which a callusing took place, which one called experience, being too dishonest to give it other names. "I would not go as far as that," he said.

"The weaker ones," said Clinton, "get shaken out, and that is all. It is a normal process."

"It is inhuman," said Helen.

"Are you," said Clinton, "trying to teach me my business?"

Mackendrick rose. "I must go," he announced. "I have a lot to do."

I am babbling, he said, what on earth have I got to do this time of night? Walking in the narrow path cut by his flash-light in the darkness, his mind leaping. From Clinton, whose rock could raze, though how deeply he did not seem aware, to Helen, whose containments he had seen breached, so that she trembled; to the lolling tongues that claimed to know the reason for abrasions and absences, piling it on a pair of shoulders. Bashiam, said Mackendrick, and frowned, and wondered. Thinking of him, this jungly-wallah. This man, he amended, being fair. Straining to look through a woman's eyes, and see-ing, or conceding, the fine construction of bone and muscle co-ordinating with spirit: the steady flow of the man, unconcerned with the jerking world outside. Then Mackendrick grew angry, it could have been out of alarm, and dragged them together ludicrously in his mind, the tribal and the Englishwoman, so that the ruthless juxtaposition could begin to work. As eventually it did, though not until he had come out of the jungle and entered his bungalow. Impossible, he said, as he settled in his chair, and adjusted the anglepoise lamp to his convenience. Or, if possible, only within the limited frame of a brief encounter. Which, being familiar, could not intimidate. Or so Mackendrick hoped, thinking about overseas spells, those febrile chunks scooped out of ordinary time, which were always crammed with brief extraordinary encounters.

When Mackendrick had gone Clinton said, distantly, "I'm sorry," and Helen said, equally pointlessly and distantly, "It doesn't matter." Both knew that it did. Helen sat blindly. Her hands were limp in her lap. Clinton glanced at her, glanced away again, quickly. He got up and got himself a clean glass, splashed soda into it, added four fingers of whiskey and drank it in one go. The whiskey burned his stomach and he waited for the mellowness but it didn't come. All it did was to add a leaden drag to his bowels. He drank more, this time neat, liquor up to the rim. Still she had nothing to say. The silence was wearing him down. He said, abruptly, "I think I'll turn in."

"All right."

"What about you?"

"It's stuffy in here," she said, "I think I'll go out for a bit."

"Where?"

"Nowhere in particular. Just for a walk."

"At this hour?"

"Why not? It's not even nine o'clock yet."

Clinton did not answer at once. His brain seemed to be swelling, he did not want to argue the matter. He simply wanted to forbid her to go, authoritatively, exercising his control over her as he did over his men. But he could not; not yet. The alcohol in his blood was running high, but not high enough, on its own. He said, querulously, "You'll get lost. It's pitch dark."

"I'm used to it," she said.

"Jungle," he said, thickly, "not a park to play in."

"I'm used to the jungle too," she said. "I'm not afraid of it."

"You're too damn familiar with it," he said, and felt something beginning to bolt, his strength, or control. "What you don't understand is that what lies out there is verboten. Not our country, not our people. Nothing to do with us."

"Then we shouldn't be here."

"I bloody well wish we weren't."

She rose to go and he seized her wrist. "Stay away," he said, passionately, and the feel of her flesh twisting inflamed him and he bore down on her until he prevailed. Then he carried the listless body to his bed.

He woke soon after. His body felt sated but his mind was cloudy. For minutes he could not remember. He lay staring into the black opal night, probing delicately for the roots of the oppression that weighed him down. Presently he knew. He had raped his wife, or as nearly as made no difference. Achieving physical relief, and some pale shadow of pleasure, at a cost. Which, not wishing to compute, he put from him and turned to bolstering, which was what was needed. She is mine, he said, stubbornly; why should I let her go? What I have I hold. But knew this to be an illusion, having touched the emptiness where she had fled him, so that the bolsters began to sag under the weight of knowledge. Then he looked round for scapegoats, and one was near at hand, which he seized. The whiskey, he said, but for which it would not have been done. But was only dragged down into darker pits and confrontations, where the overthrow of his will by an imbibed force loomed larger than other defeats and losses.

Next to him Helen lay, awake, inert. Suspended, it seemed, in darkness, but now and then becoming aware of parts of her body; her lips, which were cracked, and her thighs upon which he had spilled at first touch, not even completing. Now and again she moved, tongue over blistered skin, tips of fingers over the scales into which the wetness had dried. Burning, or seared, but cold, the two of them cold, and the breath that should have warmed rising in lone chill columns in the silence. Then each knew that something, some restraining line, had been severed.

22

THE sirens roused Clinton, but Helen slept through them.

When the wailing died the sound of the river was stronger, the gurgle and slap of the water invaded the quiet room. It's running high, Clinton thought, but could not be certain if the rise was in his imagination, or if the rains had in fact started in the upper reaches of the hills. Then he realized if they had he would know; the Roseires gauges would register, they were positioned all the way up to the topmost peak, and he would have been told. Everything under control except me, he said to himself, annoyed with the hangover that still shrouded his mind. He lay with the sour thought a few moments longer, then he slid out of bed, had a cold shower, dressed, drank his tea, and left for the site.

Smith, on early shift, saw him coming and nudged Jackson. "Look who's coming. Looks like burra sahib's getting jumpy."

Jackson grunted. He had been with Clinton many years longer than Smith and had learned to respect him. "What's jumpy about getting up early?" he said. "Something wants watching he watches it, same as you would if you was him I don't think."

"Everyday since I've been on early turn," said Smith with a kind of wonder. "Crack of dawn, out he comes. Late turn, he's the last to leave. As if he had no home or something."

Jackson scented criticism. "It's lucky for us he stays on the job like he does," he said ominously. "You and me, we can sleep in our beds peaceful, leaving him to do the worrying."

"You was restless last night," said Smith. "Tossing and turning, like you had a load on your mind."

"It's the food," said Jackson forbiddingly. "It never has agreed with me."

Clinton nodded to the two men as he passed. Good workers, he thought, good men, and knew that the feeling was mutual. But Jackson looked tired, not physically but mentally, a tiredness in the eyes like the look that Millie had carried since Bailey's death. Whereas Smith, to use her phraseology, was positively blooming. For Smith was going home. Jackson's golden boy, step light and spirits jubilant, was taking his radiant body home to his wife. Leaving Jackson deprived and alone. Poor Jackson, Clinton thought with a flicker of sympathy. Then he abruptly thrust the man and his misery from his mind. Personal relationships were private matters, not subject to third parties. His sole concern was to see that they did not distort work capacity. The two were distinct, and as far as he could he intended to preserve the dichotomy.

Mackendrick, also an early riser, saw Clinton carefully negotiating the incline and noted, with a slight sense of shock, that his gait was unsteady. Almost imperceptibly so, only a hair's breadth deviation from normal, but Mackendrick was too versed in departures from the norm in Clinton to be deceived. I know him too well, he thought, as well as he knows me . . . and because of this he said, sympathetically,

"You look a bit rough. Can I help?"

"Is it that obvious?" Clinton managed to smile.

"Only to me," said Mackendrick comfortably, and prepared to let it go, but Clinton hung on.

"It's a mug's game," he said. "Hitting the bottle, I mean . . .

only sometimes you have to, you think there's a chance it'll help and it's a chance that you have to take. Sometimes it does."

"Sometimes," Mackendrick agreed.

And there was a silence, in which they exchanged their thoughts, without acknowledging. Both knowing that talking about drinking was a shutter, hauled down to close off. Helen, said Mackendrick, and something besides, not the progress they were making, which was good, but still, something. Both sensing there were skins that had yet to be peeled.

Then Clinton returned them to the farce, which had to be played.

"I shall survive," he said heartily. "We shall survive, we have before," and he clapped Mackendrick on the back with a jarring bonhomie.

"Of course," Mackendrick responded.

After which both men looked away, their glances traveling to the river below and the flags at the site of the dams which were flapping and phutting in the wind.

When the sun came up one saw that the flags were tatty. They had flown since work began. In the long months the gunny had flapped itself to pieces many times over. Threadbare patches appeared, then holes. Then, when nothing was left except rags and tatters someone, Clinton never knew who, repaired the damage. New bright khaki gunny sprouted like beanshoots between the shreds of the old, faded in turn, and added further somber hues to the canvas. In time, the fabric of the flags closely resembled a shabby patchwork quilt. In time, too, an affection grew for these forlorn symbols, as if they were guardians of the sanctity of the dams, under which men might unite. All kinds of men, tribals and technicians, English and Indian labor and management, otherwise disparate, who might be drawn together under this tenuous bond, and perhaps were.

Now, picking his way through the orderly clutter of machinery on the bank, Mackendrick paused to give the flags a kindly salute, and turned to see Rawlings' ironic gaze fixed upon him.

"Propitiating the goddess?" he asked.

"Something like that," Mackendrick smiled. "Why?"

"Carry on the good work," said Rawlings, and jerked a thumb at the peaks of a distant range, "she'll need some propitiating, because the first rains have started."

Clinton, a few feet away, did not hear the conversation: the whine of machinery and the rumble of trucks drowned the short exchange. But felt the storm-cone forming, a still center in the general clamor, and went closer, and Rawlings unbuttoned his pocket and handed him the signal.

Clinton read it slowly. It only confirmed what he had suspected, the high note of the river that morning had warned him. It gave him a certain bleak satisfaction to know that his senses were still registering, though he had talked them out later. He said:

"How much time does that leave us?"

"About a week," said Rawlings. "A week to ten days before the monsoon proper. I've averaged out the records."

Clinton nodded, accepting the limit. Shading his eyes he looked over the river to where the dams advanced, their arms reaching out across the swollen waters. Those arms all but touched each bank: a man could have leaped the gap. But that was the surface, there was the depth below. Clinton gauged it in his mind, with an almost physical feeling for the heavy currents that scoured the concrete bastions. A week he thought again. Well, it would do, it would have to be made to do. He said to Mackendrick, continuing a dialogue that seemed to have begun a long time ago: "We can't ease up now, can we. "We've got to finish."

And Mackendrick understood that they were to be stretched further, and agreed, though only the night before he had believed they had already reached the limit.

"I'll get my end going, double-quick," he said, so that Clinton knew Mackendrick would be pulling with him, actively, not passively with a shift of the load of responsibility and an option to disengage from the consequences.

23

THE quarters allotted to Bashiam were in Clinton's Lines, a section of the barracks where the Indian workers lived. Though differently sited, its standards of comfort, under the regime of scrupulous fairness instituted by Mackendrick, were identical to those enjoyed by British technicians of equivalent cadre.

Bashiam found little comfort in the two-roomed concrete box they had provided for him and in which he lived alone, for there was no one who precisely matched his mixture of tribal and technician with whom he could have been asked to share. He lived in it for convenience, to be near the work site; and because the difficulty of identifying with any society had accentuated his liking for being alone.

Sometimes he could not. Sometimes the sides of the box pressed closer and the ceiling seemed to bear down until he felt if he stayed he would suffocate and then he had to go, wrenching open the door to be rid of the congestion, taking the path past the British quarters and the British canteen that his displaced tribe had taken.

A few hundred yards upstream, where jungle encroached, the path grew vestigial; there had not been time for tribal feet to keep it beaten down, and the booted British seldom came this way. The thin ill-defined line wavered across grass and scrub, following the course of the river round to the base of the hill where the tribesmen had built their huts.

No one thought of a hut for Bashiam. To his tribe he was a man who walked alone, sprung from them but no longer belonging, a man who put shoes on his feet and worked machines, whose feelings and desires they could not fathom. Until one day the headman saw him at the edge of the encampment looking like a strayed animal, and ordered a hut to be built for him, believing he would not know how to do it for himself. They planned it a little apart from theirs, out of consideration, straining their minds to think as he might. Out of consideration, too, they built differently; not bamboo and thatch, but a tin shack roofed with corrugated iron and sheets of plastic like the temporary shelters the contractors had hustled up for the first contingents of workers. This edifice they presented to Bashiam, with faint statements which they did not believe of its unworthiness for a man of his high status.

Bashiam agreed, and tore the structure down, returning its components to the various stores from which they had been pilfered. The tribe watched with a sad consternation. Bashiam did not trouble about their feelings. He had learned what a bar to progress emotion could become. He could also build and thatch, having cumbrously reassembled these discarded skills when, to confound him, the West had looked with nostalgic respect on what he regarded as primitive. Now he set about constructing the refuge he wanted, in the insalubrious region into which the tribe had been cast.

He had not, in fact, been aware of his want. For many years, after all, he had lived as the other workers lived, in shacks and tents and barracks up and down the country, among people whose language sometimes he could not speak, and been, more or less, content. It was only in the wake of the tribesmen's effort that his obscure longings crystalized, and he was glad when the hut was finished. Here he retreated, when he felt the constriction, like a migraine, beginning.

Sometimes it happened by day, more frequently at night. The eve of the first rains it began at dawn, and took the whole day developing. Bashiam felt the heaviness as he woke with the sirens for the early shift, and it engulfed him again when he came off duty that night. For a while he lay on his bunk, staring up at the ceiling which oppressed him, white and blank like a winding sheet. He switched off the light and it was worse, the whiteness precipitated itself closer, he felt if he breathed it would come down on him. At length he pulled himself up from clutching inertia, dressed, and went out.

It was a dark night, close, with a low cloud cover. The thin blue light of the arc lamps by which the night shift worked followed him a hundred yards along the path and then filtered out. Guided by memory and the sound of the river he walked on, in what was almost total darkness, and was glad when the first huts of the encampment loomed up in front of him.

His own hut stood aloof, on the outer perimeter, similar outwardly to the other huts. The difference was inside, in the furniture, which consisted of a table, a string bed, a folding canvas chair, a hinged cane door: comforts unknown to the others which, now, were indispensable to him. From the doorpost hung a small hurricane lantern. He felt for it in the darkness, lifted the visor and lit it, looking round the interior by the light of the steady yellowish flame. It was familiar, clean; someone had swept the floor, sprinkling it with a clay wash that kept down the dust. A plaited rush mat lay beside his bed. The perks, he thought, of having walked out on them. To lure him back? He could not set such high store on himself. Just the little courtesies due to a guest, which he had become. Which suited him. He needed these attentions: he did not wish to be more than a guest.

On the bed—more comforts—were a thin biscuit mattress stuffed with coco fiber, a kapok pillow from which someone had thumped out the lumps. A waste of time, Bashiam thought, the smoothness under his hand; by morning it would be as lumpy as ever it had been. Nevertheless he was grateful. Whoever the someone was had done what was possible. Presently he lay down, carefully dousing the lantern first. The smell of kerosene hung heavily under the eaves before dispersing to let the smells of the jungle seep in. The jungle, as familiar as a woman one had once slept with, regularly . . . . only not recently, the urgent sense of intimacy was missing.

He still could not sleep. The oppression he had hoped to escape had crept back; he had not known it to survive in these surroundings before. A woman, he said to himself, and knew one would be available, but the tightness was not in his loins. He lay quietly in the darkness, waiting with the patience of his people and the jungle, which were intertwined, while the hours went by. At length he felt the strain beginning to ease, grain by grain like the yielding of sand to water, and listened for and heard the note of the river change, and knew that somewhere distantly, perhaps only in his mind, the rains had started to fall. Then he slept.

He woke to the full blast of the sirens beating down upon the hill. The river was swollen, running high. So it had not been only in his mind: the first rains had fallen, on the higher slopes that always took the first brunt of the monsoon. The fall had been heavy, judging by the level of the river. There would be a lull now, then more rain, and another pause while the clouds gathered, then the monsoon, lashing down at full strength . . . which gave them—how long? He began to calculate, not by the record as Rawlings had done, but by a slow charting of the signs of the season, relying on his instincts more firmly now to interpret them correctly.

The six o'clock shift which should have ended at midday was extended to two.

Bashiam was dog tired as he came off work, though up in the cabin of his crane he had hardly noticed the extra hours. Tiredness was on everyone. The men who had come off work with him moved torpidly, feet and eyelids weighted. Watching them trail slowly up the escarpment toward their billets he felt the sluggishness in his own limbs, a stiffness in his muscles. All he wanted now was a bath, and rest and shelter in his hut in the village. But there were no baths in the village, only the river, which was in spate. He hesitated a little, then made his way back to Clinton's Lines.

There was a shower unit here: twelve cubicles in a block built next to the water tower at the end of the barracks. There was a long queue inside; he had been slow off the mark getting to them. He joined the line of men waiting their turn, under the sign which said, in English, Please Q. It was quiet, except for the showers. The news had flashed through to all, subduing them. Someone said, "Time's short," and someone else, "There's no time, the monsoon has started." He let the first remark pass, but pulled up the second. "The monsoon has not started," he said flatly, "only the preliminary rains. There is still time in which to finish." A low buzzing began, punctured by a hostile voice which instantly picked up followers. "How does he know? How can he tell?"

Bashiam did not answer; there was no real answer. He knew, that was all; though he also knew no charting could take in freaks of mountain weather. Absolute certainty: was there such a thing to be found? Not in any sphere, he thought wryly, it was simply another human activity, groping after the unattainable. And, so, said no more.

The queue moved rapidly; he was heading it now. There was a free cubicle and he went in, hung up his towel and got under the shower. Over the sound of the spray he could hear them arguing, some accepting what he had said, some skeptical, then someone said, "Jungly prophet," and he heard the covert sniggering. It pricked him, momentarily, then he held himself aloof. What, after all, did it matter? In a few months they would disperse, he would not set eyes on them again, these volatile lowlanders with whom he had little in common. Only the dam, my brothers, he said to them softly, brings us together. Then he ceased to listen, giving himself up to the pleasure of the water, the warm fine needles stroking the weariness from his system.

It was mid-afternoon when he emerged and started to walk to his quarters. Then he changed his mind. His hut was farther away, but it beckoned more invitingly. Turning, he began to walk rapidly in the direction of the settlement.

It was a hot day, the sun shone strongly. In the clearings his shadow danced across the scrub ahead of him, ten foot high like a giant's. Bath and a meal had driven his fatigue underground; he could not have worked again, but felt limber enough for other things. What other things, he asked himself sardonically: the cinema? carromboard in the canteen? with a crowd whose tempers had dried out to tinder? His own company seemed infinitely preferable.

Twenty minutes brisk walking brought him to the outskirts of the settlement. Only a few people were about. He greeted them shortly, to discourage them from following him as they sometimes did, crashing after him as if he were one of the herd. When he had ceased to be, had as little in common with them as with the canteen crew. Only the dam, my brothers, he said as softly as before, and walked on, circuitously, avoidingly, to reach the shelter of his hut.

Someone had closed the door; usually it stood open, fastened back with rattan strips to withstand the shock waves of blasting. He thought of knocking, but it seemed a ludicrous thing to do, and after a little hesitation he pushed the door open. And it was like a culmination, an aggregate of the day, and his feelings, and weeks and months. For Helen was inside.

"I had to come," she said.

He stood in the doorway, filling it. But offering retreat, should either care, which would be wise.

"Is anything wrong," he said, "that you had to come?"

Because she never came here, went always to the village.

She did not answer. She looked up at him. There was a frantic look about her mouth and eyes that warned him.

"What do you want with me," he said. And stood outside. Warily, because it was a memsahib who wanted. Who would use him like a blackjack upon her white and exquisite body, suck him into her vortex to taste his coarse flavors and when it was done, the rare thing savored, go. Leaving him to—what? What about me, he whipped himself, what about *me*? While her nearness wafted warm currents about him, about his body.

She rose and came to him.

"What is it," she said. "What has gone wrong?"

He said nothing; watched the sweat form, small glittering beads on her pale forehead.

"It's not like that at all," she said. "Look at me. I've never been a memsahib. You're not some kind of freak to me. We're alike, we're freaks only to the caste we come from, not to each other. I thought you knew. Was I wrong? If I was, I'll go."

He put out his hand to stop her. His thoughts had gone. All of them. All that mattered was what lay unfinished between them.

When they touched, there was a stillness. It held them, and the fire began. He felt the flame and came in, closing the door to keep the world away from what was happening, and leaned against it heavily.

"Only don't be sorry afterward," he said, thickly, "because—"

"I've only been sorry before," she cried, "feeling and feeling, and stopping. And starting again, and never finishing."

"Finish this time," he said hoarsely, and covered her. They lay on the string bed, moving to quickening beats, until he felt it drive through him and heard her shuddering cries, which were more abandoned than his own.

24

IT was midnight when he woke and the devils were howling.

Helen was still asleep. He got up and lit the lantern, and then he shook her gently.

"What is it?" she asked drowsily, and curled round to sleep again.

"Time to wake," he said. "Listen."

"The sirens." She stirred unwillingly, cursing them through half-sleep, trying to drift back to dreams, and failing.

"They call them the wailing devils," he said, "in the village."

"Do they?" She yawned, still greedy for sleep, but coming awake now. "They never told me."

"They didn't want to offend you."

"Why would I be offended?"

"In case you liked the noise. It was invented in your country."

"Not by me." She laughed and sat up, swinging her legs to the ground, the rush matting a polished coolness under her soles. "Still, it's effective."

"I noticed that."

She laughed again, the laughter close to the surface, being prodigal with it. "I sleep through them," she explained, "because they carry no message for me. If they did I'd wake up, like you and Howard do."

Then her laughter was burdened; and a little strip of no-man's-land fell sharply into place between them. Of which he became aware, but did not attempt to cross. Some time it might have to be done, but not now. Rivers, bridges, boundaries: one came to these and negotiated them if need be, all in their proper season.

"I must go," he said. "I'm late already."

"You've done your stint," she protested, wanting the laughter back, which had bubbled. "How many times in a day does your turn come round?"

"As often as one can stand it," he said. "The rains have started."

"The rains have started," she repeated impatiently. "Is that the end of the world? What does it mean?"

"It means we've got to finish."

"Which is the central thing."

"It is the central thing."

It sounded to her like Clinton, or Rawlings, or Mackendrick, or anyone who was part of Clinton Mackendrick. What they lived by, what they said. The central thing. The hub, round which the others, even living and loving, revolved. She accepted it, she had to. And got up, putting these away from her as he had done, and dressed and went out.

In the darkness she could not see but heard the stiff sounds the moving grass made in the wind; sap gone, the withered blades whispering for water.

"The rains," she said. "You're wrong. It's as dry as a bone."

He joined her in the swelling darkness, a wash of black, tidal, palpable.

"Smell," he said.

"What?"

"Rain."

There was the smell of eucalyptus and leafmold, the faint tang of pine that came in on the wilder gusts.

"I can't," she said.

"It's there. Try."

"I have tried. It's no good."

"It's far away. Two thousand feet up."

"But you can and I can't," she said. "I wish I could. But my senses have been blunted. Pavements. Something."

"Pavements?"

"Our world," she said. "The one in which I live. Things are battened down in it. Under concrete and mortar, all sorts of things. The land. Our instincts. The people who work in our factories, they've forgotten what fresh air is like. Our animals —we could learn from them, but we're Christians you know, an arrogant people, so we deprive them of their rights. Deny them. Pretend they haven't got any. Then they don't know about sunshine or rain either. Sometimes they can't move, poor things. We don't allow them to, in case they yield us one ounce less of their flesh. Where is our instinct for pity? Blunted. We've cut ourselves off from our heritage. We've forgotten what we knew. Where can we turn to, to learn? A million years' accumulating, and we know no better than to kick it in the teeth. Now I can't even sense rain, which is there."

"One has to listen," he said. "Yesterday, I could not either. One has to trust oneself before one can feel the—joinings."

"Affinities."

"When one does it returns," he said. "Everything is there. Buried. Not forgotten."

"You can leave it too long," she said. "Then it goes rotten. Bury it too deep, it never surfaces again. But we suspect it's there, the dowsing rod won't hold still, so we feel lost, feel we've lost out on something. I do. A lot of us do, only we don't let on that we do. But here—now—I don't feel that anymore. I belong, I'm not alone. Everything is a part of me, and I'm a part of everything—not just a pop-up cardboard figure."

The words rising, and brimming, and spilling; she could not stop. And felt the release as she spoke, a peace that was to do with her mind as consummation had been for her body, the fusion making her whole in a way that she could not recall having achieved before.

Bashiam listened and was moved. Then he grew afraid, not a particular fear but a general malaise that grew out of caring. Because he knew what they were like, these assaults upon oneself and what one cherished: did not want her to be subjected to them until disciplines were accepted, and she was ready, so that the wrench and tear when it came could heal cleaning, without leaving open, weeping sores.

"Don't feel too deeply," he said, inadequately he knew. "It doesn't do to feel too deeply."

Then he was gone. She heard his footsteps retreating, soles scraping against the brushwood, the slight sounds carrying despite the buzz of machinery. When they died away she went in, looked again at the hut, its neat, pared to the bone economy. Now and again, in response to distant blasting, the thatched roof raised itself slightly, all of a piece, and settled down again gently. Like some old gentleman, she said aloud, who has adapted admirably, and moves with the times. Which kept her smiling, even after the image was gone, so rich were the residues.

At length, not very soon, he prepared to go. The door, which he had left ajar, she fastened back as it had been when she entered. The lantern still burned. She took it down and blew out the flame, but when she went outside she could not see to walk even a few steps. Cloud cover had thickened, destroying the luminous quality of the night to which she was more used, in which she could walk in the darkness without strain. She felt for the flashlight that she sometimes carried, but it wasn't there. She tried to do without, and went forward, but the blackness into which he had walked as if it were light had, now, a kind of animosity that made her retreat. She had not, so far, felt this mood of the jungle. After a little she groped her way back to the hut, and relit the lantern.

Bashiam, heedless of jungle or mood, his mind on the work waiting for him, aware of being late, hurried back at a jog-trot. Then, when the blue artificial glow flickered through the trees illuminating his path, his speed slackened. Other considerations crowded him now, and he had to push his limbs to keep them moving.

It was past midnight, near one o'clock. Clinton, continuously on site since the morning, felt the tiredness clogging his faculties. Pack it in, he said to himself, and started walking slowly up the escarpment as Bashiam, equally slowly, began to descend it. As their paths crossed, briefly, Bashiam saw the purple rings under the older man's eyes, accentuated by the steel-blue glare. Whatever Clinton saw he gave no sign; his control had returned, iron-clad since its recent lapse. When they drew level he raised his eyes to Bashiam, as he might have done to any one of a dozen workers, and moved on. The jungly, he said to himself, blindly invoking the protective phrase. But the shrinking medicine, infallible before, had lost its potency to reduce to negligible size.

Das, dozing fitfully in his stifling godown, heard Clinton's boots on the gravel and sat up. He had no idea of the time, except that it was late. This did not deter him in any way. Groping around in the pitch-blackness he found matches and lit the lantern. Then he unwound the shawl in which, despite discomfort, he swaddled himself against the unknown, and put on his white robes. His turban, already tied, reposed on a shelf: he lifted this down and set it on his head, pressing it down firmly to anchor it in the rising wind. Feeling respectable now, he unfastened the door and opened it, gasped a little at the bootblack solidity of the night, then launched himself into it and flew as fast as he dared along the path leading to the kitchen. Once inside he returned to normal. The room was reassuring, its familiar surroundings belonged to the realm of respectable bungalows, whatever lay outside. Filling the kettle he set it to boil, turned up the electric stove to maximum heat, then methodically laid out the tea tray. Master, he knew, would like a cup of tea. Das would too, though that was not the primary matter. The master was, and Das was prepared, night or day, to give him the service he needed.

Clinton heard the flurry, followed by the clink of crockery. Das, he thought, as usual on tap. He looked into the kitchen to make sure it was, not the bungling cook who had a knack of getting on his nerves. Then he went to the bedroom. The door was closed, and he hesitated a little; then he turned the knob quietly and let himself in. Helen was not there; he could feel the emptiness before he switched on the light. He had not really expected her to be. The blow was no less formidable for that. He had to sit down and he went back to the living room and threw himself into a chair. His boots were chafing him, but he made no attempt to remove them. Whiskey, glasses, were on a salver on the teapoy; he reached for the decanter, halfway withdrew his hand, no longer being certain he could stop, once started. But found another frame, which more or less fitted. I need all my faculties, he said, primly. With one week to go, it is no time for drinking.

"Tea, sahib?" Das materialized at his elbow.

"Yes," he said. "Yes, please." Anything, to please.

Das put down the tray, removed the mob cap that the teapot wore and poured.

"Memsahib," he said with pity, "not come back, sahib."

"No," said Clinton. "She hasn't, has she."

He felt too tired, or it was too late, to pretend, to make out that he didn't care. Where was the need anyhow. Das was a servant, moved on a different circuit. It was when you were on the same run that you had to be careful. Or was it? One could jump the rails, so to speak, go to the devil that way.

He drank his tea, dialogues crowding his mind. The brew was well made, fresh and fragrant, even to lips that would have preferred whiskey for instance, or the mouth of his wife. They grow good tea in the hills, he thought, and remembered it was Helen who had told him. Helen, at the heart of his homecomings, whose serenity could reach out and wrap you in warm blankets, shut off the rasping day . . . yet gradually a wrongness about it, the way she could be, rapt, month after month, absorbing invisible unguents that made her bloom while other women went berserk, like Millie, ripped off the sheaths and exposed their nerves. And increasingly the sense that all was not right: becoming afraid, aware of the eyes that she turned upon him, probing, asking for something that he could not give . . . withdrawing when he could not, the tranquillity shot with terrifying strands, its center a spinning core of restlessness that took her away from him, led her into this and that. Dabble in everything, get your hands muddied. Hands that belonged to him, whatever. So holding her down, physically, enjoying the leap and twist under him and thrusting deeper and coming to nothing, spirit gone and womb closed, only a paper thing in his arms.

His cup was empty. The watchful Das refilled it, throwing the cold dregs into the encroaching lantana outside. Then, squatting on his knees, he pulled off Clinton's boots. It was not his job really, it was the boot-boy's job. But he could not bear to see the master as he was, he had to alleviate what was alleviable even if it was only a small thing like removing boots. Anyhow there was no boot-boy; he belonged to the world of orderly living, certainly not in these wilds. Das pursed his lips and hung about to see if there was anything more he could do but there was nothing. At last taking the initiative he said respectfully, "Good night, sahib."

"Good night, Das."

"Sleep good, sahib."

"Oh, I will," said Clinton. "I will. Presently."

When Das had padded out he rose and switched off the light to get rid of the midges that had slipped through the mesh and were pinging against the bulb, and stood at the window looking into the darkness until he saw trees rocking frantically in the lantern light. There were weights on him now, he could not shift them. Except for a hand, which remained free for a purpose. Which slid stealthily along the wall to the switch and snapped on the light as she came in. Despising himself when it was done, hearing her gasp, and questioning the purpose which was already wasting away. For the truth was not to be got by shocks, being his for the asking. Only he did not want to ask.

"I'm sorry," he said, and noticed her paleness and extended his apology. "I hope I didn't frighten you, I didn't intend to."

"It's me, I'm jumpy." She shook herself impatiently. "It's a bit murky outside."

"It's this blasted country," he said, laying it where it belonged all at one door, hoping she would join him so that all that was wrong between them could come right. But she did not and he knew he had not expected her to. In a way if she had he would have despised her. Knowing they were matched in this, that neither would choose the easy way out unless it happened to be valid. He waited a little, though he could not say why. But no words came, nothing that would do, and presently, heavy-eyed as if pennies had been laid on his lids, he went in to sleep.

25

IT was the changing pattern of the wind that they noticed most now. Where it had risen and subsided gently before, cool breezes by morning to a fair wind by nightfall, now it took to whipping down the hill at runaway speed, short sharp squalls that stripped the leaves from the trees, and raised dancing columns of debris on the site.

In the settlement by the river the headman silently contemplated the season. He could no longer sit in the open, where the sharp wind sliced at his bare shoulder blades; but he dug himself in at the entrance to his hut, in a hollow lined and rounded to fit his haunches. From here he could see, despite the tears that spurted from his eyes at each onslaught of wind and grit; and he saw a good deal more than most people looking at those milk-blue old-man's eyes could credit. What he could not see, he sensed. He knew about the rain, and the rise of the river, each day accelerating; about the Englishwoman, and the plight of the lowlanders who had come up the hill on the trail of money. He saw the dust from the dams like ash on his tribesmen's faces, and the growing neglect of the village as more and more of his men were sucked in, to whirl like cogs around the restless core.

"Go ahead, get as many as you can get," Clinton had said to Mackendrick. "We've got to finish on time." And Mackendrick, his recruiting at base at a standstill with the worsening of the weather, barely able to restrain his labor from beating a sensible retreat to the plains before the roads grew impassable, turned to the tribe, milking it for what he could get and abandoning all selection. And the long lines of cheap labor could be seen, working ineptly, in a way that consolidated every atom of contempt in which Clinton already held them, alongside highly efficient costly machines, carrying away in shallow trays on their heads all manner of detritus, gravel, clay, the gray sludge from the riverbanks that oozed through the wicker and wattle onto their naked backs.

Helen, distressed, saw with the headman's eyes the visible deterioration: the uprooted palings lying where they had fallen in muddy troughs of their own creation, the unfilled subsidence craters left by intensified blasting, the ragged come-apart thatching. In a matter of weeks the damage was plain, a perpetuating circle that gained momentum as the dams drained men from the tribe. She could not, however, speak of it either to her husband, or to Mackendrick, or even to Bashiam, recognizing there was nothing to be done. All of them were bound, shackled between a modern juggernaut and time, the ancient enemy armed with teeth and a new ferocity.

The headman remained. He could, if he wished, have exerted his authority, compelled unwilling men to return to a skimped care of the village—the elemental care which was as much as it had ever received or would receive at the hands of his harried people. He did not. At one time Helen would have railed at him as she had railed at Bashiam, goading him to action, her Western dynamism galled by his bloodless acquiescence; but now she was quiet, her mind slowly filling with glimpsed truths, nebulous understanding no less valid for its lack of form.

In the wordless sympathy that existed between them each knew what the other was thinking.

"When there is nothing to be done one does nothing," he

said, "but it is also necessary to guard the inner feeling. Because, you see, one is shaken to pieces if there is inaction without and a hurricane raging within."

Helen nodded. The country was shaping her, working in all of them like an unnamed, diffused drug. It could not alter the soil, composed in a northern continent and climate, but it modified the form so that what had been thrown out as inalienably foreign now found acceptance, a place. Where it could not, it set up currents: those crosscurrents which Clinton and Jackson, Rawlings and Henderson, those who resisted and fought back, felt beating about their heads. This blasted country, they frequently said; and in that were closer to the truth than they imagined.

"You see, you have changed," said the headman. "Between then, and now, you are a different woman."

Helen agreed. "I know, but is it for good. I don't know, I hope it is. I wouldn't want to change back, when I return."

For neither questioned that she would return.

"Most countries provide a place for outsiders," he said, and began to chuckle, "an uncomfortable one."

She smiled despite herself. More and more, of late, she had come up against an errant humor in him which she had not earlier suspected, a discordant amusement sparked off sometimes by his own discomfiture, more often that of others, most frequently that of his unfortunate clan. She saw them one day, a half-dozen shivering members of it, attempting to salvage the roof of a hut which the wind had lifted bodily from its crumbling base and dumped in the river. The thatch was sodden. Fronds broke away from the parent hulk, and the grappling lines refused to bite, slithering off the surface of the disintegrating remnant. While the men sweated and grunted, up to their thighs in silt, the old man rocked with laughter, from the vantage point on the bank to which he had tottered expressly to watch, hugging his bony sides at each disaster. That laughter, she thought, with a sidelong glance at the convulsed figure, there was a ripe spicy quality to it, like malice. Well, malice was a better safety

vent than many for the heartburning his men must have caused
him, defecting from their duty to him and to themselves, which
he must have felt for all his serenity, the calm whose priceless
grains had been meticulously isolated over a lifetime.

"I don't suppose they find it all that funny," she said, nevertheless. He wiped his streaming eyes. "They are comedians.
What else are men who will allow the roof over their heads to
be taken from them for want of a little care?"

Roofs and ceilings were also on the minds of Jackson and
Smith, over in the British quarters.

"Few more gales like what we've been having," said Jackson,
"we shan't have a roof over our heads."

Smith blew more smoke rings at the cracked ceiling of the
canteen under which they sat.

"Who cares?" he asked.

"I do," said Jackson, and his brows drew together. "I'm seeing it through, aren't I?"

"Meaning I'm not?" Smith stopped blowing rings. "If so say
so, straight out."

"I don't mean nothing of the sort," said Jackson, heavily and
not too promptly. Smith, he thought, was becoming decidedly
unpleasant, bit off your head, these days, no sooner had you
uttered. "You done your time, I suppose you're entitled to your
home leave."

"Suppose is right," said Smith. "I don't fancy ending up like
that poor bleeder Wright, what they ought never to have sent
out here in the first place."

"You wouldn't, you're built different," said Jackson, nervously. He did not like talking about Wright, who was indis-
solubly linked with Wilkins, whose face at last viewing had
looked like a squashed tomato.

"Maybe I am," said Smith, complacently, and held up his
hands which were absolutely steady.

Jackson's hands were steady too. It was his guts that twisted
and slipped, doubling him up when he thought of the nights
ahead. Sometimes he could have screamed with the pain.

"What I can't stand," he said, tentatively, because Smith had taken to being quite brusque with him, "is the nights. They sort of hang on your neck, if you know what I mean."

"It's the wind," said Smith obligingly. "Gets right up your arse."

"Gives me a pain," said Jackson, stumbling in the coils of his own dark experience. "Right here, Smithy. Like nothing I ever felt before and I hope to God," he said violently, "you won't neither."

"What're you bellyaching about now?" asked Smith.

"The pain," said Jackson.

"The wind," said Smith, not quite thinking of something funny, on the brink of it if only he could remember.

"Pulps you up," said Jackson, staring at this blond, careless, godlike young man with the succulent body, who would not understand what he was talking about unless, say, he were able to take that thick thatched head between his hands, split the skull and implant the needle. Call puss, puss, and pussy will come, soft-shaven head lopsided, gladdening the man all white-coat and brain, a hole where heart should be. As Jackson knew from what they faded out on the telly.

"Them thatch roofs," said Smith, glad he had remembered, unconscious of the electric seed that sped past, bombarding him. "Coming off like toupees, they are." He laughed callously. "Off of the natives' huts. There was six of them fetched up in the river last count."

"Them blacks can stand anything," said Jackson indifferently. Thus returning, in Smith's mind, to sanity.

"It's like venom," said Rawlings queerly. "Those bush boys, they knew it all. Slit the skin, pick up a vein and ping—the stuff goes straight to your heart, before you can count three, so they say. Only a pinhead, mind, what you can scrape off the point of a thorn. Next time a bit more. How do they gauge it . . . I wouldn't know, I'm not sprung from the bush . . . when they've finished you wouldn't feel a black mamba. Not I, man.

They. They don't feel a thing, after they've had the treatment. I wish I'd had the treatment . . . but it's deadly stuff, you can't really trust them, can you?"

"Not to do you in, do you mean?" asked Mackendrick.

"Well, yes, that," said Rawlings, and his eyes swam mistily, clouded by the debris that the river had brought down, planks and spars, and lopped limbs and puffy torsos bled white like calf meat, the dragon's teeth they had sown sprouting, sharp and pointed and able to kill, and killing. "There's that," he said again, "and there's the other thing too. They're subtle devils you know . . . you'd think you were safe, you'd be gone before you realized. Black mambas act fast."

"There are no black mambas here," said Mackendrick. He was tired. Tired of Rawlings, who came at night with his African fears riding his shoulders like ravens, and tried to let them loose here in his bungalow. Tired of hauling him out of the bog, when his own joints ached, and he knew that the knotting that went from his swollen hands to his windpipe and choked him would not go until he was left alone to his own kind of peace.

"But there are cobras," said Rawlings. "Frightened of cobras, aren't you, Mack?"

"What the hell has that got to do with you?" said Mackendrick.

And clenched inwardly, because of the spark that could run through them like a forest fire, destroying. Their tight tabernacle, split open because of a climate, a feeling, before the task was accomplished.

"I'm only saying," Rawlings brooded. "I'm saying how it gets under your skin, this country . . . right under, I mean, into the bloodstream. Goes round and round inside you, without you knowing, some damnable poison that stops you reacting. Properly, I mean, in our way. Not theirs, what good is their way to us? Only you don't realize, how can you? That's the subtle devilish part. Unless you look out for the signs." His eyes swam again, behind the thin fluid his pupils were fly, a pair of bright vigilantes. "They're lighting candles," he said, "out

there in the bush, every single night. What are they afraid of,
that's what I'd like to know. What are they afraid of?"

Mackendrick shut his eyes tightly. To keep sane. To keep out
the rabid invasion.

"What they're afraid of is their concern," he said patiently.
"Let us light candles for what we are afraid of. If we are. Are
we?"

"It's this wind," said Rawlings, and got to his feet. "It rattles
the windows. One hears nothing, beyond."

"There is nothing beyond," said Mackendrick, lacing his
fingers into a supporting basket for his head. "For what are you
listening?"

"Someone must," said Rawlings. "Or else, if we shouted, who
would hear? But, you see, the wind would carry it away."

"We must have a party," said Millie. "Something. It's not gay
here anymore, is it? Something to tide us over."

She bit her nails, fretfully, spitting out flakes of red varnish
that belonged to the past.

"Who would come?" said Helen. And chafed, because they
had gone over this before, they went over it every day, only
Millie was not aware, her memory cells were malfunctioning.

"Yes, who," said Millie. "They work, and they fall into bed
and get up and work again, and no one comes up the hill because who would at a time like this? One wants men," she said,
and lifted her eyes, whose lids were heavy, like hoods. "You
know what it's like without. But you don't, do you. You're lucky.
I've tried to work it out of me, I go down to the barracks and I
sketch, all those lovely birds they have there . . . but it won't
wash, it just won't wash."

"Get away for a while," said Helen. With compassion, supple
in her own rounded flesh, but subduing its radiance, which was
barbed for others.

"Yes, where," said Millie, and stared at the grave marks on
the backs of her hands, liver-colored smudges that ran into each
other, and almost obscured the skin's citrous surface. "There's

nowhere, really, now. There's been nowhere, since poor Bailey went. He was good to me," she said. "Really good. The consolation is, I always knew, it made each minute longer. . . . What I don't know is what I shall do now. Grin and bear it, I suppose. I've done it before, I ought to be able to do it again. But when you're older it doesn't come easier, does it? Same old grind, only harder."

She forced her lips to smile, a terrible rift that showed her teeth, which were yellowed, tinctured pale lemon like her eyeballs, the jaundice spread right through the system.

And Helen, who would not quarrel with truth, was silent. Looked round, nevertheless, for sweeteners, in the shape of Das, who would offer comforts unashamedly, quite small ones, limpid eyes and murmurings, and food and drink and cajolings, which would not lighten the spirit, but cushioned the desolation whereby, surprisingly, it grew easier to bear.

But Das had retreated discreetly, leaving the memsahibs to indulge their own langugage. From the kitchen he kept watch, through the crack insinuated by wind between door and jamb, ready to spring out with offerings when memsahib signaled. The older memsahib, who gave such signals; so that it was her he watched, not seeing the younger memsahib's frantic eyes, while the hot spicy milk cooled under a wrinkled skin, and the orange flesh flagged on the mango which, he was coming to think, he should not have stoned and skinned so early.

From watching he settled to waiting, translucent sacs sealing off the memsahibs while his mind opened to himself, yielding arch after arch under which he passed, pleasurably, away from the encircling hills to his own congested warm flat pad in the disheveled city.

In the next room Millie, boned and upright in the silence but listening, limbs upon the rack she had fashioned for herself and head slightly bent, said: "It's the threat. Like something over you, I don't know what. You don't feel it, do you, but it's there. Sometimes I feel it all the time, I can't feel anything else. One could forget, if there were men, but there aren't, are

there? That's really what one went for," she said, "to get rid of
the threat. Do you know what I mean? But it's over now, so I
don't know where I shall go for a bit of peace."

And got up, restlessly, to search.

Lefevre felt the climate lash at him and likened it to an ocean
and was exhilarated.

"We are a seafaring people," he said to his friend Gopal. "We
understand winds and tides.

"A little," he amended. "Because, you see, at no point are
we more than fifty miles from the sea, so naturally we learn."

"We are a river people," said Gopal delicately. "Or, I would
say, an inland people who live by our rivers. I would say, also,
that this river is a demon."

"There is something in the air," said Lefevre. "Catching. We
go down one after another. Now you."

"One has natural fears," said Gopal humbly and innocently.
"Haven't you?"

"Have I denied it?" said Lefevre, and strode about the room
rattling bottles and tubes in their racks along the walls.

"I only say that this river is a demon," resumed Gopal, treading brittle, as if on glass. "I do not say it cannot be tamed."

Lefevre ceased pacing and sat down upon an original orange
box which, sentimentally, he still preserved among the furniture.

"I'm a river man too," he said. "I've made myself one. It will
be finished."

"Of course," said Gopal cheerfully, and went to dote over his
model, where the sliver of glittering mica ran like a Lurex
thread, showing the river, or the strip which was all that was
left of it at the end of the striding dam. Here, presently, Lefevre joined him, and the two faces, which had been whittled
away almost to the bone, filled out again in each other's strength-
ening company.

"I shall go away and not come back," said Shanmugham

tiredly, shutting his eyes to the tossing forest and feeding in tapes of the lush, level green paddy-fields that his father owned, "when the coffer dams are completed, God willing, very soon."

"God being so," grunted Krishnan, "they will not lose face."

"Nor shall we," said Shanmugham, and opened his eyes. "We shall keep face also, phase one of our project being completed on time the country will sing our praises. Is this not good for all of us?"

"Of course, of course," said Krishnan, and stroked his temples, inside which old embers smoldered. For there was a problem, unresolved: the cord that threaded through them making them one, like an ill-sorted bundle of sticks that stood or fell together. Whereas, in times which were still livid to him, the cord was cleanly severed, between each side which heaved and fell independently, giving the triumph to one or the other. Krishnan smoothed his skin, feeling the passion that went through the bone to his marrow, and looking forward to a time when they could walk, ride, fly, and build solo, gathering strength and pride and thereby grow mighty.

Instead of shuffling one step behind, yoked to an arrogant buffalo.

Shanmugham saw a whiteness in the eye, like an opaque third lid, and shifted nervously, his own vision clouded by his companion's.

"It is not like that," he ventured, his green fields vanished, the tempestuous jungle once more jogging his elbow.

Krishnan tightened his mouth, purplish lips over strong white teeth, and considered.

"It is like that," he said precisely. "It is to be the Clinton-Mackendrick Dam."

"No, no," chattered Shanmugham. "It is our dam, what we call it, the Great Dam, the Bharat Dam—"

Presently he grew still.

"It was their brain," he said, "after all."

"Our need, conception, money, flesh and bone," said Krishnan, his carved god's face idle, immune, the pressures packed into words alone, which fell on Shanmugham like hail and chilled him. "All that, and there is no name to be put to it?"

"There is," said Shanmugham, and felt his cold, cracked lips, which smarted with pain whenever the wind rose.

"It is a joint achievement," he croaked. "Is that not what we want?"

But did not receive the endorsement that he sought from Krishnan, who was hung on his problem. Who only said, opening dark hands which had pinkish palms: "That is to be seen."

So that Shanmugham was left with uncertainties, which tormented him, taking turns with the pain of his poor peeled lips.

26

TO those to whom it was new it was miraculous. Not only the actual achievement, but the means of it: the puny, perishable men whom the rocks and the hills could have pulverized at the lift of a rib, absorbing the fall like imprudent amoeba. Whom one saw nevertheless, insignificant specks upon these ancient faces, advancing and remolding the landscape.

They came to watch, all those upon whom the great net had not fallen: the weak, the old, women and children in their idle moments. Even those who participated were not immune from the wonder of what they were hatching, coming in their curtailed free time to line the high plateau, among the tawny rocks, to view from there the gaunt slopes at whose base the fruit of their labor was emerging.

This fruit was multiple and simultaneous, and dazzling. Twin dams, whose solid thickened arms were seen, and seen to be holding the river across the whole of its width less a narrow pass, the last exit through which the jumbled waters poured. Twin quadrants of the bypass channel, cut between rock, its walls of towering granite, the broken rockbed fifty feet below void and dry in its new creation, awaiting the drafted waters. Double sand-blocks, constructed but awaiting destruction, one at each end of the curved channel reinforcing the natural rock barrier they had left to seal off the river from its new course. And between them all, visionary but marked, the piebald flags which showed the founding line of the main dam.

To Clinton it was not new or miraculous, except inasmuch as each birth is so. It was, perhaps, something more, a coming culmination that would set appropriate seals upon protracted effort in which flesh had melted on the whitened bone; that would stretch farther, becoming springboard and rejuvenator for the next long haul which waited the turn of the season. He immersed himself in it, this swelling intimation of approaching, and profound, pleasure, shutting off those abrasive encounters which drained him in his relations with his wife.

Not drowned, immersed; and not so much as not to notice flies in his particular ointment: the idle watchers who cluttered his line of vision, and fractured and spoiled his contemplation.

He considered ordering them off his earth, but did not because accomplishment was near and he would not risk it. Also because there were implants within him, invisible seedings from the containments and silences of Helen of which he was not aware, which subtly questioned his imperious rights and held him back. But mainly, perhaps, because he saw that it did not work, there were always people, sometimes he felt that the very ground spawned them, to take the place of those who were bawled off.

As Rawlings and Henderson did, their Adam's apples gobbling, their vocal cords frayed and tangling with the strands of imcomprehension wafted to them from the amazed spectators, across the rocky canyon. Impudence, they called it, rank disobedience to—something, if only they could find the right name for it; and they took their problem and laid it where they felt it belonged, squarely in the lap of Mackendrick, who managed men. Who would handle this for them, though the image that dimly formed in their minds was not of a pair of hands, but rather a wholesale contrivance like the one which swept away ninepins at the end of a bowling alley.

Mackendrick seethed with them, and went off the boil when they had gone. He had no authority over the tribes, except when they labored for him, and this was no time to tease the weave, risking the overall pattern by which they could work, whatever the knots and tensions below.

No one sensed the danger except Clinton, whose mind no longer being as clean and hard as a diamond but cumbered with reason and doubt, did not allow more than the hem of fear to brush against his consciousness. But there was, as well, the solid mass of his experience, from which there now arose emanations that he could not ignore.

"One day," he said, training his gaze on the jungle people assembled on the distant ridge, and frowning with displeasure, "they'll get themselves blown skyhigh, and have no one to blame except themselves."

"In which case there will be no trouble," said Mackendrick, not because humans were expendable, but because he had taken the measure of these men.

"But still," said Clinton, and listened to the tapping at his breastbone, which grew fainter the more he tried to trap what it was he heard.

"A few days more," said Mackendrick, his eyes on the tops of the fluctuating trees, like a green sea it had seemed to him those ages ago when he came chopper-borne to chart the beginning.

"A few days, it will be finished. How many hundred deaths can there be in that time that have not already happened? Besides there are the warnings. One would," he said, repeating himself, "be bent on suicide, not to hear the bells and cymbals."

"There is always time for an accident," said Clinton.

In an instant that was pure light, he saw the split-second happening. It faded as quickly as it had pulsed. Then, because it would not have been rational to do so, he did not insist further.

27

ON the first half-day's rest that came round to him that month, Bashiam made a journey to the upper reaches of the hills, borrowing from the old man of his village a woven jute mantle to withstand the cold of those heights, and a palmyra umbrella whose stiffness matched the mantle's, to ward off the monsoon wet.

He came back with his calves scraped raw by the jute, his hair hanging in watery tongues, and the headman's umbrella taken hostage by the wind. The season seemed to have trailed him. There were strange lights in the bulbous cloud, and the squalls that lashed the trees were laced with metal, spiteful tags that split the bark, glinting palely where they struck.

Bashiam sought out Mackendrick, straight down from the mountain and still in his borrowed gear; or possibly Mackendrick sought him out having heard of his trip, for they met in the middle, between bungalow and hut.

"Shall we finish?" he asked, dripping, the water oozing off his hair landing cold, like grubs, on his dark neck.

"Of course," said Mackendrick, and raised his voice above the squalling of the blue gums that had blown this finely sinewed tribal across his path. "How long do you give it?"

"Four days," said Bashiam.

"Then four days is how long we shall take to finish," said Mackendrick.

They stood thickly, like teak trees in their strength, each admitting the power of the other but neither naming it. And together heard the pulverizing blast that made the ground ripple as if veins were splitting at their feet, and rose and expanded into great clapping wings.

Then there was silence.

All that men had made, the clamor and banging, the grinding and jangling, ceased. It was silent, except for the wind and the trees, and the clash of the clouds.

"I don't see how it could have happened," said Henderson, shaking bewildered jowls. "It was no different from any other day, was it?"

"Your not seeing doesn't mean it didn't," said Rawlings. "And, clearly, the day was different." He opened and closed his hands, which wanted to squeeze Henderson's incessant throat, to stop him repeating himself. As he had done since the happening, and now the light was gone.

"I mean in the beginning," said Henderson. He massaged his neck, which felt something, some pressure, that he put down to the dust which had invaded his tissues after the explosion. "In the beginning it was a routine day."

"It began one way, it ended another," said Rawlings, flatly, his face flattened, like a spade, in violent, repressed rejection of quivering jowls and wagging tongue.

Like a snake, thought Henderson, momentarily relapsing, but the need for communication being strong he got rid of the thought, preparatory to having another go at the conversation.

Because the end was near, and he could not keep away, Clinton saw what happened. As far as anyone could.

It began as Henderson described, ordinarily.

Bore-holes in a neat pattern along the natural rock barrier

upstream, which they were thinning, skiving to the thickness of a plate which they would smash on the nearing day of the dams' completion, so that the river would turn as told and flow over its new bed. Charges of dynamite laid. The fuses. The sweat began to swell from his pores and run whenever Clinton came to this point, as he had done over and over again since. Because of the confusion, things being there which should not have been, occluding; and others being absent and neglecting to warn.

For he had seen the red tongues flicker, and when he looked again the signals were dissolved, whether by trick of light or the hoaxing wind, no one would ever be sure. Nor would they agree about the whistles, which some heard shrilling wildly, others feebly or not at all, according to the vagaries of season and their own response. Clinton, listening, heard the whistles, and waited for the sirens to follow and heard these too but thinly, on a backward wash, the attenuated wave coming at him where he stood on the overlooking promontory. While on the contentious ridge they were gathered like gulls, ready for flight at the first assault of sound. But waiting. Lulled, it seemed to Clinton, his body erecting frightened frills of skin and hair; or inscrutably pinioned while their fates overtook them. Which happened very soon, in the shape of the blast waves, in an obscuring welter of granite and grit. Except for the pair whom Clinton saw, in a great clarity above the flash, ascending and falling like starfish, in a neat parabola that ended in the river, smack.

Then there was the silence that involved them all, except for the wind and the trees, and the banging clouds and perhaps a few echoes swept back from the mountain on streams of turbulent air.

"Like a trip wire," said Smith, wonderingly. "I never saw nothing like it. Regular fireworks, whoosh, bang-bang. Now what d'you suppose made it go up like that, considering it's never happened before?"

"There's got to be a first time for everything," said Jackson. He nursed his jaw, which felt stiff and was beginning to ache, in anticipation of the coming inquisition. "Ask me, we've been lucky it's never happened before this, and I ought to know, I've been in the business best part of my life and I wasn't born yesterday. Lucky," he said, and hitched up his voice a few decibels, so that he could be heard bearing witness, "and some might say deserve to be. Because God hisself could not have been more careful than we was."

"Are you saying we stopped being?" asked Smith curiously.

"I'm not," said Jackson, and brought his teeth together sharply, as if a stick of rock had been between them, to exhibit the words of innocence that ran right through to the end. "All I'm saying is human is human, and there's no call to expect humans to act as if they was different."

"What do you mean?" asked Smith.

"Who knows?" said Jackson, laboring. "We got to wait for the dust to settle."

But Smith was not willing. He had got out his probe, and did not intend putting it back unbloodied.

"Them that checked the fuses," he said. "Stands to reason, they couldn't have done it proper."

"I seen them doing it myself," said Jackson somberly.

"And it was done proper?" asked Smith, wielding bluntly.

"Must've been," answered Jackson, moving slightly to foil.

"And them junglies," pursued Smith, "that ought never to have been where they was—"

"Leave them be!" cried Jackson, violently. "They've been blown to kingdom come, now you leave them poor heathen alone. In peace, see? If you don't mind."

"I don't mind," said Smith, and moved his lips which wanted to utter something injurious in retaliation upon this barking ape, but difficult to find. "I'm going home," he said significantly. "Maybe you ought to too. I mean because you don't sound like yourself. Sounding off, I mean, about them jungle apes, as if they was us."

"Maybe I ought," said Jackson, edging toward recantation, because it was queer, thinking about it, not at all like himself.

But not making it, for some reason or reasons which blocked solidly, though they refused to come out and be named.

The man who had lost the most said least.

The old man, who had been waiting, rose from his hollow when it happened and tottered to the site supported by two of his stalwarts, who were past it themselves, but the pick of those to be found in his village. His eyes were running with moisture, which being usual, they did not notice. Except one or two, whose impulses had been fined by disaster, who saw where the old salt runnels lay, in grooves which were different from those now being worn. The rest were stunned, and would quiver when the pithing rod passed but now were still, which the old man saw but was silent. Though he felt; and drew the thin shawl that his brittle bones would not support once more round his frame, to protect, against the wind and the chill in those faces, and hid his own which he feared would show the weeping rictus.

Then someone came to ask, or perhaps to be reassured, tweaking at the cloth that covered the bones, and the old man raised his face, in which something seemed to have clarified, like blood turned to wine or flesh become spirit, which made the questioner conscious of his intrusion.

"They ask," he faltered. "It is necessary to know. If it is possible to tell."

"Tell them two score," said the old man, and moved his mouth gently over the first words he had spoken until then.

And so indeed there were, when they had matched members to men, and counted, after the dust had settled. Forty human beings, less two who marinated in the river, at the upstream section of the dam.

"It was a triple failure, or error," said Mackendrick. "Who would have thought?" Speaking disjointed thoughts, in the hope that a shape might form, a plan to which they could all rededicate themselves. Instead of the present division, whose splinters sharpened the air, even if they had not yet pierced the flesh.

"The signals were not working," said Clinton, "efficiently. Some not at all. It was also a premature blast. A runaway," he said, precisely but thinly, because some of his substance was gone.

"At this eleventh hour," said Mackendrick.

"The inquiry will show," said Clinton. "Only, of course, there is no time for luxuries."

"There is no time for anything, much," said Mackendrick. "Except to get moving."

"Yes, that," said Clinton. "Like shoving snowballs uphill." And smiled with bloodless lips, which suspected, like Mackendrick, but would not give names to shapeless fears.

They went in company to inspect the area of disaster, a tight small band of men whose worries were sealed beneath blanched white faces which had never given anything away. Not even pity, felt the amazed onlookers, whose numbness was yielding to—what, they did not know, something with needles in it that pricked their eyes, and formed hard angry knots and clots in their chests. Because the dead were pitiful, scraped up from their scattered landings and assembled, in a broken, rag-doll kind of way, along the bank which had borne such weights before, and was stony.

Rawlings, who had put on a safari hat and carried a knob-kerrie, walked down the row of dead with Mackendrick, who had put on boots, counting, with the aid of his knobbed stick which scalloped along, halting briefly over each extinct head.

"Thirty-eight," he announced, making it final, and affixing the official seal, though the count had been taken before. "Ten, I would say," he said, "are our labor. The rest are theirs."

The rest who were old men, women and children, whom the dam could not use, but whom it had nevertheless taken.

"Correct, bar two, who are in the river," said Mackendrick.

"The corpses will rise," said Rawlings.

"I don't think so," said Mackendrick, and made his boots

squeak, one upper rubbed against the other, to crack the small hard kernel of silence which had formed again.

So they went to see, walking along the flattened crest of the sand-block as if on eggshells, which was unnecessary, for the bar was of solid sand, and would need dynamite, as they knew, to disintegrate. Nevertheless, going delicately.

Clinton led, in the natural order of things, which not even disaster could disrupt. As they were glad to see, under lowered lids which did not show their pride, though the essence of it rose and wrote similar sentences in their minds. Clinton read, and was consoled by the solidarity that knit their little island, and felt the in-flow of strength replenishing his substance which the day had thinned and depleted, so that his back grew straight, almost, and from this recovered and commanding height began to notice again, and compare. Unfavorably, with a curl to his lip that could have been distaste, or even a remote pity, the marbled containment of his own against the others who flocked and flapped, surging about on the riverbank among the dead.

Then they were at the edge, peering down. Not far, for the rock-filled dam loomed up, all but breaking the surface of the water, and had been destined to do so in a matter of hours, but now was halted. By the corpses of foolish men, who lay on the rocky bed, pinned by the rock boulder, their limbs flowing with the tide though attached to the trunk. Waving like seaweed, or the pale tentacles of some hindering fate, at which they gazed with repulsion, through two feet of swirling, yellowish floodwater. Then it was left to Clinton, who being nurtured on royal jelly would have the strength, to say. Who would, though other strengths were making themselves palpable, which pressed at his sides and whitened his gills but did not control the content of the resolve that was forming. Coldly, in crystalline chambers of his mind which he would not allow to be buffeted, or invaded, or clouded by the bitter absinthe of the mourners on the bank.

Until Rawlings, who hated the guts of the wind, and wanted to see the beginning of the end, began to rap with his stick the steel of the inlet gates which the explosion had left intact, to remind. While Clinton, who did not need reminding, and would not have his decisions rushed, grew irritable at the sound of the tapping, so that the rancidity broke like veins on the surface of their marble, threatening the inner cohesion on which they leaned.

"Two dead men," said Mackendrick, for the sake of saying, to reduce these threats before they could damage, at which he was good, though what his hasty search had produced he could not feel was his best.

"Gummed up the whole works," said Rawlings, and listened vengefully to the silence, below the natural sounds, of their idle machinery.

"In time the currents will free them," said Lefevre, wiping the spray from his eyes to gaze down, seeing through tumbling waters the sea-change, wrought already in his mind, of dark uppers and pink soles bleaching in soak to the color of the underbellies of fish.

"In time the fish will have them," said Henderson, who caught what was in the air and was pleased that he had, since it did not often happen.

"But there is not the time for any of this," said Clinton, with the bleakness of the crags that surrounded them upon his face, battling with them to prevent them crushing, closing in before what lay in his mind could grow, accumulating power and inevitability.

Or was his conflict with men, standing as he could see like windblown scarecrows on the opposite shore?

Then his strength which had been in flux began to mount, from watching them, in inverse proportion to their frailty.

"We'll be days getting them out," said Rawlings, not declaiming any more, nor even subdued by Clinton's restraint, but gathering the facts like reins into his capable hands.

"Must weigh ten tons, if an ounce," said Mackendrick, answering his cue, sizing the granite laid upon those chests. "It will not be easy to shift, under water too."

"Floodwater," said Lefevre, anguish under his lean contained flesh, which coolly took note of the currents. "Though it has barely begun."

So without knowing it, or perhaps subliminally aware, they smoothed the way for Clinton, in whom the notes of jubilation were cautiously sounding, for those truths which had always acknowledged that the fibers of his strength were concerned with carrying his side with him. Which was easier if they accepted a part of the load.

"There is no need," he said, "to shift the boulder. It rests on the dam, and can be molded in."

"The men," said Mackendrick, sickly.

"Or the men," said Clinton. "Their bodies can be incorporated. Into the structure."

Then he went away to his bungalow, which promised to be empty, and indeed was, for Helen had left for the village. Except, of course, for Das, who bowled out of his godown like a puffball, robes fluffing, to tend his master.

"Bad business, Das," said Clinton, tranquilly, for the poison tooth of disaster, its delaying potential, had been drawn, or soon would be.

"Yes, sahib," said Das, whose shining face wanted to mirror the tranquillity but could not, because of certain signs he could see. So instead he drew off the master's boots and socks and creaking on to his knees began to press and pummel the pale calves, to loosen the knots he could feel. Which was a wife's job, certainly his wife's, whose massaging fingers he missed, though from what he had seen of memsahibs their hands from pride or primness never went below the neck muscles. Thus defecting, in his estimation, from pleasurable duty. So now he kneaded, his eyes gone to a glaze, like an amiable and conscientious baker.

Clinton, whose hackles had stiffened at first acquaintance

with these sensual attentions, had since learned to derive pleasure from them. So now he relaxed, in the verandah chair whose canvas curved supplely round his body, while he waited, senses alert for the throb and hum, for the great wheel of construction to begin its ponderous revolutions again.

28

OVER in the settlement Helen sat beside the pallet on which the old man lay. He had fallen, in the strong wind they said, or perhaps it was from some inward loss, and had been carried to his hut by the same two stalwarts who had supported him to the abyss. Whose knees had buckled when they saw the fall, from consternation for the future of the tribe, or perhaps an anguish for their own harsh-pressed bodies. Which the old man noticing, would have asked them to let him lie where he was, in a passing weakness, except that he found he was without speech. So he gave them their way, allowing his bones to be slung between them while his spirit wandered, at ease in the forest whose seasons were phases of his life, and its tumbling lights drifted down as softly as mimosa, melting under the eyelids to tender golds.

It hurt him to wake up.

"He is coming to," said Helen, who kept watch, in the space around the pallet they had cleared for her.

"Coming to," echoed the villagers, who crowded the entrance to the hut, and had squashed themselves against its sides and piled up against the rafters to allow her this spacious pre-eminence. Because of the blankets and medicines she brought, not thinking spitefully beyond to the money and power that were behind such largesse. Thinking simply, and falling back.

The old man heard their voices and opened his eyes, on which those yellow flakes had rested. He was dry. Denuded bones scraped thinly against each other, and flesh had fallen away from the bones as if dried out in some oven. He creaked when he moved. So he lay still, looking at all of them, and listening. To the voices in the hut, and beyond to the calling and keening of women, and beyond still, for something which did not come.

Then Helen, misunderstanding, said: "You must not worry. What is done is done. The dependents, I will see to it, will be cared for."

Sponging the cracked skin, to ease the agony, or to deliver speech, which presented its breeches and was stuck.

The old man tried again, as was his duty. When he could not be turned away from them into himself and began listening again, and presently heard the great silences which gave his inner being repose.

Which seeing, they tiptoed away, some to console, some to snuff out the candles they had lit after the warnings had carded their skins, to ward off, and in case, which God's will had not permitted the wax to do.

Except Helen, who had her duties too, and bore a weight whose nature she sought, which might have been guilt or responsibility, though Rawlings would have found no difficulty in pinning on the correct label.

"God knows why," he said, this reddish man Rawlings with the blue suspicious eyes, to Mackendrick, "why we insist on carrying the white man's burden."

Mackendrick was incredulous. In this day and age, one did not know, one held beliefs from which such words could spring?

"Because of the filthy lucre?" he suggested. He could be brutal, and now was, partly because of the lead that lined his stomach.

"Ah yes, well, there is that. Yes," said Rawlings. And paused to consider this man, whose skin seemed to him brown, from the sun, or perhaps from the notions that lay under, pigmenting it. "Though we give, ounce for ounce, flesh for gold, I would say more than we get. Though possibly," he said, patching, because he was greatly afraid of rifts, "it has not always been so."

"Flesh for gold, that is funny," said Mackendrick, and managed to laugh. "It is precisely what the other camp is saying."

"Which you would know about," griped Rawlings. "For myself, I prefer not to associate. No good has ever come of it, and none ever will."

"One has only to think of Helen," said Millie, who came in briskly at the tail-end of the conversation, shaking a debris of blown leaves and severed creeper from her, to be rid of the alien society; and she thought of her, the process deviating, despite herself, from a rounded righteousness to ripe images that brought greenish tinges to her hungry flesh.

Then Mackendrick grew very tired, and fell to stroking his arms, which felt thick and reliable under his cotton shirt, in contrast to the helplessness that held him. When confronted by walls, or was it fences: solidly constructed, with no chinks to let in light.

So they sat, laboring in each other's company, and not even a drink to help them along, for Millie had run out, until presently Lefevre drifted in, for no special reason except to be there, though he had little to contribute to leaven the atmosphere. Followed by Galbraith, who like Lefevre had looked into this empty bungalow and that, and his wife Betty, and then Henderson and Scott. All of them, congregating, though none with very much to say. So that Rawlings, constrained, brought out his blunderbuss to clobber the unnatural ice.

"It's the weather," he said, "that depresses us. Rising and falling, you never know where you are with it."

"The humidity. Like wet blankets. You may laugh," said

Millie to Lefevre, who had barked unwisely, "but that is exactly what it feels like to me."

"It is at least predictable. Even the rising and falling," said Mackendrick, with memories of the quirky deluges of his native land.

"The monsoon is due," said Henderson, heavily, and loudly, for it seemed to him they were in danger of forgetting. "Any day now. We ought to be getting a move on. What are we waiting for? Does anyone know? Or care?" Because he cared, passionately, in those passing sobrieties that allowed him this freedom.

"We are waiting, as always, for them," said Rawlings, returning to, and doubling, his briskness. "The schedules are ready. We move the instant they finish. They are mopping up," he said, "their dead. It takes time. There are thirty-eight of them."

"And two in the river," harped Mackendrick.

"They are no problem," said Rawlings. "It has been decided."

"To concrete them in," said Mackendrick, opening a cage it seemed, or perhaps only the door of some experimental laboratory, kept out of sight in the basements of humane hospitals, where the smooth men in white coats worked. So that they had to look, and saw the twisted thing, that made their bowels jump and kick, in a silence that squirmed like a wormy cocoon.

Until at last Rawlings said, uneasily, "There is no other way."

"Unfortunately, no," said Mackendrick, his steady voice returning them to themselves, safe home after rounding a dangerous cape, which some felt aggrievedly he had quite unnecessarily made them negotiate. All that fuss. When the dam came first, hundreds of lives depending on it or would depend in the future.

"The dam takes overriding priority," Henderson put it for all of them.

"No time to muck about," said Galbraith.

So the air grew congenial again, blue with smoke and mur-mured reminiscence, as they relaxed in chairs, or on cushions which Millie threw on the floor with girlish abandon.

"There was this croc," said Rawlings, and they prepared to listen, for on lucky days he could be a good raconteur. "River just swarmed with them. Lay up on the bank like logs so you had to step carefully or else wham! they'd have you in, no mat-ter if you were an ox. Now this croc, she was a real man-eater, seems she had worked up a taste for human flesh. The boys were scared stiff of her, believed she was the devil incarnate, because she had one green eye and one brown one. Appar-ently," he laughed indulgently, nostalgic for paternal days, "that was the infallible mark. Well, one day there she was, cruising along, only eyes and snout above water. And, sure enough, one eye green and the other brown. Well, I let her have it, both barrels. And I got her, those days I was a better shot than I am now. Smack between those wicked, glittering eyes." He paused, to linger and perhaps warm himself in the sunshine of this carefree past, and instead dark shadows fell, of happen-ings on this same river, which had ceased to be full of crocodiles, or if there were one no longer saw them, saved one's shot to protect one's own skin. Rawlings fell silent, and had to be prodded to continue and did, but the heart had been taken from it and they were not held. Listened for want of better, but were not rapt, until he finished and then Mackendrick be-gan.

"There was a foundry, when I was a boy, Inverness way," he said, taking them back to understood backgrounds, on whose common fields they could lie peacefully, they thought. "Where they used to cast bells, big ones, mostly for export in those days. When the war came they had to switch to guns, which didn't please anyone, but they knew they had no option. There was one order, though, which they meant to complete, for the local kirk, whose belfry had crashed and mangled the bell. Small job for them, two tons, where they were used to twenty and more; but still none too easy, a lot of their experienced men had gone into the services and copper was short, for what they called inessentials. The pastor was a decent man, when he heard he told them to give up, he would manage with hand bells. But they were determined, they got the copper, they made the molds. We saw the molds, this was our bell, we saw the shape of it in the melting metal. Then—nothing. We knew the bell had been cast, though we did not see. But nothing."

He stopped, and those who were listening drew back, heat from the glowing bell-metal fanning their faces, and felt their scalps tighten, for no good reason.

"It had been a long time cooling, they said," said Mackendrick, "when they eventually got it out so that we could see. They put it on a padded gun-carriage, and the padre consecrated it, and it was strung up. But the note was wrong," he said flatly, "they took it down and honed the edge, but whatever they did they could not make it right. It never pealed, it tolled. After a while no one would ring it."

Faces were gray. Mackendrick did not see them, because of the light, the long shafts of sunlight that slanted through the bell tower and struck the silent bell, struck terror in the heart of the watching boy that he had been. Who saw flesh colors in the dull bell-metal. Who knew.

"Though no one would say," said Mackendrick, "they were a tight-mouthed lot. It seeped out, you might say. That all that was left was bones, as they saw when they hauled it up."

Marsh gas writhed through the room, or it could have been the rancorous whorls of their thoughts, dealing soft insidious blows which they parried by moving. Restlessly, picking things up and putting them down, for no good reason except the invisible one.

"Avoidable accidents," said Rawlings. "Careless buggers."

He crushed out his cigarette and threw the hot stub into the tin of water in which a leg of the liquor cupboard stood. The other three tins were empty and he thought of fulminating but let it pass. Insects were ascending the wood, and he began picking these off, fretfully, with the toe of his shoe. "Bloody things," he grumbled, eyeing the mess they made, dark smears which disfigured the furniture. But did not desist.

Millie felt the air thick in her nostrils and rose from her chair. "Fresh air," she mumbled, and opened a window which the gale seized and flung wide, with a wrench at the hinges. Which held, but a pane was gone, through which the outside entered that they had jointly labored to keep out, even after the window was closed. So that there was no point to herding, and little comfort. Cane and canvas creaked, under their afflicted bodies, and presently Henderson stood up, easing his heavy thighs in the khaki shorts which had ridden up and were cutting his crotch. Then they were all going, leaving Millie with Rawlings, who was no use to her. Who shivered, in the cotton dress whose violent flowers died away in the liquid light that flowed through the windows, at the sounds that came in the wake, or van, of the distant storm that was swelling, she felt, to destroy. So that she began to scream.

"Boy!" she shouted, "Boy! Boy!" and when the nervous servant appeared, pointed imperiously to the jagged hole through which it came, she pretended. "Mend it, at once, at once!" she cried. As if he were a glazier, but did his best, with brown paper and paste, and sacking to mute the buzz-sawing of wind against paper.

Then it was as quiet as one could expect it to be, especially by comparison, until the drums began. Which was not new, they often rataplanned, though governed in their rise and fall by the clamor of the dam, so that one rested easy in the confidence of machinery to whose power the drums were subservient.

But now heard clearly, in the troughs of the tossing forest. The throbbing, like an ache in the air. Then Millie opened her lips, which were discolored from being pressed together, to foist her fear.

"That man," she said, "gives me the creeps." Of Mackendrick, who had been gone an hour.

"What, old Mack," said her husband. "Yes."

And pretended, listening to the beat of the drums which carried a message, he knew. Though what, he could not have said but wished to be told, to put up defenses. There was no one, however, neither Mackendrick, nor Helen, nor Bashiam, nor anyone whose wider horizons could have enlightened him. Only the servants, who clustered and cowered in their go-downs, with shawls muffling their ears, so that even a cup of tea was not to be come by.

29

"THERE is something not quite nice about it," said poor Gopal. Trying not to think about these beefy men, the master builders, who could stomach anything, flesh and blood and kidneys that reeked as he knew from watching them feed, and now this concrete thing. While his fastidious body flinched.

"Hrrmph!" said Lefevre, who thought the same thing. "It may not be nice, though one had been given to think that what you bloody Hindus cared about was the soul." And he went out, striding with long legs, out of the bungalow which had had a joint vision, to be with those who would see things in the same narrow beam as he did.

Leaving Gopal who fidgeted and grew morose, glooming over the little dam whose works were jammed. Until the magnet began to function, drawing him out to congregate with those he hoped were his own, to whom he repeated, it is not nice.

To which Krishnan replied, "It is only the body detritus," absently, while his mind continued harshly its engagement with another matter, and his hands lay still in the folds of his snowy muslin lap, into which he scrupulously changed each evening when he was done with the khaki.

"One would not have believed," pursued Gopal, hopelessly, "that they would countenance such a thing. Or even think of it, thinking as they do."

"Who knows what they think?" said Shanmugham. "They do not know themselves."

"Except that they think differently," said Krishnan, "when their own kind is not involved."

"Though one would not say that the lost two are our kind either," said Gopal, and found that he could not raise his voice, which had thinned and dwindled in the tussle between truth and the proclaiming of such unworthiness.

"They could be, it would depend," said Krishnan. "But the dam. That," he said, not to remind but to test its cohesive power, "is our first consideration."

"Our dam," said Shanmugham, tilting the word slightly, to prop it up where it sagged, and to quell the apprehension that was mounting stealthily.

"Not so," said Krishnan. "It is the Clinton-Mackendrick Dam."

"No, no, no," cried Shanmugham. "It is a joint effort. Theirs and ours. Otherwise it could not be."

"Nevertheless," said Krishnan, and plaited his fingers together, like overlapped wattle which does not give, or break. "The plaque has been cast. It is blue, and the letters are golden, although they will go black in time. They do not record a joint effort."

"It is not fair," said Gopal, thinly, because of the striding legs, or it could have been those arms that held the river, to all of which he was close to love.

Then they were silent, Gopal and Shanmugham and the rest, huddled together in the circle of Krishnan's power, or strength. Waiting for whatever it was to happen, and listening to the drums whose message, though not of their vernacular, was becoming apparent.

Until presently the five men came whom the crisis had thrown up, a confused junta to take the place of the speechless old man. And stood and shuffled, resolution wilting, dusty bare feet scuffing the cement floor which played on the nerves of those waiting, curling their toes and the vulnerable roots of their teeth, which clenched. Krishnan unclenched them, to say, sharply, "What will you do? For what have you come?"

"We will do nothing," said the spokesman for the five, and chattered a little, because of the happenings of the day, or perhaps because of the sharp white teeth that confronted him, at which he did not look but was vividly aware. And continued stubbornly, despite the rigors. "No work, until the bodies of our dead are returned to us. So that the rites may be correctly performed, and their souls depart in peace."

"No work, you think they will notice?" asked Krishnan, disregarding, using his words like whips. "They will work harder, and they will make us work harder to make up for you."

"If such a thing is possible," said the spokesman.

"For them it is possible," said Krishnan. "So what will you do?"

"We will do nothing, for there will be nothing to do," said the spokesman, with dignity, but bowing his head.

Then Krishnan despised them, as much as anyone had and more than he had ever done, the disdain welling up from the depths of his heart and mind but contained within the mask of the idling god. While he thought, and reeled in the lines to which lives were attached, onto the bobbin he held in his powerful hand.

"If you withdraw your labor, so will we," he said, "since we are one kind, mixed and formed from the same soil, unlike those others who would do this thing without regard to our feelings, and in pursuit of their own glory."

"The dam is its own glory," said Gopal. But was not heard in the effusions of roused emotion, and the sounding of triumphal roundelays, and the scraping of chairs and feet that make up the business of upping and going.

So the two wings clapped together, whose independent

articulation had been a source of Clinton's strength, though both were necessary to him; and the sound wheeled over the torn valley and the stricken dam distributing its message, like a flock of screeching parrots.

"I cannot think what is holding us up," said Henderson untiringly, to Mackendrick upon whom he had fastened, in lieu of Rawlings who had bluntly requested respite. "Or what they are up to, to take so long. Though it is pretty well impossible to think with the bloody racket those drums are kicking up."

"The ceremony of death," said Mackendrick simply. "It is usual to mourn." So transforming the sinister notes which, unconverted, nosed along like ice floes in Millie's throbbing veins.

"Banging and banging," said Henderson. "It is uncivilized."

"Tolling," said Mackendrick, whose mind had returned to the foundry, whose business had been the casting of bells, "is not uncommon. One hears St. Paul's. And elsewhere. It is a matter of country. Bells, cymbals, or drums," he said, "one takes one's choice."

But Henderson did not consider it was a question of country, and still less a matter for levity. Mackendrick is odd, he said to himself, and it is barbarity. We are not communicating as we should, he said, and at last was silent. Continuing to be with Mackendrick, for company, any being better than his own, or none.

Then in the silence, perhaps because of it, he became aware. Of something in the air, and groped for it, clumsily like a drunken man after a nimble fly, for this was not his forte, and at length touched a tenuous wing.

"That banging," he said, "seems to have changed. Perhaps it is the rhythm that is different."

"It is different," said Mackendrick.

"In which case, it is not mourning anymore, but something else," said Henderson.

"Right," said Mackendrick, who had seen the faces, and

whipcord in the strained calves of the men who waited on the riverbank, and suspected and now heard his suspicions confirmed.

"They will strike," he said, discarding withdrawal of labor, and withholding of services, and other cheap phrases which petty men use, or dishonest men, to titivate a declared intention. "Unless we restore their dead to them, which we cannot do, they will strike."

For the drums were very clear.

Presently, quite soon, Mackendrick laid his hands on his bony knees and jerked his spare body up. "I must go," he said to the fleshy face that was Henderson, and paused to focus his vision and said, with a kind of heaviness, "Perhaps it would be as well if you came too. Since we are in this together."

"It would be best," agreed the fleshy face.

In his drafty hut, in the depressed land fringed by uncurbed scrub and rustling thickets of the trusting forest, the old man lay, still waiting. For death they said, muting their voices to ease the passing, but their chief, who had tested himself for loosening of flesh from the spirit, knew better. He waited, straining to hear above their murmurs, looking at marigolds and greenery they had twisted into the thatch, where the smoke writhed and coiled from the *sambrani* burning in a corner, fragrance to honor the presence of death or perhaps suppliant to it. But the old man smiled, insofar as lips could that had slid out of his control. Sometimes he slept, brief moments that opened out in his mind to wide pastures and great reaches of time, so that when he woke and saw that the light was altered so little he could not believe. But was refreshed. And listened again for the sound of the turning wheel, which did not come. And slept to gather his strength, but it would not come. So presently he accepted his weakness, and allowed the jumbled lights of the jungle to wash over him, and basked in the warmth they brought to his old, friable bones.

*   *   *

Clinton waited for the same thing, in the impregnable box set squarely in the clear patch of defeated jungle, whose unbridled plumes tossed and lunged a bare stone's throw away. The box felt empty, having been constructed for two and containing, now, little more than the husk of one. For Clinton was dry. He could feel himself wither, and the grating as the juices thickened and the crystals formed, as he waited on the edge of his chair to pick up the sound of the growth of the dam which did not come. Now and then he moistened his lips, of which the skin felt glazed and brittle like crackling, dipping a finger in whiskey and running it over to bring them to life. But achieving only arider deserts. Water, he said, is essential, and his mind for no reason returned to that suffocating session in Delhi, an era ago it seemed, when other men had said, and he had not listened. Bored by their passion, stifled by the emotion which spilled over into their eyes, which still remained opaque for him but would, he knew, become clear in this suspended moment if he wished. But did not wish. Beggars, said Howard Clinton explicitly, emotional beggars. And drank from habit not hope, the molten priceless liquid behaving like a decoction of lead.

And continued to sit even when Helen entered.

For they shared a roof, and bed and board, and the services of Das, though this was less evenly distributed. Only the selves remained apart, not by will alone, but by an irresistible process of drift. So that the distance between them widened, whose presence Clinton had decreed and precisely defined as essential to him, passing out of the control of both.

"It has been terrible," said Helen, in the flat voice of her kind, or perhaps of exhaustion. The darkness of her vigil circled her eyes, whose lids drooped from a saturation of what she knew, he felt, but would not reveal.

"A high price," he said, and creaked in his chair, "will have to be paid."

"A high price has been paid," she answered.

I do not know her, thought Clinton, and looked at the thick

smooth brows, above those fallen concealing half-moons. I do not know this woman, who is my wife. But he tried, putting out a few tenuous filaments.

"They asked for trouble," he said. "They got what was coming. Naturally they are upset. It is upsetting."

"Naturally," she said. What language, she asked in wonder, did we use before that was common to both, of which we have now lost the art? But she too tried. "It is not the dying," she said. "Lives have been lost before. They are used to death, it is everyday and they see it, having no hospitals to cover up. It is not that."

Now he was really at a loss. He could feel the thin weave of it, shoddy in place of the substantiality he usually wore, rubbing his naked shoulders. Of which she grew aware, if only through the chair's canvas and timbers, whose creaking had risen like a storm-running ship's.

"If it is not that," he said, to whom death was an end, "then I do not know what it can be."

"The bodies," she answered, "which are to be incorporated."

"Bones," he said, and thought of calcium, the chalk that went to the making of cliffs and the framework of men.

"They are not so easily reduced," she said, "by some people. Not always by us. Never by them. Who believe the spirit will not be freed, until its body has been reverenced."

"Are these sane beliefs," he said, shaking, his sights upon the desert that stretched as he spoke, "beliefs of sanity, to which I am asked to pander?"

"They are beliefs," she said. "One does not walk over graves wearing jackboots."

Then they were both tired, of each other, and this thing which presented differently, blinding to one though light to the other; and the filaments put out began to wither, like severed vines in the sun.

Now there was nowhere to meet, except in the open. For sensibilities had been wrought to so quivering a point that brick and concrete, and even thatch, took on the character of those it housed, and so became suspect.

"Why the hell should I go to their miserable hovels?" asked Rawlings, lobbing the question like a daring deed into the midst of his sympathizers. "We have to talk, right, we talk in my bungalow. Which is civilized, and draft-proof." And he glanced at the window, whose brown-paper pane buzzed like a bee.

"I will not," said Krishnan, "negotiate on alien territory. The emanations being strong, and inimical to our purpose, which rise from these little bits of England." And his eyes considered, to see if they were with him, how much farther he could take them. For he could tell there was still some way to go.

The junta shivered, ashes daubed on their wornout faces, spines stiffened only by Krishnan, and the imperative nature of their demand.

Mackendrick sighed; an echo of the sighs that trailed away down the hill and over the months, or perhaps it was years, to the beginning. Something in him bled a little, for the uselessness of it all. Then he went away to search out pockets of goodwill, which he was certain existed, which accordingly manifested themselves. So that presently there were guy ropes and pegs, and a tent that heaved and creaked to the tune of the season, straining at its tethers.

Here they could assemble, and did; keeping face, in discomfort, in a glare of emergency lightning, and something that was close to hate.

Though why, said Gopal, it is difficult to know, for we are a gentle people, and he looked down at his hands, over which Lefevre had exclaimed for the capability residing in the delicate, birdlike bones.

Apes, said Rawlings, riding high but false on the stench of crushed-down memories, which nevertheless rose. It is time for us to rap them down.

Try, said Krishnan, and opened his face to allow a glimpse of the cutting blades housed in the smooth nose cone.

So that Mackendrick felt that for two pins he would have risen and spelled out DAM, in letters of some white fire that would burn painfully, and perhaps purify, leaving only what mattered.

"We have no time," he said bluntly, "to bring up the bodies. The rains are due. The dam is at risk."

"It is a question of hours," said Krishnan.

"I am thinking in hours," said Mackendrick bleakly.

"One has to think of the men too," said Krishnan. "Who will not resume, for reasons which have been made clear."

"And you are with them?" asked Rawlings.

"The men are behind me," answered Krishnan, and his lips were ripe and round, as if they enclosed the wafer for which he had long petitioned, though mind and muscle were substantially involved in the prayer.

Then Rawlings began to swell. The veins in his neck were like warnings, or threats, though the time for these was past as Mackendrick knew and perhaps Rawlings too, but he could not help himself.

"Are you aware," he said, thickly, "of what you are leading these men into? The consequences?"

"I am aware, perhaps more strongly," said Krishnan, "of the spiritual torments they will suffer if I do not."

Rawlings drew a long breath, to give himself time. This man is subtle, he said, and resolved to be wily.

"Spiritual torments," he repeated. "Since the two are dead, and their spirits have gone, and the bodies are nothing, what would these be?"

"The same as you would endure," said Krishnan, "as you once described to me, if you were unable to afford your dead decent Christian burial."

Then Rawlings knew, and told himself, the man is a devil.

But continued to have dealings, doggedly, and because there was no other way.

"It is merely a question of disposal," he said. "The matter is as simple as that."

"It is a simple matter of equality," rejoined Krishnan, "the same done to us as to you. Whether in life or death."

Mackendrick had withdrawn. Now and again their words frothed and burst against his skin, spindrift that he brushed away. For they were without substance for the day, they did not relate, except insofar as something was being worked out that had not begun this morning, nor would see an end there. The sins of the fathers, said Mackendrick remotely, and he traced the glittering thread back as far as he could follow, and forward to where it was still being spun.

Rawlings meanwhile had talked himself out, or almost. I am exhausted, he said; stupidity is physically exhausting and Mackendrick who has reneged gives no help. Feeling the ulcers form, but quelling them to make one more effort.

"You will be a laughingstock in the bazaars," he said, "if we do not complete on time. Whether you like it or not, we're together. Hamstring us and you hamstring yourself as well."

"That is as may be," said Krishnan, with his flush-fitting face, and his rounded mouth with the purplish lips, at which Rawlings could not bear to look.

"But you will not succeed," said Rawlings. He meant to say, but it ended as a shout.

After this Krishnan went away to be alone. When he was he could feel his bones jutting, and the gauntness of his face, whose disfigurements he knew.

For he was in agony, and it rendered down the flesh leaving only the frame.

They will find a way, he said. When all will be well, for it is a common aim.

Only if we break, he answered, and we will not, for it is our turn to be strong. Power can shift. They must learn that it has, it is for us to teach them.

But either way there was no peace. I am a stranger to it, he said, twisting, pressing his knuckles to his feverish eyeballs, as perhaps all men are. Since it is man's condition to manufacture anguish. From which presently he drew, or there rose, a strange, fatal, weary calm.

30

CLINTON, who had to be aloof, was alone too.

Until Mackendrick came bearing news. Towing defeat like an empty trawl, and looking to make sure that Helen had gone, to spare her, for these merciful attitudes still lingered, sometimes to plague him.

For a while the two men sat quietly, steeped in the flavors of what was happening, sharing the bitterness, and something of their thoughts. Then Clinton said, as he had said to Helen, passing a hand over his eyes to clear his vision but not achieving the purpose: "I do not understand. Such preoccupation over something which is lifeless and irrelevant, when there is so much at stake."

"They mean us to eat humble pie, which we have made their staple fare," said Mackendrick straightly. Who understood motivational force, but was unable to pass on his understanding.

"I cannot think why," said Clinton. And rose and leaned against a pillar of the verandah, from where he could see the solid achievement, or imagined he saw, between the fissures of the plunging forest.

"One builds," he said. "A ship, a bridge, a dam. What it is

built of, is plain to see. Iron, steel, glass, concrete, would one not say? But not at all. It is built out of oneself, one's blood, brain, nerve, guts, spleen and marrow. And spirit. Whatever goes into us, goes into it. The making of the two," he said, and smiled, with those thin denuded lips to which Mackendrick was growing accustomed, "is not dissimilar."

Then Mackendrick felt something within him contract, his heart maybe, he said, though it is many years since I was made aware so strongly.

"There is the chance," he said, and stopped, it was so frail a thing to offer, having died more than once in his hands.

"Of the rains holding off?" asked Clinton.

"Of clearing the obstacle before the rains begin," said Mackendrick.

"It is a matter of several days, not hours," said Clinton, "to blast underwater. The rains will have swamped us by then."

"If the boulder were lifted whole," said Mackendrick, and paused, from a difficulty with naming the name. "Bashiam," he said, "Bashiam considers it feasible, and is willing to try."

"It is not within his power," said Clinton.

"Who knows?" said Mackendrick. "These crane men, they can work wonders with their machines. One might almost say," he said, and dropped his eyes, to disconnect himself from those who said, "perform miracles."

"It is impossible," said Clinton.

"It is a chance," said Mackendrick.

So it has come to this, said Clinton, and stroked the line of his jaw, whose strength was demonstrably an illusion. That I am to be beholden to this man. Grasp the line which is offered, studded with thorns though it be. Then the suns which had scorched and singed before, showed themselves boldly, burning brilliantly, and excoriating him.

"Let us take the chance that Bashiam offers," he said through blistered lips.

*   *   *

Bashiam could have said why, after some thought, if he had chosen to, but did not choose to reveal the wherefores of all he did. He went down to the river, not only to gauge, but because it was something he lived by, wound into him through the years, its hold strengthened with his absences. For other reasons also, whose whorls, for the moment, he would not consciously enter.

He, too, needed to be alone, and had to wait until the crowd and clutter of the riverbank had retreated beyond the boundary of consciousness, leaving him isolated in his cell, which was lucid, and brilliantly lit. Then the scanner began to work, of its own volition, taking in land and water, the slope of the bank, the capacity of the crane, and the sweep and reach of its arm; and joined this knowledge intricately, with dovetails, to an awareness that had grown and hardened into shape, and was to do with rights and responsibilities. So that he had to recognize, and said, it can be done.

And paused to gather strength, for it needed strength, and said, I must do it, since they are my people, whom I cannot shed although I have tried. My people who are the impediment as they have long been said and are now proving themselves to be, which it is for me to remove. I will, he said, and felt strong, and looked at his young man's limbs which were smooth and strong but would twist so easily, frail under metal, breaking him with them for he possessed nothing except his strength. Then he wavered, and trembled for the loss before he had sustained it, and would have withdrawn (notwithstanding his people, and obligations through them), but that the shadow fell that was Clinton's, whose wife he had taken, to whom a debt was owed.

Though she came to me, he said, and blew out his cheeks to relieve his mouth, whose walls had cracked as if dried in a kiln. She came to me. But the act, which was ours. It has delivered me to him, he said, and felt the tightness in him and round his body, like bonds. Wetted rattan thongs, which would contract when the moisture was gone, as it would soon do from the fever that afflicted him, and begin to eat inward.

If I am to be free there is no other way, he said at last, with an immense weariness, but an easing of the bonds. Then he fell to stroking his limbs again, as if for the first time, with love, and realization, and awe for the great skill and power that had gone into creating them, and agony.

Eighteen hours had gone by since they had last assembled. By the clock that is: though everyone knew it was years, they felt aged by that length of time.

Clinton and Jackson stood a little apart from the crush, and Jackson said, clutching the yellow sou'wester he had donned against the threatening rain, "Lucky we can start up, sir. Reckon we haven't got long."

"If we do," said Clinton.

"Though I wouldn't have old jungly's job," said Jackson, "not for all the tea in China."

"It doesn't arise," said Clinton, coldly. "He is a crane operator. You are not."

"I'm going by what Smith told me," Jackson sniffed, offended. "He knew about cranes, he did. Ought to have been on this job like Mr. Rawlings wanted him to, only he wouldn't touch it. You won't catch me up there, he says to me, the gate's not been recast proper. Or it might have been the lugs. That's right, it was the lugs." Jackson sucked his teeth, which were false, while he brought up the grains. Of what Smithy had told him, only it was not easy, what with the trees throwing themselves about like maniacs and the burra sahib breathing down his neck and cranes not being, so to speak, his line of country.

"What," said Clinton, grown tired of waiting, "is wrong with the lugs?"

"Who says anything's wrong?" Jackson's eyes bulged, then subsided because of his memories of Smith, the less exacerbating of which were now uppermost. He almost smiled.

"Nothing's wrong. Just Smith, you might say, Mr. blooming pernickety Smith."

"What did he say?"

What's he on about? asked Jackson. Irately but silently, his patience rubbed thin while Clinton's grew, his grip like a worrying terrier's.

"I can't rightly remember," he said.

"Try," said Clinton.

"About the shape of them lugs not being the same as before," said Jackson. "Not that that would of made any difference, far as I can see."

"What shape were they before?"

"There's a thousand tons of equipment," said Jackson, suppressing righteous emotions, "what pass through works. Or more. I wouldn't rightly know, sir, or like to say, what their exact specifications was."

"Ask Smith."

"Smith's gone home. He's on his way now."

"And you don't know."

"It's like this," said Jackson, groping after the geometrical patterns that formed in his mind. "Either they was rectangular before and we had to put in square not having the right sort in store, or it could have been they was square originally and we put in different. Because of the time being short," reminded Jackson with asperity, "and Mr. Rawlings wanting the crane working on site pronto. Which we done, recast the gate and all, which come up busted. And got it working on site," he said with a flourish, "pronto."

"After testing, according to the regulations," said Clinton.

Could be Smithy's ghost speaking, swore Jackson, bottling the oath because it was the boss, and continuing to be hampered by it.

"Was it tested?" asked Clinton. Repeating, dangerously.

"It wasn't," admitted Jackson. "Because, like I said, of not having time. Though," he said, and felt the earth growing firmer under his perspiring feet, "it has been working satisfactory and there's been no complaints what I've heard of since."

So that Clinton, almost, allowed himself to be convinced.

Over on the riverbank Bashiam stood by the Avery-Kent while the steel nets were laid. Which would hold the two corpses swept downstream by the swollen waters when, it was hoped, the boulder was raised. As it will be, said Bashiam, not to bolster but making a statement of intent, watching the weighted curtain drop length by length into the foaming mouth between impeding dam and shore, and the heavy sweat on the bodies of the working men which sprang from their pores quicker than the roistering wind could dry. And so, absorbed, did not hear Clinton approach, who therefore had time, in this incongruous hour, to notice the fine build below the lumberjack shirt which wind plastered to body. Which comes from sufficient food, he said with surprise, not only from birth as this body has had the same birth as those scarecrows in the village. Then he felt a strange regret, akin in its way to what Bashiam had felt, and closer relation still to the emotion that might have overwhelmed both at the sullying of some splendid machine that had been given into their keeping. Then Bashiam turned, and his eyes; and the feeling faded and Clinton said formally, asking himself: are there depths below that blackness? or nothing? said formally, holding his voice on the ice-edge of neutrality so that no man afterward could accuse, "Do you wish to go on?"

"I wish to go on," said Bashiam. And waited; or appeared to be waiting, it seemed to Clinton in whom voices roared. But who kept silent.

Then Bashiam was gone, into his cab, into normal routines of testing and checking controls. And Clinton was released and could notice, and saw the name "Devi" painted in red on the crane's yellow arm, and the green light of the safe-load indicator flickering.

Left alone Jackson felt the hollowness forming, like some blooming potter putting the hole in my clay, he said to himself, inaccurately, and sought out the nearest company. Which happened to be Helen, though he did not take it in in time.

"One does one's best," he said, to this creature that was human, he hoped, not a steely trap in disguise.

"Of course," said the creature, humanly, so that he was emboldened to continue.

"Then to be jumped on like that," said Jackson, whom jumping on had flattened, though it could have been the absence of Smith, or perhaps the sequence of events, from the runaway blasts that rolled the boulder down the crest to the crane that Smithy would not touch. "As if one had failed, or neglected," he said, bleeding for himself, pulling the crackling sou'wester closer round his battered form.

"Neglected what?" asked Helen, who saw the flickering green light which meant go, but was suffused for no reason that she knew by the vivid colors of alarm.

"Nothing was," said Jackson, crushing with his heels the rank grass and the shoots that sprang. "Only what there was no time for, we got no time for going by the book in this kind of jungle. So I told the burra sahib," he said, and saw that it was the burra sahib's wife, and he began to unsay but she had gone.

Wielding the controls Bashiam felt the swell of power as the hook glided down, smoothly as honey running in the sun, toward the hawser girding the rock. Devi, goddess, he said as he engaged, and he tried to be humble but the flame reared high, beyond the discipline. They are depending on me, he said, not to feed but to quench with cold jets of responsibility, but the fires grew stronger with the vision, though it could also have been a view from the glass of his cabin, of the multitude that waited, in a silence they had created for him.

In the tight grouping of crisis Clinton watched, with Rawlings and Henderson and Mackendrick who were involved with him, and the crowd whose involvements were of another kind.

It is not the first time, he said to the crisis, which swam

nearer, and seemed to have developed a head, I have ridden out other crises before, which have threatened no less. But still it loomed, not crushing but scooping, sucking out portions of him that he could ill afford to lose. So he turned to his empire, the flesh and the steel that were spread in the valley before him and would answer his command, but they slithered away as he looked, pouring down the funnel whose outlet had narrowed to one. To be dependent on one man, he said, and gazed at the face which would not be read, any more than his own.

Then Mackendrick moved, not to prevent breakdown which he knew would not come, but to relieve the atmosphere.

"The man," he said, "is entirely reliable." Dealing, in his innocence, the appalling blow.

"Yes," said Clinton, thickly. "Yes," he mumbled, "the man is reliable." Managing to stay upright though something had begun to buckle, his body, or it could have been the great boom from whose metal the intermittent sun struck sparks, though he could not be sure because certainties were lost, dissolved in the shifting light and, finally, by the shrilling alarm. Then he shaded his eyes to clear his vision, and saw the safety light turn to amber and then to crimson, and heard the ringing bell.

It rang and rang, a jangling sound that ripped away whatever protective sheaths they wore, as it was meant to; and the red eye glowed, dangerously, until the automatic level fell cutting off hoisting power. Then the rope which had been taut for lifting began to slacken, it hung and dangled, and there was a shivering void in which they heard the dull clang of the hook falling against the boulder and the sounds of metal dragging and scraping on rock.

Clinton passed his hands over his eyes, on which a film had formed. He would have clapped them over his ears to shut out the sounds, which to his empty state resembled a ghost's heels scraping, but that the act could not be contained within the shell of sanity, as all must see. So he searched for something that would sustain, but found nothing other than what was obvious.

"It is too heavy to shift," he said, simply, "and that is all."

"It is not the first setback," said Mackendrick, gently, who saw the pain, and forgot about his own.

"But this one is crucial," said Clinton, and paused to consider though there was nothing left now for him to consider, but nevertheless needing the pause.

Into which Rawlings flew, empurpled, enraged by a helplessness which might overcome other men, but from which he believed he had been assigned the right to exemption in perpetuity.

"Those black bastards," he said, choking, the blood channels like blocked conduits in his neck, obstructing him, "God sod them, they've won."

"Or one might say," said Mackendrick, flatly, fearing a burst vessel, with which he felt a disinclination to cope, "that a man has tried and failed."

"It is not the man," Clinton brought out. "It is—" and stopped, and was saved by the sound, which none had thought to hear, of the crane working again. The throb and whine, both gentle, as power came on, and a grinding across granite and the smoothness as the hook rose clear.

"He has," said Clinton, who realized first, "simply bypassed the load indicator."

"Switched it off," said Rawlings. "The light has not come on. Or else it is not working, though it was, only minutes ago. Perhaps," he said, grasping the let-out which offered, "it is not working properly."

"It is against safety regulations," said Mackendrick, "to operate without the safe-load indicator." And took a step or two.

"He knows what he is doing," said Clinton, flatly, and raised a restraining hand, which could have been brushed aside, but was not.

"I hope he does," said Mackendrick, and waited with the others in attitudes of frozen action, and would be grateful like them when the time for it had passed.

As very soon happened.

For now the crane was lifting. Slowly, it could have been in millimeters, though there were those who believed their eyes were deceiving them.

Bashiam, controlling, knew the truth of it. He could feel the strain running through cable and wheel to his arms, man and machine being one, he believed. Easily, he said, gently, sweat falling from seared skin onto hot metal in the joint exercise of power; and felt the shadow, or shudder, as the members took the weight which the silenced bell had refused, and held and steadied. It lies within the capacity, he said, or his mind formed the words which he could not utter; it is not beyond our strength. And started to float the load.

When the rock rose they divided, seeing different things. The crowd saw the corpses, which had risen, and were now being rushed, bobbing and jostling like logs in the current, toward the nets. Overcome, laughing to ease the strain which had bent their backs and could, they felt, have broken the bone, they ran along the banks, shouting in triumph which had still to be rounded, and outpaced by the rolling logs which had once housed men.

Henderson watched the race, and his gray face twitched. "Look at them. Gory savages!" he said, and so did not see where it bent, the metal become plastic.

"He's slewing," said Rawlings, puzzled, who had expected the jib to stay but saw the movement. "What for? What's he slewing for?"

"He's maneuvering," said Mackendrick wildly, hoping. "To settle the boulder back on the dam."

But Clinton saw the slipping vision, and this time knew.

"The jib is breaking," he said.

Quietly, because it was expected of him. Also because there was nothing, really, that could be done about it now.

After that they watched the towering arm of the crane whose strength had flagged, or so it seemed, the metal of its members gone to fluid under some intolerable strain. It curved and bent, this steely structure that had become supple, and began to fall, sideways and relatively slowly, restrained by the yielding and bending of the main booms. But falling, and grounding, straddled between land and water, and imprisoning in its crushed cage the man who could still be seen at the controls.

31

SO they could complete the coffer dams, the impediments having been trapped and lifted, and dried off for the burning, and
wrapped in cerements which would help the flames, while the
waxed cloth contained the fluids which still, despite the pressing
and pummeling of laying-out, continued to drain from bodies
as if from watermelon flesh.

This time, as the tribals had done for Bailey and Wilkins, so
Clinton, Mackendrick and their following did for the two,
standing shod and civilized, and a good foot taller, next to palmyra humps under which were the shivering hill men. Uncomfortable among them, and suspecting barbarity in the flames
which consumed so openly, or greedily, where decency decreed
a casket that could be consigned and concealed in white heat,
out of sight before the assaults could begin. Though whether
upon themselves, or upon the corpse, they could not have said,
nor even questioned, but stood silently, shoulder to shoulder
in public view, with one eye on the weather.

When it was over, duty done, though the flames would not be
finished for a long time yet, they returned with relief to the
coffer dams. Over which they had schemed and slaved, and

planned jubilant culminations, all of which, as everyone perceived, would now be out of place. So they completed the dams
quietly, ready to strangle hosannas which, in fact, did not rise
strongly in worn-out throats. And each man felt oddly done out
of, as if he had been cheated, but kept it to himself, only asking
for what purpose he had humped all these flags all this time,
which had now to be furled and put away together with the
hoarded hopes of flourishes.

When the last rock-fill had been dumped they blasted apart
the sand-block, over whose residual gobs and lumps the river
swirled, licking and ingesting, then gathering force it turned
and swept into the channel they had cut for it, and climbed up
the sides in frenzy, the thick muddied waters lashing and froth-
ing, and tinged with red.

For the whole air was red, lit by the effulgence of the coming storm. It fell on them all, this scarlet light, made up of sunset, and burnished leaves, and reddish earth. Shrimp flesh
grew lurid, and tanned hides, being impermeable, glanced
off their surfaces shafts of liver-colored light. Under the falling
sky the jungle glowed like a garnet, balefully, some said, who
knew the moods of the season, but others too, whose fretful
minds suspected every manner of radiance.

"Just look at it," griped Millie, ceaselessly shifting, but caught
in the cornelian aura. "Like spitting blood. I've never seen anything like it, what does it mean?" Straining after meanings, in
the Chinese robe which Bailey had bought her, a kimono with
dragons on the back.

"Why should it mean anything?" answered her husband, rancorously. "Clouds mean rain, which is all one needs to know.
Why, on top, should color mean anything?"

"Color means everything," said Millie significantly. She
thought of black, and under this hue marshaled all shades from
cinnamon to cocoa. "Helen," she said, and smoothed the silk,
which tended to ruck where the ridges were, over the pelvic
tissues, "is taking it badly."

"What badly?" asked her husband, who ached, from the soles

of his feet which had stood flatly from morning till dusk to the crown of his head he ached.

"That tribal she fancied," said Millie, and rubbed herself, small surreptitious movements to ease, or subdue, the fibrillating flesh. "Who is broken."

"Who will mend," said her husband, "though he will not be as good as new. It was," he said, reluctantly, because he had been forced to recognize a quality, crawling through twisted steel to chart the rescue, which recognition he would have preferred to leave lying undisturbed, "a magnificent body."

"But still who would have thought," said Millie. "It is disgusting to think."

Rawlings thought, and tried, but could not find it disgusting, and was silent. Because of the women whose shining skins had gone from copper to ebony, whose breasts had filled and overflowed his hands, whom he had mounted in unparalleled passion, exercising double mastery over the woman, and the serf. As they had all done, unfitting themselves in the process for the pale equal clefts of their wives. He would have liked it again, thought Rawlings, and wetted his lips at memories. But it would not be the same, he said, in this country, where something has gone bloody wrong, and the spirit is different, and traced it down to the freedom which, he believed, had been delivered on a plate. Which makes people uppity, he thought, following the loose coils of his mind, one cannot crush, and the pleasure is lost. And he stared at the dragons on his wife, who had turned her back.

"I must go," said Millie, who felt something pass, like filleting-knife between ribs and flesh; but not for that reason restless. "To help," she said, over a shoulder, over which she often tossed her mind, finding it easier to communicate with her husband by this method.

"In what way?" he asked.

But Millie did not know. Envisaging Helen, who locked herself away in the cool containments of an ivory casing, the vague ideas she had nourished began, in fact, to acquire a shape.

"It is usual," she said, nevertheless, "in an outpost like this, to—" And stopped, the shape having rounded, and presenting a cipher. "To stick," gasped Millie, struggling to drag the tacky thing out, "to stick together."

Then she had to go, and took off her silk robe, and donned her wind cheater, and went.

But Helen was not to be found, or aided, or comforted, by Millie.

She walked alone, in the carnadine glow, in her blood-caked khaki shirt, through the forest which was silent, waiting.

Though not entirely alone, for there were men who watched, hardened into the redwood of tree trunks when she approached, or merging in mottled shade, keeping their distance, yet close enough. Because of some danger which she could not see, being as she was. Respecting her state, and the woman who walked unheeding in her stiff shirt and thin-soled shoes in jungle which was not her country. But vigilant, moved by a concern for themselves as well as for her, knowing what outcry there would be if a white woman . . . closing their ears against the terrible sound as both jaws of the nutcracker, black and white, met over split shell and squeaking kernel. So they went on padded feet, the dark guardians, to prevent or circumvent, alert for movement that snaked through the undergrowth or lay in wait, vicious in this oppressive waiting time.

Helen was not aware. She strode blindly through an airless vault, aureoled by light, her throat bare where she had wrenched at the shirt, which chafed, being encrusted with the dirt of days and nights though how many she could not exactly remember. For now the anguish which had washed over each in turn was upon her. As if some crime to which we have all contributed has been committed, and is to be paid for, she said stiffly, and drove herself. Through memories of shattered steel, and the reeling sky as the tower fell, and—using goads now, to prevent herself bolting—crawling under, and clasping, to hide the shuddering waves of repulsion that the disfigured body roused, round which she had locked her recoiling arms. So it was to do with her body, she said, bringing out scourges since there was no other way. Nothing else: the rest, which had meaning, was in fact delusion. Going through purgatory, which at times she wondered whether she were creating, at other times differently convinced. So she turned to the jungle, opening her turmoil to the stillness in which it was wrapped, and entering partway saw the strange burning light, and the leaves of trees, worn to fretwork but cupped upward, it seemed, in the certainty of the rain which would come. Then was able to say, whatever it was, will come later, will be revealed, and at last stopped her pacing and went, exhausted, to the hut where the old man lay, his frail hands composed upon his breast, and someone brought a pallet upon which she lay down and slept.

It was, in fact, the second night. In the morning she returned to the bungalow.

Clinton, unconscious of his protesting buttocks which had been flattened between bone and the damp canvas of the verandah chair for the best part of the night, was composing a report which he would never write.

The collapse of the jib of the crane in question, he wrote, a 15-ton Avery-Kent model AK.614 mobile crane, serial No. 9861, was due to two factors, viz., (1) the abnormal forces produced by the incorrect procedure adopted in setting up the lifting operation, subjecting the structure to unduly severe stresses, and (2) the disconnection of the safe-load indicator, resulting in the mechanism being required to hoist a load which was beyond its capacity.

With regard to (1) there seems little doubt that, although the lie of the land and the nature of the operation probably precluded any alternative siting of the crane, the effect of the 1 in 30 slope in producing severe lateral forces, which must be regarded as a major contributory cause of the break in the jib, was not fully appreciated by the operator.

With regard to (2) the action of the operator in disconnect-

ing the safe-load indicator, as witnesses have described, must
be ascribed to an error of judgment in calculating the margin
of safety available following the flashing of the warning light
(this apparatus functioning in fact within a tolerance of four
percent), and in estimating the weight of the load it was required to hoist.

It must however be placed on record that, within the limita-
tions noted above, at no time did the operator proceed in other
than a careful and cautious manner.

When he had finished disgust began to well, an inexorable
fluid whose property it was to bring into view the invisible
writing that ran, or lurked, between the lines of his composition.
At which he would not look, then could not avoid, but laced his
fingers across his eyes to prevent a total view, and at last said, it
was not like that.

It was not like that at all, he repeated, aloud, to the lonely
listening room. Because the man knew what he was doing, he
knew the lie of the land, he knew what his crane could do provided it was what he believed it to be. Only it was not, he said
starkly, the lugs being defective which he did not know, and so
broke his back. Though by now he was not sure if he meant man
or machine, so formidable were the blows that weariness dealt
him, which he would have countered with alcohol, and indeed had lumbered up out of his chair, but that Helen had
come in, and was standing in the doorway. White-faced under
the grime, the black rings around her eyes matching the darkness surrounding his own, the flesh flabby from the long wake
as, putting up his hand, he knew his own to be.

The two hideous worn-out strangers stared at each other, recognizing the signs, though held in some petrifying mixture
that would not allow, beyond the simple recording.

She said: "He was not told, and could not know, since it was
a concealed defect."

He answered: "He could have withdrawn had he wished, but
was prepared to take any risk. As his own action showed."

Running around the perimeter, when there was a heart to this matter.

Then it seemed indeed as if both were converted to stone, such was the quality of the silence between them; but something was struggling, which could not be allowed to die, which presently emerged.

"I did not wish to destroy," he said.

"If you are sure," she replied.

And he could not answer that.

32

SO the rains began, the first heavy drops leaving imprints like
pug marks on the earth where earth showed, between the tussocks of yellowed grass, and along the banks of the river which
they had stripped of their cover, and in the clearings where the
blocks were built, and in the land basin where the tribe had
camped, from whose stony soil the season had ripped the last
scraggy lichen and spear of grass. Soon the pug prints enlarged,
and ran together, and blurred and obliterated themselves in a
wash of water that seeped and scoured, forming a brownish
mush. Into which, from time to time, they reluctantly de-
scended, in order to continue. Though what, they could not
convincingly have said, since all seemed at a standstill. Or was
waiting, it sometimes appeared to them, when they paused in
the damp round of necessary tasks. Though for what, again, they
could not exactly have said, but were united in naming a cessa-
tion of rain.

Which continued to pour from inexhaustible skies, falling
in plops in which one sometimes discovered little green hapless
frogs, and sometimes in long, determined, densely packed needles that shortened their already reduced range of vision. But
whatever the shape, the common quality, as they were discover-

ing, remained an irresistible penetrability. Against which, nevertheless, they donned defenses, so that the hillside was flocked with scurrying figures in ulsters, sou'westers, oilskins and rain-repellent coats.

The tribals, who did not possess and had not been provided with any of these, wore palm-leaf cloaks whose colors, having been mixed and weathered by the seasons, merged them indistinguishably into the waterlogged landscape. Making for shocks, and encounters, where shiny rain-repelling forms scraped against solid murk, looked into masks that streamed.

"Gives you the willies," said Jackson. "There ought to be a law. Loomin' up like effing ghost ships. Makes you jump out of your skin." And he felt his skin, doubtfully, as if it were not proof but let in water, there was a watery feel to the flesh.

"Rising up out of the ground like," concurred Jones, who had taken the place of Wright. "Right by your feet, as if they was not human or something."

"You give me the creeps," said Jenkins the giant, who replaced Smith. He aimed a dart. "More, any day, than what they do. Christ," he said, "the frigging thing's on the wall. It's this light," he complained, "it keeps flickering, I can't see proper. You can't tell me I'd have missed the board, otherwise."

"There's nothing wrong with the light," said Jackson. "It's your eyes, if it's anything, wants seeing to."

Jenkins threw down the two darts that remained and came over. His eyes, which had been impugned, were clear, but stern.

"You want to make something out of it, do," he said, and breathed heavily. The sleeves of his shirt were already rolled up, as they always were this time of evening, before the midge and flying-ant invasion, sparing him the necessity.

"Oh, bugger off," said Jackson morosely. "I got troubles of me own."

"Who hasn't?" inquired Jenkins. "Only the rest of us don't hold with off-loading like you do. On to all and sundry," he said, bitterly, "indiscriminate."

"I wasn't doing no such thing," said Jackson. But mildly,

because he had shrunk, being alone: his burly frame had dwindled—he hoped in a way that no one would see—since the going of Smith.

"You was," accused Jenkins, aware of strength, though its source remained obscure. "Ghost ships! And those poor bleeders working like blacks, if you're gonna be fair."

"Whose side you on?" asked Jackson.

And knew that at last he had picked a winning card. Because in spite of the tugging and linking that had gone on, by one or two from either camp, the split had widened. Especially since Bashiam, who would not have wished to have a part in such fissiparous matters, but had no choice.

Though, of course, they continued to work together.

Laboring and floundering, side by side in the mud, as they strove to oil and grease, and repair where the wind had rent, and cover and tether their exposed machines which the weather had bonded, the bowed figures acquiring the same anonymity as sheeted steel, except for feet. Which the ooze had coated brown, a uniform brown, but the shapes and sounds were different some being boots and some being bare, the boots sinking deep and coming up with grunts and gasps from quaking bog while the feet being lighter rode higher, the brown paste squelching up between toes.

Gopal, who was sober and civilized to a degree that could still surprise his friend Lefevre, felt convulsed when he looked, and had to force himself on to the site, whenever it became necessary.

"It is only a little mud," said Lefevre comfortably—even comfortingly, for the two had advanced beyond, or perhaps transcended, the rift that separated others, and had once split them. And passing over it had drawn closer into a sphere which each knew existed, where there was a falling away of inessentials, the clutter of color and skin, and the acquiring of badges to pin on, and the donning of blinkers to abet in base deceptions. A falling away, and the wide clean space that stretched like fields that were open to meaning, and the ushering in of a reverence which each recognized from its pulse and shape as the heart. A reverence for what was created, all its forms: and the spasms, transmitted from spirit to flesh, when the blight of destruction placed this crucial domain in jeopardy.

"Only a little mud, true, but it makes my toes curl," confessed Gopal, "to see it squirting up, over the nail and under the quicks, only they don't seem to mind, as far as one can tell." And he averted his mind from the sight, which moved on, and he would have drawn it back then, even to a renewed viewing of the sludge, but was too late since the consciousness was common.

"It could have been mud," said Lefevre, putting it in words, "that made him go over. The crane would not have tilted from a firm base."

"If it could have been," said Gopal, wearily, with a longing for the scapegoat which would have eased them all, broadbacked to carry away burdens and sins. "If only it could. But, you see, the rain had scarcely moistened the surface."

Then Lefevre knew that he had to attest, not simply within the rare communication that they had achieved but in open court, and wondered only that he had taken so long to come to it.

"Bashiam was used," he said, and felt the shuddering waves of relief wash over him. "For that is what it amounts to, whatever the end, or the object, or the motive. He was used, and it was a violation of his rights."

Then both men sat quietly, among the vials and the orange-box furniture, and their faces were illuminated by the bluish sheets of lightning that flickered through the panes, or perhaps by the bands of thought that ran between and joined them.

There were others, too, to whom the mud meant little.

The nun, for instance, who came up with the mobile medical team that Clinton Mackendrick had summoned, money being no object, within limits circumscribed by reason. The gentle Sister Theresa of the nursing order, who squelched through the slush without a care except for her patient, raising the hem of her habit only to save herself tripping, and showing the thick knitted stockings under the straps of her shoes which the soil had stained permanently brown. Fearless, and strong. For else, questioned Das, how could this woman with the puny wrists and the pale fragile hands lift and tend a stricken man? Watching her, the oval olive face framed by the wimple, whose European cut and pleats did not square with the features whose conception and carving were Indian. And the cross that dangled from a black cord upon the flat bosom. And the garments that concealed or repressed, from throat to ankle. Then Das looked down at his own, which were not unlike, and began to wonder, and considered the design and queried the motives of memsahibs as he had never done before, which he could not believe were concerned with denial of body for spiritual ends.

But rather, he said, to do with purloining. A man's self-respect, he said, brooding through the rain-filled days, continuing to serve and tend the other man who was also stricken. Continuing to make beds and light mosquito coils, and wiping green mold from damp surfaces, and blowing at the coals in the *sigri* so that the cook could cook when electricity failed, and bunching his skirts in his hand as he ran, as infrequently as he could but rain had ruined his bladder, to the trench latrine behind the servants' godowns which was boggy, from contents which had foamed and overflowed.

Then one day he shed his bell-shaped robe which was voluminous and gathered like the nun's, as well as the girdle whose dangling tassels had been, he now came to think, a bane of his life, and put on trousers and shirt. And dared to appear, half free, half fearful, and waited anxiously for nemesis. Which, to his alarm, did not overtake, so that he was consumed with fears for the changing nature of his world.

"Das has taken to wearing sensible clothing, at last," observed Helen, waiting until he had gone, as she had learned to do.

"I had not noticed," said Clinton, speaking obliquely to his wife as he had fallen into the habit of doing. Since the straightness was gone from their marriage. Which had re-formed to en-able them to continue, providing falsetto voices and gestures to tide over every occasion, while the empty center expanded, whittling away at the watery rims of substance that remained.

Sometimes, after they had eaten, and long before they could decently take to the separate halves of their bed, and rain had blotted out the separate lives they had etched for themselves, they had nothing at all to say to each other. Then Clinton would sit, and fidget, and drink his Scotch, and watch the thin smoke ascending from the pungent green mosquito-coils, until finally his mind would balk, as if at some stony, dried-up river-bed it had been asked to negotiate, and turning away flow relievedly down easier channels. Which opened beyond the smoky blue panes, and the frenzy of green, and were to do with his empire of concrete and steel.

He could not see it of course, from his salubrious bungalow in inclement weather. But would rise, and put on weather-proof clothes, and nod to his wife, and go squelching down the hill to where it lay, waiting, humped under canvas or tarpaulin, or hulked below long, corrugated-iron structures upon which the rain thudded and drummed. And would walk, his head held low because of the force, straightening a flap, or threading a maddened rope through a flailing eyelet, for the pleasure of touching. Until he was brought to the coffer dams, whose whitened ribs could be seen holding up the rising river, as it was planned they should do.

"The rain is heavy, sahib."

The solitary watchman, to whom they paid derisory sums, though for what purpose no one quite knew, detaching himself from the murk of mud and solid falling water as he never failed to do. Piping above the wind, his reedy voice whipped clean from his lips as it formed.

"It is," said Clinton, and felt his way, which was not easy, since communicating was not his line. But obscurely aware of his need, strangely fastened upon this figure in its sodden and bedraggled fibers.

"Let us hope it will not last too long," he managed.

"Do not worry, sahib. The dams are strong and will hold," said the dripping figure, meaning to comfort, but entering regions which Clinton considered entirely his own, so that he said, forbiddingly, "There is no question. Only one has no wish to extend one's stay in this country."

And continued his contemplation alone, of the twin coffers upon whose rough-cast crests the deluge beat and broke.

Then Helen, whose release came with departure, would also rise and go out, choosing a time when the fluctuating storm was at its lowest ebb, to save being swamped. Since feelings were reviving, and she could not stride as she had done, numb and uncaring through the forest. But walked with an enlarged awareness, of oils and essences that the season distributed, eucalyptus and arum and broom whose particles were suspended it seemed in the flying globules of moisture; and awareness of the endurance of structures, webs that clung, and trees whose supple stems could arch and bend without breaking, and inhabited anthills, the conical earth scored and fretted by rain into Gothic edifices but persisting, providing shelter for the creatures that scurried in before each fresh onslaught.

Sometimes she paced the compound, coming upon the bones of the birds that had died upon Jackson, one after another in their cages, that he had brought here and buried, and those tribal shards which the downpour washed up in quantity, which had also provided an awakening, though of another kind. Or took the obliterated path to the hut were Bashiam lay, next to which they had hustled up the prefabricated cube to house the nun who nursed him.

Bashiam could speak again, though he could not walk; had drifted from coma to consciousness, from suffering to sedation and back, preferring pain that exploded in sharp bursts under the flesh to poisons that fuddled and unhinged his mind. Now he was done with drugs, except at night when personal defenses slipped, and weakness nibbled at lifelong disciplines, and his brain began to whimper, asking him questions which no one could answer. By day he lay quietly, husbanding his strength, flat on his back except when the nun rose, regular as clockwork, to turn him.

"So that sores do not form," she said, rubbing the vulnerable points on which he rested, elbows and shoulder blades, and buttocks and heels, her hands and her clothes smelling of alcohol, or sometimes of talcum when the skin would not tolerate. Smells that rose sharply to the eaves of sodden thatch, wrinkling the noses of the tribesmen who came, cautiously, to visit another of their number whom the dam had laid low. Though this they did not say, knowing the passions and attachments of the man on the pallet, which they might not hold with, but would not thwart.

But melted away; the nun, gathering up the rosary whose beads clicked softly through her fingers like the hours, and the tribesmen, furtively depositing the gifts they had brought, when they heard the Englishwoman approach. Helen, whose gathering knowledge lay heavily, a weight against her breastbone. But which she could feel yielding and lightening in this small hut through whose rafters the wind went whistling, for all that it was one of the better built ones. So that one day when the occlusion had dwindled, allowing her to breathe, she finally said, "Why did you do it?" Twisting her fingers, and hearing the joints grate, because of that part of the answer which rested with her, as she knew.

"There are some things which one has to do," he replied, also withholding, since after all there were regions which must remain private to each, and racks always ready for those too eager to unburden, weak slack lips that allowed spillage into some cheap confessional.

Then each understood the other had gone as far as it was possible to go, for the present or perhaps even forever, and were quiet. Until Helen, who saw the other loose end, grasped it, willing that it should lacerate her if need be.

"What will you do," she said, "afterward?"

"We must wait till the rains are over and see," he replied,

marveling at the itching-powder that entered into substance, making these people so restless.

"When we are gone," she said, steadily, but raw, the linings were raw from the chafing and scraping that went on.

"I shall go too," he replied, to spare her. "There are many projects. It is a big country."

And in a way was soothed, because, after all, it could be the truth.

33

AS the wet season advanced the plateau, and even the hill, seemed to lose its identity of land and take on, rather, the characteristics of water. Pocks and hollows filled, and spread, merging their surfaces in lakes. Rivulets broke from the lips of pools and wandered, sprawling over ground too soaked to absorb them. The camp was awash; guy ropes fouled, and gray damp coating the canvas of tents, and the bases of the concrete blocks standing in water like the legs of furniture, with water blisters forming.

"Like soused herring," said Henderson, wringing drops from cuffs that clapped wetly at wrists and ankles. "That is exactly what one feels like stranded up here. And waiting. How long? Does anyone know? I have forgotten, and shall be glad," he said primly, "to remember what it feels like to be dry."

Mackendrick did not remind. There were things that he, too, would have liked restored to him, like the textures of tranquillity, but accepted that it could not be.

"It is a bad year, they say," he said, and watched the islands breed, or it could have been water that created by inundating; and the creatures that crawled, precariously clinging to the remaining peaks; and the sand grains that swelled, intimating disaster, before caving in to fluid.

"Who says?" complained Henderson. "One has only to ask and they shut their traps. It is enough to make a bloody saint swear."

Then Mackendrick came near, but contained himself, because he could see that Henderson meant no harm, although he might inflict it. He simply got up and went away, leaving Henderson to become convinced, more than ever, that something was up with old Mack. He's got the wind up, he said to himself, that's what it is, he's got the wind up.

And could have been right, though not quite in the way he understood it. For Mackendrick was afraid, and could not bear to look inward but riveted his gaze on things that lay outside, while within the fraying went on.

"I suppose all this," said Krishnan, sharply, to Shanmugham, "must remind you of your precious paddy-fields."

Shanmugham recoiled. "Indeed, no," he said. "Not at all. There is no comparison."

Krishnan was pleased to have roused him, this blithe man whose depths were a paddling-pond to his own subterranean soundings. For he knew, though would never bring himself to accept, that these piddling victories were all that Clinton and Bashiam from their twisted union had left him. Which could have been substantial. Might have been, he said, and was cruel.

"All these wet acres," he needled. "Just like paddy-fields, for which you have thirsted ever since you came to these hills."

"But they are much different from this," said Shanmugham, in a pale way, though his wan face took on strength from reflections of green. "They are controlled, and there are bunds to contain the floods. Whereas here—"

"There are the coffer dams," said Krishnan.

"But the waters are uncontrolled," said Shanmugham.

"Which is the point of the dams," said Krishnan.

"If they will hold," said Shanmugham, trembling.

"If one can gamble on them holding, you mean," said Krishnan, "the counters in the game being lives."

"It will need courage," said Shanmugham, moistening his lips.

"It is easily come by," said Krishnan, "when it is not one's life that is gambled upon."

Shanmugham, who did not know, and dared not enter the shattering labyrinth Krishnan had constructed for him, looked away. From the dark face that compelled to the ridged highlands where the officers' bungalows were built, whose flanks were scored with the courses of streams that drained the hill, leaving foundations firm. And saw, not only the safety, but also the brimming wells of loneliness in which men could drown. For there were unexpected views at every turn as each of them, in this time of waiting, was beginning to discover.

"So here we are," said Rawlings grimly, "marooned on top of a ruddy hill," and he unbuttoned his shirt, because glass and mesh between them shut out air, and the air-conditioning had failed.

"I do not know what it is, but something," said Millie restlessly, moving her neck fretfully inside the turtle collar. And fanned and fanned, with the palmyra fan that belonged to the bearer, which the man had given his memsahib out of pity for the signs he detected in her strung-up face.

"It is the humidity," said Rawlings, moving to escape the stale ellipses of air she created, "that makes one feel so clammy."

And he wiped and mopped, under the shirt that clung, lifting the matted hair, and dabbing between the creases of flesh where a paste of talcum had formed.

"Something," said Millie, watching and fanning. "Something is building up."

"What?" asked Rawlings, and was only able to think of the river, whose levels had not stopped rising.

"I don't know," said Millie, and threw down her fan. "I am stifling," she said, and went to the door. Unthinking. Her hands

like claws upon the wire mesh. Releasing the double catch, and
opening, and falling back as the air grew full. The filtered air
congested, filling with soft filmy wings that beat against her
face and brought up the nap of her cringing skin, and tangled
in her hair, grubs and gauzy scales caught in her hair, which she
could not free. So that she began to shriek, and jerk, and put up
her hands blindly to protect, while the ants which had dropped
their wings and could not fly began to crawl, under the sleeves
which were wide to allow air, and down the turtleneck, leaving nacreous streaks and debris of obnoxious powder. Or so Millie imagined, as she sobbed, and shuddered, and tore from her
wildly as she ran.

Was mad, her husband was convinced, who rose to his feet to
prevent, but was pushed, or fell, among the wings and the glittering insect bodies. From which he pulled himself up and hob-
bled to the verandah and stood on the edge of the glistening
stone, shouting to his wife, and for the servants. But his wife
had slipped into the dusky envelope of jungle, leaving behind
the shreds of her turtleneck dress, and the servants who came
bunched round him and cowered, except one brave man who
ran to the end of the compound and beat the shrubs that bor-
dered it with his hands as if for some small concealed mammal,
but soon returned to the prudent group. Then Rawlings cursed
and threatened, and even took necks by their scruffs, but could
not prevail. As he had suspected he would not, from an ebbing
of his strength which made it impossible to assume his role, leading and striding in regions into which they would not venture,
but might conceivably follow. Fears of which grew as he stood,
on the edge that felt like a brink, and listened, to the water
that dripped from lanceolate leaves, and the creaking teakwood
trees, and the tap-tapping of bamboo, or so they said, which
never stopped. Then his voice died away, and he shivered in
the evening air which seemed to have thinned, and turned back
into the room which they had swept and cleared, and prepared
to wait.

While Millie ran. Running to escape the fears that had

shaped into wings, in her thin slip and house shoes, whimpering, into areas of jungle she had never entered before. As presently she recognized, through the blown gray curtains of moisture and dripping coagulated green, and stopped to retrace but the trees had closed. Stood round her, she saw, thickly, in a sameness of bare trunks and soaked bark that rejected all marks of civilized identity. Then her breath which had been stifled came faster and looser and she would have run, but the bog had sucked off a shoe. Groveled in the mud and among roots of trees to find, crouching and poking, but it was gone. Gone, she said, and tilted her head like a dog, but throttled the terrifying sounds and lumbered up, treading as well as she could but stalking and limping until she saw what hampered and tugged at the remaining shoe which clay had caulked to foot. And continued bumping along, in wet rags of stockings, watched by the men of the forest who made it their business to track. Whose bodies she glimpsed in the wavering trails between trees, but could not be sure because of her mind, which was flickering. Until her breath began to grate from some failure of spirit, and she swayed, grunting from the pain of bleeding soles, and fell on the tussocks of matted spear-grass. Then they came close, and she saw they were not the forms of her fears, or imaginings, but men, surrounding her. And screamed and screamed, twisting upon the grass, her swollen flesh bursting from slip and skin, at the blacks whose hands were on her. But moving under the screen of sound, under forces she would have resisted but failed, toward a kowledge that formed as she felt the hands, and the muscles of the lithe bodies lifting, and her own heat that was melting her; and crying louder for the self-inflicted outrage, or perhaps to conceal, until she was exhausted beyond the possibility of her face betraying her.

It was not only Millie.

All, it seemed, were inching toward discovery, though whether of their own volition, or dragged, none could be sure.

But suspected the latter, from the way in which they found themselves bloodied, and the firm flesh pounded to jelly, which could only have come from resisting.

Though why? questioned Mackendrick, who was troubled, who ached from the bruising, and his bewilderment. I am not afraid. Truth has never been a rod for my back. But felt the pressure on his bones, and lay staring at darkness, through the long span of nights, waiting it seemed, or listening, afraid, for the first crack, like the splintering sounds of a rabbit's neck breaking.

Then knew that he could not go on, like this, not knowing; only you see, he said, there are blocks. Since one does not know oneself, or others: where one stops, or, rather, how far one will go.

"One could rest if one were sure," he said to Helen, to whom he was moving close, so close that there was no possibility, nor perhaps the capacity, to hide his haggard face. "But how," he asked, "can one be sure?"

To which she could not reply, she whose cool casing was cracked, and could be seen to be here in the hut with the dying chief. Crouched beside him, her whitened hands upon the pallet on which he lay which was decked like a bier, her body bent from loss, and the heaviness of knowledge shared silently with Bashiam. And having no reply, took her hands from the bright jungle flowers and laid them on the old man to claim his attention—ruthlessly, such were the dimensions which a joint need had reached—repeating the question in tribal language which had acquired as much meaning for her as her own. But the old man did not listen, being preoccupied with the loosening of coils, which still bound his soul here and there to his crumbling bones. Yet if he could not listen, still heard the accents of distress and struggled back, the habit being strong, from a view of the cool valleys that invited at the rim of his contracting horizon to the heaving, stony plain.

"It is enough to look within," he croaked.

Straightly, so that they should not think he was wandering, but heard them say: "He is wandering," and fell back in exhaustion.

When there was a commotion as Millie went past. Slung from a pole, to which they had lashed her ankles and wrists, unable to devise other methods of bearing through bog the writhing and witless woman. Who had fainted, seeing herself ignored, seeing herself borne, as she sobbed to herself while her senses reeled over the precipice, like some slain animal. And hung, the heavy rain slashing down upon her lolling face, until pity welled, and hands supported the small of the back of the swinging body, and the skull from which the wet hair streamed.

But now had revived, and screamed and abused, and accused, filling the openings of the huts with the people who had been huddled within, while the dark eyes alighted with contempt upon the scraggy flesh which made assumptions in these rising tones.

Then the nun, whose first impulse to her shame had been to stop up her virginal ears, rather than go to the aid of the soaking nymph, slid the beads of her rosary reluctantly into the pocket of her habit, and went out to see. What little could be seen, in the obliterating rain and obstruction of bodies, through whom she waded with a strength of purpose which astonished, people having grown used to her gentler aspects and unsuspecting. And reaching the center, slapped with the firmness of her training to restore some measure of calm before attending to healing.

Which, she began to understand as she washed and tended, in the hut in which they were now alone, could only come from within the woman herself, whose form lay exposed and flaccid upon the string bed. But doubted, from the pale eyes that followed her hands, which were sane, but touched. Sister Theresa could not have said exactly what: but something, she said, some unnameable disease or distorting of spirit, as she continued dabbing and disinfecting the torn soles of feet.

34

ALL this time the river levels rose.

Three feet, five feet, eight. The crests of the coffers, which had ridden high and proud over the flow, no longer seemed so mighty. Nor did the riverbanks, whose walls had been built up into canyons. Reduced, they said, or dwindled, assigning reality to illusion as they watched the waters mount, reaching and engulfing mark after mark that was notched in the granite, the inches and centimeters and yards and meters by which they had measured their achievement.

Between the dams the height of the pool that was left also grew; but slower, in inches, fed only by rainfall and unable to match the bounding pace of the river, gorged with the floodwaters of streams that poured down the mountainside. So that those who still came to see, and ventured on to the crest, forgetting their personal peril in the larger anxiety, gasped and retreated, scarcely able to comtemplate the drop.

"It is always a strange thing," Rawlings put it for them, "to see a river running at different elevations, which have been created by dams. Especially when the difference is so marked."

"The size of the drop," said Henderson, and shivered. "There is a limit," he confessed, "to what one can stand."

243

"If you have reached your limit as you appear to have done," said Rawlings, "there is no need for you to look."

For the time was past, he felt, to put up. Even if the man was one's own kith and kin. For I have had a basinful, he said, I can no longer lay on soothing mixtures, I have not the energy, or what I have I need for myself, as reserve.

And he glared, or so it seemed to Henderson, who would have withered, hide and all, but that he felt he could explain to them the reason for this savage usage. But desisted, so powerful were the rays, or emanations.

"I did not mean a human limit," he said instead, and became aware that this was in fact the meaning he had intended and dropped his eyes, which enabled him to continue. "I meant, plainly, that there is a limit to the stresses which structures can withstand."

Then there was a beam so concentrated and intense that Henderson could feel the skin and bone of his forehead seared where it entered, and he tried wildly to retrieve, hunting among the carbonized cells, but they could proffer nothing beyond a few charred platitudes. Which, seeing that they would not do, he fell silent, searching the assembled faces for crumbs but seeing from the stones and cinders that they had nothing for him either. So then there was little left to do but get up, and put on his coat, and go out into the preying loneliness that awaited, he was convinced and so conjured into being, those who stayed or were banished beyond the confines of their circle.

Leaving the door open, which banged and banged, it took two of them to close it, such was the strength to which season and storm had grown, with no sign except of worsening. And came back and sat glumly, in the circle whose segments should have supported each other and sustained the ring, but aware only of the breach that had been made in the powerful front which had never before allowed the strength of design to be questioned in public. Then Rawlings could feel it building up in him as Millie had done, and he said, passionately, "Mouths

should be sealed. There is the danger, otherwise. Men have been
shot, before the panic could spread, to stop the rot."

"There is no panic," said Mackendrick. "But one must consider. Whether one persists at all costs," he said, recalling the
steel that ran in the man alone in his bungalow refuge, "whatever those costs may be. Or whether one gives way."

"It depends upon the costs," said Rawlings.

"In what coin they are computed," said Mackendrick.

"Is this the time?" cried Rawlings, unused to nakedness, and
crawling for cover.

"It is, if it is not already past," said Mackendrick, blocking
with the blunt tones of affirmation, which would not allow bolt-
holes to breed.

Then Lefevre knew that his time had come too, and said,
flatly, "It is not the dam, which will hold, that is the danger,
but the cost of holding if these abnormal conditions continue.
If they do," he said, stiffly, and with pain because fibers of heart
were interwoven, "the coffers will have to be breached, or the
river will burst its banks. The whole land-basin where the tribals are," he said, pale, but publicly attesting in the only way
that now held validity, "is in risk of inundation."

"The banks have been strengthened and reinforced," said
Rawlings, still resisting, but feeling himself reduced from the
splitting that was taking place among them.

"But they have limits as well," answered Lefevre.

Then Rawlings turned to reserves, upon which he had
hoped to rely, but found that they too had been thinned and
drained. From the way in which we have been laid open, he
said, though whether by them or us or the country, it is difficult to tell. And rose, a weariness bending his back, to put off,
or perhaps because of loyalties.

"I must go," he said. "Millie," he mumbled, "I must get her
away from the settlement, where the tribals have taken her.
After a fall," he said, his voice like a reed, "in which she sustained some injuries."

So he buttoned and lashed, and launched himself into the deluge and fought his way down the hill, leaving Mackendrick the shorter run, the few yards between the bungalow in which they had assembled, and the citadel in which Clinton waited.

But Rawlings had miscalculated, or so he swore to himself.

Floundering down the hill, between cascading streams and toppling walls of water, with the slurry gushing up over the rims of his boots, he began to think that Mackendrick had had it easier. And grew convinced, in the depression where the sludge was piled in glutinous slabs, morbid against his legs and the trunks of trees which were assuming shapes in the greenish gloom. Then he turned to retrace, forgetting each step had been reclaimed by mire at moment of forming, and stood in the morass intending to reorientate, but listening instead to the scurryings of terror. Though why, he said to alleviate, it is nothing but a forest and a storm; and plunged on, finding that now he had to pluck each foot from deepening bog, while the wind tore his breath from him and sweat ran, and sometimes blood from colliding with bark, being part blinded by water. Until he began to falter, seeing that little was to be achieved by going forward in this manner, and confirmed in old suspicions that no one would hear his cries, and so was brought to a standstill.

Here he was spotted, among the soggy shrubs and fallen trees, by the only man to be out sampling the weather: the solitary watchman, who had emerged from the dugout in which he had taken shelter, owing to the imminent danger of drowning. Who hesitated, from fear of getting the sack for dereliction of duty, of such importance was his job to him, to go to the help of the sahib; but at length overcame these venal obstacles and did.

So Rawlings came to aid Millie, though really, he felt, in no better shape than she. But rounded out somewhat, the proportions of his old self dribbling back in the order and calm that prevailed in the hut. Which was now wrecked, as he set about organizing the efficient transporting of Millie up the hill.

Millie watched the loud stranger who was her husband.

Risen it seemed from streams, with water trickling from hair, and boots that leaked, barking orders above the noise of the gale that were as much to do, she guessed, with the restoring of himself as with arranging for her. Lying supinely, prepared to go along with him until they were ready, he and she and the coolies he had pressed into service mustered in the open doorway about to lurch forth, and then she resisted. Clinging to peaceful hands, which would not accompany, and crying. Creating, said Rawlings, and turned upon the nun.

"Come along, come along," he said, crackling with irritation. "Can't you see that Madam apparently needs your attention?"

But Sister Theresa was not within his reach.

"Madam has no further need for my services," she said, quite firm, "I have, besides, my other patient."

So they proceeded, with their trussed and sheeted burden, to begin the return to safety. Except that, a few steps on, Rawlings felt constrained to turn.

"It would be for your safety," he called to the figure in stained robes.

Who merely replied, "There are others besides myself," shouting to make him hear, and the beads of rosary dripping through fingers.

35

IN the bungalow which had become a citadel they sat over whiskies, from the necessity of preserving surfaces. Clinton and Mackendrick, and Helen who had come up the hill for reasons that bore down more harshly than safety. No one else, the others having come, and spoken, and gone, leaving the three alone. Who were entangled in themselves, and each other, and in issues which had arisen rather than been raised, billowing out into full-blown spreading fungi by processes they could not have exactly described. But suspected air-borne seeds, or even their own constitutions, nourished for some time on foreign soil, or some enlargement of health or disease of organ or mind. Of which they could not readily speak, words being difficult to come by, so sat, shredding their spirits, and revolving moist glasses in tired hands.

Until Mackendrick managed, breaking the silence as it seemed to him it had become his lot in life to do.

"The gauges," he said, and cleared his throat, "are registering an inch every hour."

Innocuously, waiting for it to build.

"I am aware," said Clinton, "that rainfall is phenomenal."

And he too waited, while eroding waters swirled which would, he knew, discover the merest crack or cranny, enlarge and undermine until the stability of structure was threatened.

Which is necessary to me, he said, since I am a builder.

Invoking the strength-giving formula, and indeed even inducing an inflow, but aware from some thinness of quality that it was still open to testing.

Then Mackendrick, whose senses were honed to a glittering point, also became aware. Of the accumulating strength of the man against whom, he said, I have nothing, except that one has duties. And would have moved to prevent a further consolidation, pitting his own weight solidly, but was held back, or desisted for a while, rooted in the misery of the occasion. So that Clinton, from a great need that lay within himself, mistook the nature of the silence.

"We have," he said, "survived other crises before."

"It is not a question of our survival," answered Mackendrick simply. "It is a matter of extinction of the entire land-basin. Which," he said, "will form the bed of a lake, unless the coffers are breached."

"It is not," said Clinton, and felt arteries break, the fine network that nourished his eyes. "It is not possible," he said through the grayish blur. "If there is a breach, scouring cannot be contained, but will be total."

"Nevertheless," said Mackendrick.

"Entailing the destruction of both coffers, down to foundations," said Clinton. Who could not believe that this could be asked of him. Who could not bear to contemplate, nor initiate nor assist at an aborting, seeing only the beauty of structures, and a birth that was cradled between. The dam, which would not arise without its guardian coffers: the great dam, which already bore his name, whose conception and completion had long ago been underwritten by him, which he would not now revoke.

"Because you see," he said to Mackendrick, this solid monolith against whom he would have liked to lean to ease his back which bore a burden alone, "they are molds into which we have gone, been melted, and poured in."

This Mackendrick would not dispute. Only, there were other considerations.

"The people," he said.

"The tribals," began Clinton, but did not continue for barriers began to fall, metal shutters separating them whose reverberations outdid the furious season. Which Clinton would have halted, and indeed even inserted a shoulder to try.

"It is a calculated risk," he said, "as sometimes one is forced. Which one has to take, since there is no other way."

But Mackendrick would not allow. Because of the insidious slope that stretched, tempting with offers to soothe and ease feet that would have preferred, on the whole, not to labor uphill.

"It is not," he said bluntly, "we who take the risk. We make the calculations, it is they who run the risk."

And a coldness began in him, the chillness of shame and fear let loose by dialogues of them and us, which crept like a miasma over the three ruined figures, which were already pocked and pitted, not being indestructibly fashioned with such poisons of atmosphere in mind.

Then, at last, Mackendrick accepted that no further exchange was possible. Knew that the time had come to leave, and did not wish to loiter, now that the decision was taken, and the moment of departure before him. But continued to sit as if his limbs were locked in traps. Feeling mangled, because of all these years, the weight of them.

So it was Helen's turn. Who rose, her body casting long shadows across the room, and the man. Who became aware. Of anguish. Of his mind leaving him, as he watched her prepare.

"Are you," he asked his wife, " are you not with me?"

She did not reply. There was not the strength for replies which ended lives. But gathered her reserves for the question which still remained, which had to be put, and answered.

"Is there to be," she said, "no line drawn, at which one stops?"
Which needing strength, Clinton could not answer.

I am exhausted, he said. Physically exhausted, that is all. So
he turned to his will, which was clad in iron, to serve him.

"No lines are possible," he said.

And acknowledged then that there were indeed no limits, no
frontiers which he would not cross or extend, so long as the
power lay with him. Whatever the departures or deaths, the sui-
cides in baths of repentant water, one would continue.

Krishnan, who had his spies, learned of the goings-on and
baited Shanmugham.

"Now you see," he said, "into what our leaders lead us."

"What?" asked bold Shanmugham.

"To me it resembles homicide," said Krishnan.

But Shanmugham would not admit.

"There is no option," he suggested.

"Because we have allowed the power to pass," said Krishnan.
Accusing, and this time getting the charge to stick.

From joint panes the pair watched thick mists swirl up from
the ravines.

"The dams were built for the benefit of the people," said
Gopal, out of an instinct for mercy.

"They have created their own dangers," answered Lefevre.

"These have existed before," said Gopal.

"But have been magnified by us immeasurably," said Lefevre.

"There are the higher reaches," proffered Gopal, "which
would, if one could gain them in time, offer a degree of safety."

But Lefevre could not accept, his views being clamped to
truth.

"One would not get far," he said, "before one was swept to
destruction. Or perished of exposure upon those slopes. Besides
which there would not be the time."

*   *   *

So Mackendrick and Helen prepared, as Rawlings had done, donning capes and hoods and tightening drawstrings, watched by Clinton, who had no more to say, and Das, whose mouth had rounded to a dismayed O, which could tell, but never would, out of loyalty to master. Whom he would continue to serve, or perhaps to sustain, if only by his presence, though suspecting that such royal sustenance as he perceived was needed the sahib could obtain only from his own kind.

While the two, now girded and laced, opened and closed doors, and went out onto the verandah, and into the compound among the blown leaves and flapping rags of shrubs, and along the path which had returned to jungle, and worked their way down the hill through swaying trunks and thick churned earth. In silence, except for turmoil that the weather created, but communicating through a community of purpose.

And so came to the chief's hut, which had become a focus, as if all who wanted strength could think only of the weak old man to draw upon. Here space was made for the two, who rested legs and bursting lungs while exhaustion slowly drained, which had come from the labor of their savage descent, as well as some inroads upon spirit. These had been substantial, Mackendrick began to think, as he revived, and looked about him, and looked at Helen. Or, rather, was confronted by her, by this woman whose face was worn, its bones reminding of skull beneath from some wastage or consumption of flesh. Then a sharp fear for her rose again in him, whose frantic coursing only a purpose, and an issue, had subdued.

"There is no need," he said, out of regard for her, this pale woman whose battered form enclosed such powerful qualities of cell and matrix. "There is no need for you to be involved."

"I have forgotten," she replied, and raised her blanched face, which was streaked with rain and water, and caked with mud and whitish crystals of salt. "I cannot remember a time when I was not."

This he accepted, but still could not settle and searched his mind which was distracted, by the humid smells of earth and the fears of men who had gathered, and the guttural sounds the dying chief made.

"You must go," he managed. "It is pointless." Not to shake a resolve, whose cladding iron he recognized as counterpart, but to spare himself burdens.

This she, equally, accepted, but cast around nevertheless, and remembered words she had heard used which it seemed to her would fit, even though they might not explain.

"There are some things which one has to do," she attested.

After this they continued to sit, since there was no more to be said. Until Mackendrick, who could not endure the passivity, got up to pace, up and down in the few feet of room, disturbing the dying man. Who stirred, feeling these airs of anxiety, and began to pluck at the sheet that covered his form. So that Mackendrick, becoming aware, stopped striding, and looked down at the old man whose eyes were cloudy, but open: whose brittle skull, pellucid in this light, enclosed a knowledge it was necessary to extract. Or so Mackendrick convinced himself, and began to itch and burn with a desire to penetrate the egg-shell cranium, and finally bent, placing hands under armpits and hauling, meaning to raise to a position from which those eyes could see, but jerking the figure bolt upright, so weight-less had the frame become, or so pressing were his demands whose imperative nature he had failed to judge correctly. Then Mackendrick felt the wave that rose and broke against him, recognizing from some similarity in quality that this was what had beaten upon Clinton; but resisted, stubbornly, telling himself that his own back was broad while he kicked the flimsy door open and braced his arm to support the flopping neck and bony column, continuing what was begun.

"Look at it," he said to the tilted waxy face, above the wind and driving rain that the flailing thatch revealed. "Bucketing down. Where is the end that was promised? Do you know, do you care to tell? Or does it mean nothing whatever to you that we are all about to perish?"

Unfairly, but going on, such was the madness. Closing his mind, his ears, to the clamor outside and in, in himself, in the shocked voice of the nun, and the silence of Helen.

While the mind which had been absorbed in its own with-drawal opened to these auras of affliction, and the neck which had lolled like an overladen stalk miraculously steadied, as the old man looked out as he had been hitched up and bidden to do. At earth and sky, and hills which had been his familiar from birth and over the long reaches of his life to these last mo-ments of its running out, and would have conveyed a seeping knowledge. Tried, while the skimmed white light advanced, dissolving remaining coils that bound him.

"When the ridges rise clear," he managed.

As they are beginning to do, he wanted to say, but the light was upon him, dazzling, and he cried out in wonder, a great shout of deliverance and joy as he gave himself up to it.

"He is gone," said the nun, who recognized the choking sounds of release, or rattle.

"He would in any case," she said, considerately aiming the words at Mackendrick, "have passed away in a matter of hours," and she leaned forward to wipe the black fluid that trickled from the fallen mouth.

Then Mackendrick, who felt or imagined a stiffness, laid the husk of the old chief down. Feeling a coldness now, and a debility of arm that seemed to have withered, making him in-capable, so that Helen had to come to his help, drawing up the sheet that bore her monogram to cover the face as he had meant to do.

There remained, apparently, only the vigil and the waiting. So they settled to it, the two who were linked by this last service, while dusk deepened and the long night stretched. Until, gradually, a ferment began to stir in the numb man, who raised his head from his hands, and perceived that the dark-ness was split, or illumined, by meanings which grew from words that had been uttered. Then Mackendrick stood up, succumbing to the pricks of incipient rebellion, and brushing off webs that festooned his mind strode to the door for a view. Meaning to thrust it open, but suddenly hampered, from some declension, or the weakness that again assailed his arm. Fumbling nevertheless, and failing, and turning to Helen to release the rattan that bound the door. Clinging to her, since he saw that she was the stronger, and blinking to clear his vision which was blurred, by the season, or even perhaps the country.

"Do you think," he said, above the creak of thatch, and peering at the line of hills whose peaks were merged in sky, "that the ridges are clear of rain? Because if they are," he said, carefully, so that the thinness of voice, or hope, might be disguised, "it will mean, if the old man was right, that the rains are ending."

"It is not light enough to see," she answered, out of respect for truth, and the solid structure of this man who had come, crushing down fears, to this watery basin, prepared if need be to perish in it from some bravery or standards of mind.

"When will it be light?" he asked, wearily.

This time she did not answer, only stayed with him, and kept watch.

At dawn she looked again, and saw that the curtains of rain that had joined the tops of the hills to the horizon had lifted.

"The ridges are clear," she said.

"Are you sure?" he asked, doubtfully, squinting into distance, where the peaks still seemed to him to be tangled with sky, so accustomed had he grown to this persistent view.

"Quite sure," she replied, having kept her vision whole, and being able to rest upon it.

Soon it was clear that the rains were ended, finishing as they had begun on the upper ranges of the distant hills, the chain continuing to the valleys.

The monsoon is over, they said, soberly because of memories of craters upon which they had lately been perched, but unable to subdue some gaiety of spirit as they emerged to flounder in the soused and boggy countryside.

"The monsoon is over," said Mackendrick to Helen, also soberly, but enclosing her hand in two jubilant palms.

They picked their way out, into the watery landscape and through the aftermath of storm to the river to look, and saw that the banks held firm and the water levels were falling, which was of moment to them. While others who looked, their concerns being different, saw only the coffers, whose formidable ribs rose bleached and clean in the washed air above the turbulent river.

Kargudi 1967—London 1968

DATE DUE